Praise for RITA® Award-winning author Catherine Mann

"Catherine Mann's picture should be in the dictionary next to 'superb.' Military romance fans rejoice!"
—*New York Times* bestselling author Suzanne Brockmann

"Catherine Mann delivers a powerful, passionate read not to be missed!"
—*New York Times* bestselling author Lori Foster

Praise for *Blaze of Glory*

"Mann's skillful writing propels readers into these complex and vulnerable protagonists' perspectives. This talented author crafts a story of smart dialogue and expertly blended romantic suspense."
—*Romantic Times BOOKreviews*

"With danger around every turn and sizzling tension on every page, this is one book you won't be able to put down.... This is classic Catherine Mann, and on my keeper shelf for sure."
—*Bookjunkie Reviews*

Praise for *Code of Honor*

"Great read in the first of a new Special Ops series."
—*NoveList*

"Catherine Mann proves that her military thrillers are top notch!"
—*Romantic Times BOOKreviews*

"Loaded with action, a vile villain, and a terrific romance, fans of suspense thrillers will enjoy this fine tale!"
—*Review Centre*, 5 stars

Praise for *Anything, Anywhere, Anytime*

"Talk about m̲_____veaves...
just the righ_____trigue
and come_____d!"

Also by Catherine Mann

Fully Engaged
Blaze of Glory
Awaken to Danger
The Captive's Return
Code of Honor
Explosive Alliance
Pursued
Joint Forces
Anything, Anywhere, Anytime
Strategic Engagement
Private Maneuvers
The Cinderella Mission
Under Siege
Taking Cover
Grayson's Surrender
Wedding at White Sands

CATHERINE MANN

ON TARGET

HQN™

ISBN-13: 978-0-373-77212-4
ISBN-10:   0-373-77212-2

ON TARGET

Dear Reader,

Thank you so much for picking up the third installment in my Air Force Special Ops series! If you're new to the stories, *On Target* stands alone, but I hope it will send you searching for the earlier books. I'm also pleased to announce we have more in the works for these flyboys!

While my other Special Ops books dealt with world crises, *On Target* has at its heart an issue closer to home. Given the heavy deployment schedules of late, even some of the strongest military marriages have felt the stress of long separations, yet another sacrifice our men and women in uniform are making for our country. Shane and Sherry O'Riley's battle to repair their marriage—while combating a foreign threat to their family—requires a tenacious strength and daring beyond anything either of them has faced before.

I hope you will also check out my next two stories this year, both of which feature more of my familiar flyboy characters. Look for *Bet Me* (Harlequin Special Release) in August and a novella from Silhouette Romantic Suspense in November that features the long-awaited story for General Hank Renshaw!

Happy reading!

Catherine Mann
P.O. Box 6065
Navarre, FL 32566
www.catherinemann.com

To deployed and TDY military members who carry
photos of their families while waiting to hold
their loved ones for real.

To military spouses who hold down the home front
with grace (and certainly some frustrated tears)
while praying for their loved one's safe return.

To military children who e-mail the excitement of making a
soccer goal or an A on a math test to their faraway parent.

May our gratitude lift you up.

Acknowledgments

As my bio makes clear, I'm one of those military spouses
who holds down the home front while also holding down
my writing career. I couldn't manage it all without
an awesome support system of fabulous people who lift
me up—sometimes tapped to do so on a daily basis!

Bountiful thanks to my critiquers, readers and also
treasured friends—Joanne Rock, Stephanie Newton
and Karen Tucker. Your insightful and speedy feedback
keeps me on track and on time.

Much appreciation to my editor Melissa Jeglinski
for encouraging me to "dig deep and go for broke"
with this story.

Many thanks to my agent Barbara Collins Rosenberg
for your fantastic guidance.

My deep gratitude for the generous mentorship and
friendship of Suzanne Brockmann and Lori Foster.

Hugs and love to my sisters Julie Morrison and
Beth Reaves for being, well, sisters. Need I say more?

And as always, most of all, my unending love to
Rob and our fab four!

ON TARGET

CHAPTER ONE

Over the Caribbean Sea
Present Day

"BLACKBIRD 33, BLACKBIRD 33, this is Sentry 20 reporting a pirate ship at your ten o'clock, twenty-eight miles."

Pirate ship? The improbable radio call from Sentry rattled around in flight engineer Shane "Vegas" O'Riley's headset as he manned his station of the CV-22 aircraft. He couldn't have heard what he thought.

Sure they were out over the wild and wooly Caribbean, but someone must be screwing with them. Air Force crewdogs were well known for their practical jokes.

Except today, he couldn't be any less in the mood for gags. This flight to deliver supplies served a dual purpose for him. He would make a stop at a tiny godforsaken island where his wife worked teaching in the latest needy village to cross her aid group's radar.

There, he would also hand over divorce papers for her to sign.

But back to these freaking pirates. Since the weather was dog crap, he was in charge of the radio while the two pilots had their hands full with the bouncing airplane.

Shane thumbed the radio "transmit" key, sweat burning his eyes, his flight suit sticking to his shoulder blades in the unrelenting summer heat. No AC could keep up. "Sentry did you say a pirate ship? Is Johnny Depp onboard with his swashbuckling costume? Do you want us to land this puppy on the poop deck and get his autograph for you?" Since the CV-22 took off and landed like a helicopter, then rotated the blades forward to fly like a plane, they actually could manage just such a feat if there were a pirate ship. "I'll tell him it's for your daughter if you're embarrassed."

The jerking craft jarred his teeth, hard, faster than the roller coaster ride he'd taken with his two daughters at Six Flags last summer.

In front of him sat the two pilots. Aircraft commander Postal gripped the wobbling stick while newbie to the CV-22 copilot Rodeo took wildly fluctuating system reads off the control panel. Shane glanced over his shoulder back into the belly of the craft to check on the three gunners— and yeah, thank God—they'd strapped their butts down tight.

Their radio crackled in the inclement weather, words sputtering through unevenly, "Pirates... guns at... cruise ship."

Some theme cruise perhaps? A pocket of turbulence whacked Shane's helmet against the overhead panel and rattled his brain worse than a baseball bat upside the temple. "I'm so not in the mood for this 'Argh' and 'Shiver me Timbers' garbage. We've got a weather emergency here."

"Sorry," the radio voice claiming to be Sentry 20 responded, "not yanking your chain, Blackbird 33. We have a message relay from Southern Command Headquarters. Ready to copy?"

Shane straightened in his seat. "Really? No joke?" he said, still only half believing. "We'll play along for the heck of it, ready to copy."

The radio crackled to life. "Blackbird 33, proceed to one-eight dash zero-five north, zero-six-three dash five-nine west to intercept a pirate vessel, suspected to be terrorists threatening a passenger cruise ship. You are ordered to disable the pirate boat—" the connection went staticky for another two jostles "—or destroy the pirate's vessel, a cigarette boat, if you or the cruise ship are fired on. Copy?"

An order to shoot a cigarette boat that just happened to be tooling around in the water? This could be the worst kind of setup for an ambush in such a lawless corner of the ocean. Unease prickled up Shane's spine as he could already see all his crew members' faces plastered across the six o'clock news.

That would be a helluva way to end his career and his marriage in one fell swoop. "Who is this?"

"Listen up, Blackbird," the voice barked back, "I authenticated the communication when I got it and I think you should do the same."

Well, they got that right. "Rodeo, dig out the code book."

"Way ahead of you, Vegas. Here ya' go." The copilot's normally easygoing demeanor was nowhere to be found as he passed back the book before quickly returning to the controls. Rodeo had his hands full running both his copilot's position and checking Shane's flight engineer regular duties, monitoring engine and aircraft health since he had to deal with this buccaneer BS.

Vegas thumbed through the pages until he found what he needed. "Sentry, authenticate foxtrot-mike."

"Sentry authenticates with zulu-tango."

"So, Sarge?" Rodeo's voice shot over the radio to Tech Sergeant Shane O'Riley. "Is that correct?"

Holy crap. Shane verified it once, reread again. No movie star autographs in their future today. This was the real deal. "That is the correct response, sir."

The aircraft commander, Postal, cursed into the interphone. "Well, spank my ass and get me an eye patch." Clicking over to radio to broadcast beyond the plane, "Good authentication, Sentry, we are headed that way… Rodeo, give me a—"

"Already on it," the copilot interrupted. He might be new to the craft but the man was a freaking genius, a quick thinker on his feet to boot. That worked well with a gut instinct player like Postal. "Come left to heading one-seven-seven. Showing time to intercept at eight minutes. Target is now twenty miles ahead."

"Copy all." Postal's normally wired façade faded at the very real threat ahead—a flipping terrorist pirate ship, no less. "Crew, lock and load, cleared to fire a burst. Let's make sure those babies are working in case we need them."

Brrrrrp. Brrrrrp. The sound of quick bursts from electrically powered mini-guns hammered through his helmet just before the smell of gunpowder drifted up to linger in the cockpit. The right gunner, left gunner, back gunner—Stones, Padre and Sandman—all checked in ready to go.

Both pilots looked out to the horizon searching for a sign of the boat. Shane kept his eyes forward, his thumb on the radio and tried not think about the divorce papers in his flight bag. There wasn't much to divvy up, not with Sherry living her life in one NGO tent after another. Most of her gear consisted of easy-to-pack toys for the kids while she left a few things back home.

His little girls. Ah hell. He wanted to settle

down, have a real family life. Sherry insisted she was living a real life around the world and he was welcome to join them anytime.

Where the hell was the compromise in that?

His aircraft commander cranked the craft in a flawless bank. Postal's wild eyes stuck to the horizon, his hand on the stick. "Work that radar hard, Rodeo. Let me know when you've got a good bead on him."

"Roger that, start a right turn, shallow bank. Roll out. Straight ahead five miles."

The air grew heavier. Some might say with humidity, but Shane had been around, fought in enough conflicts to know that the minutes leading up to battle sucked emotions out of a person and pumped them into the air where they couldn't distract a man. Inside, he could stay emotionless. Six years he'd served, since he'd given up the early beginnings of his pro baseball career to enlist after 9-11.

He'd never regretted the decision. But both careers spoke to the core of who he was, a good old fashioned picket fence, baseball and apple pie family man. He thought he'd found that with Sherry and the girls. He wanted to be the big strong dude who built a home for his family and protected them.

And by protecting, he'd meant from burglars. Not freaking pirate ships and tribal warlords that attacked tent villages. What the hell was she thinking hauling the kids around to unruly corners of the world like this?

Postal leaned forward, the air getting a good pound or two heavier until he said... "Okay, I got 'em visual. Start a turn to go around them. It's a cigarette boat. Get the infrared cam on them and see what they look like."

Rodeo nodded, sweat glistening on his dark bronze skin. "Got a lock. Zooming cameras for confirmation...and ah hell, big guns on that boat. I would say the pirates."

Pirate Captain Jack Sparrow didn't have a speedboat like that.

The infrared screen display bloomed upward. Gunfire from the boat. Aimed at the CV-22. No more questioning how to respond.

Heaven help them. This was it. Open combat to the death.

Rodeo yelled, "Incoming, break right."

The aircraft banked into a hard turn. Bullets *tat, tat, tat* punctured the skin aft of the pilots before... *Boom.* In the back.

Shane glanced back over his shoulder. "What the hell happened back there?"

Stones, a burly man with *cajones* that had earned him his call sign shouted in frustration. Pain. "Holy crap a round went through a box of flares and they're popping off all over the place..."

Ah man, it was like the fires of Hades back there

with Fourth of July sparklers exploding too damn close to Stones—and rounds of ammo. Much more of that and the whole CV-22 would ignite.

With all of them going down in flames.

Vegas reached for his harness to unbuckle. Don't think of the kids. His girls, yet not legally his daughters. They were Sherry's, adopted during her first marriage—Cara from Vietnam and Malaika from the Sudan.

Once the divorce went through, he would lose all rights to them. The pain of that burned hotter than any flares. And yeah, he couldn't dodge the self-deprecating notion that sometimes the scary shit came flying back at man like a rogue missile once the battle raged.

Nothing left to lose.

He bolted from his seat. "We've got to get that the hell out of the plane. I don't want to be the finale of the fireworks show."

"I got 'em," Stones shouted, body blocking the container of sizzling flares, a boxy dude who stood for no argument regardless of any blood loss. "Back up and take care of those bastards with my gun. I got this covered. You'll just be in the way."

Shane didn't need any more urging than that. He'd been a gunner on an AC-130 gunship before becoming a flight engineer in the CV-22. His training might be rusty but he could hold his own. "Rodeo, can you keep on manning my station? I'll take the gun."

Rodeo keyed up the mike, "Absolutely. Those bastards fired on us. Smoke 'em."

Or we die.

The words went unspoken but not unheard.

They had young pilots up front. That could work in their favor—more malleable, wild cards willing to take risks. He'd enjoyed the hell out of flying with Joe "Face" Greco, but the man had been conservative with the stick. Postal would fly a plane up a tree just to see if he could.

Rodeo was new to the aircraft, having worked in cargo planes before. In fact, this was his first flight without an instructor looking over his shoulder. A helluva initiation.

The craft dipped under Shane's feet into a sweeping turn toward the racing boat. He slid behind the mini-gun at the open side door with an easy familiarity. The wind tore at his face. There was something timeless about this, like the aviators of old in their open cockpits.

In his peripheral vision he could see Stones shoveling the flares out the back ramp with gloved hands while the other two gunners cleared the way. Deck clear, the old gunner collapsed on his butt, staring at his hands, the gloves a mottled shade of pink and red that made Shane's gut ache just to look at.

"Ah, holy crap, dudes," Sandman gasped over the interphone in jerky tones as his gun jackhammered in his grip. "His gloves are melted to his hands."

"I can't man my gun," Stones gasped in a tight voice. "I can't man my gun."

They had a pirate ship with serious firepower after them and they were down their right gunner for good.

No more delay. Shane was in place for the duration. The tearing wind in his face on the dog crap weather day stirred the rightness of the moment. He was meant to be here, needed to be here. "Sit tight. I've got it covered."

"Heads-up in back," Rodeo's voice popped over the headset. "I've got 'em in my sights and apparently they've got us in theirs in spite of the weather because they're turning toward us. Open fire."

Hell. The CV-22 guns were the only thing standing between the pirate-terrorists and a cruise ship full of civilian passengers. The cigarette boat bobbed in the churning waters, the spray not high enough to reach the CV-22, but he could swear the salt spray saturated his senses.

Go for it.

The guns kicked in his grip, the reverberation unforgettable. The heat. Lethal strength. Focus. But vulnerability as he put it all out there because the enemy knew exactly where he was. Mini-guns fired, first from the side gun, and then from the gun on the aft ramp. Water spewed up the sides of the boats. Debris churned into the air as the boat returned fire.

No time for regret over missing. He didn't have a choice. Focus.

They'd been so damn close. But not close enough. He raced through options. Aim angles. A sweep from the right would be fastest. Time was tight. Mortality close. He couldn't think about Sherry and the girls that would soon no longer be his.

All that mattered: keep his crew alive, the cruise ship afloat. Beyond that for him…

Nothing to lose. The insidious mantra chiseled at him.

Shane shouted in his mouthpiece. "Bring her around and take me lower. I've got 'em, this time."

"Crap, Vegas," Postal barked, "Much lower and you'll be able to tell if the guy's circumcised."

"If that's what it takes."

"All right then. You've got it." If anyone could take them in that tight, crazy ass Postal was the man.

The cigarette boat drew close. Spray spit higher. Waves roiled upward.

He took aim. On target. With the other gunners turned away from the gunfire, they would be fine. He would keep the cruise ship afloat. His crew alive. Because of the truth tearing at his soul.

Nothing left to lose.

Apparently his resolution carried through the

waves. That was all a part of being a crew anyway. Working as one. No hesitation. The boat grew nearer. He could damn near see the color of the driver's slicker. Red. Bloodred.

And yeah, in a part of his mind the men in the boat took on the persona of Sherry's slimeball ex who made his child support payments on time, but never took even a long weekend to see the girls. Always had a convenient excuse.

What could be more important than letting the kids know they're loved? Shane narrowed his sights. And now he would lose that chance forever because even though he'd been their daddy in every way that counted since they were one and three, legally, they weren't his.

Distracting thought. Ditch it. Now.

Training. Aim. Let it rip.

Brrrrp. Brrrrp.

Smoke drifted from the engine compartment. Acrid. But he barely had time to process the sensation before…

As quickly as the engagement started, it ended in a massive eruption of flame and black smoke below. The cigarette boat split in half. The gas tanks blew, frothing the ocean.

The boat parted the water, sinking. The sun highlighting not only the vanquished enemy, but the distant cruise ship—and the small speck of an island where his wife waited. Except this time, there wouldn't be their typical welcome home dive under the covers.

More likely a dive *for* cover.

FROM THE COVER OF A palm tree, Sherry O'Riley checked out her husband's progress in the air and hoped he was in better shape than she was.

She didn't plan to stay clutching the roughened trunk of the banana tree for support much longer for his plane to appear. No way did she want Shane to know she was basically a flipping mess since the alert alarm had sounded a half hour ago. Just dumb luck she'd been in the compound command center checking on Shane's landing time so she could have the girls clean and ready to meet him on the flight line when he landed—not that she suffered any delusions his visit had positive implications.

Hearing the attack begin over the airwaves… Her stomach rose up to clog her throat. She'd dashed through the dusty compound to gather up her girls in the tent classroom and settled them in the bunker with her friend Keisha.

Sherry knew in her head she should have stayed put, too. But her heart hauled her feet back across the shoreline to the airfield. Oh, she'd been smart enough to grab her .38 caliber revolver, but she had to be at the epicenter where the alarm still blared. As if somehow the steel of her will could bring Shane safely to the earthen runway, hot packed dirt steaming after the afternoon's sporadic thunder-storms.

How often had she walked the floors at 2:00 a.m., pacing her way through wartime deployments on the same principle? Don't sleep, *will* him alive.

She stroked her Lady Smith revolver. Shane had bought it for her three years ago for her personal protection—lightweight, less kick, and red, her favorite color. Red, like the cloying blooms all around her.

Red, like blood.

God, she was a mess of random thoughts—locking in on anything but what could be going on in the air. She really should get back to the bunker, except she couldn't give up her post peeking from behind the banana tree, foliage brushing her face.

The base security cops already knew she was here, only twenty feet from the runway, but she didn't want Shane to see her. She only needed to know he was safe, then she would leave.

And there…she thought she saw…maybe a speck on the horizon…

Larger.

Yes. An aircraft, the sound muffled by the alarm.

Her heart squeezed tight and forgot about its job of beating, taking a coffee break for about twenty light-headed seconds. Lucky for her, she had a banana tree handy to keep her from sliding to the ground while she waited for oxygen to return to her brain.

And watched the CV-22 fly closer.

Opaque plumes of smoke streamed from the aircraft in an ominous black cloud. Her heart pounded in time with the *whap, whap, whap* of the rotors. She'd lost count of how many times she'd waited for him to come home from war, from test missions—from places she had no idea where or what he was doing.

Then came the frantic sex. Because of the separation. Or the need to affirm he still lived. Or simply to let off steam from their arguments over how she refused to stay in the States all the time and how he couldn't support her frequent work overseas.

Today, there would be none of the forgetfulness through sex. A damn shame, because that part they'd always gotten blissfully right.

Of course sex should be the last of her concerns right now.

She'd faced the possibility her husband could die on more days than she'd woken to the assurance he was safe. Yes, her heart stopped beating and then pounded too hard. There were days she could still hurt over this man. Although sometimes she wondered if she'd gone completely numb from scar tissue inflicted on that hammering organ in the middle of her chest.

Some days she wished she *could* stop feeling.

She wasn't a wimp by a long stretch. She'd grown up in mission camps around the globe—

worked as a teacher in relief camps now. It took a lot to stutter her pulse rate.

Those coal black bursts belching from her soon-to-be ex-husband's aircraft left her grabbing for support. She would leave and go back to their children once he landed safely. He *would* land safely, damn it.

The looming gray craft slowed over the earthen runway, roaring, stirring the soil and trees in tornado-like swirl. The engine and rotors rotated upward so the craft hovered like a helicopter, no longer a plane. The swirl of dusty mayhem increased as the craft started its descent toward the ground.

Almost home free.

As if to mock her overconfidence, fire trucks screamed toward the rustic airstrip. An ambulance trailed.

An *ambulance*. Ohmigod.

Sherry resisted the urge to squeeze her eyes shut, as if somehow she could hold the CV-22 and her crew members together by the sheer power of her determined stare. Besides, if she blinked, she would cry.

No tears. She'd gotten that message from Shane loud and clear early in their marriage.

Show me a smile, Sherry baby. Tears will only distract me and I can't afford distractions.

As if her tears could cause his death.

What a heavy responsibility to carry into a farewell. She hated him for that sometimes, even as much as she'd loved him, back before they'd numbed each other with fights and separations. In the early days, Shane had evoked strong emotions that way. But no tears allowed in his presence.

Today, she wanted more of the numb. Better yet, she should haul over to the underground bunker—

Too late. Somehow in her musings, the craft had finished its shutdown and the crew was abandoning the CV-22 ASAP.

Shane leapt from the back hatch, whipping his helmet from his head. Soot smudged his poster-boy handsome face, a face so good-looking she'd turned him down the first time he'd asked her out because she'd been certain anyone that perfect must be conceited. His normally dark blond hair was brown with sweat. It hadn't been a good day.

But he was alive. Walking on his own two feet, unlike one of the crew members who was being strapped to a gurney. A shiver rippled through her. Who? Even knowing Shane was safe didn't stop her fear for the rest of the crew, all friends, a family of sorts even when they added a new member now and again.

Thank heaven at least they were all alive. She would cling to that.

She could leave. She would leave. Okay, move feet. The ramshackle Jeep she'd commandeered waited…

Then Shane turned toward her, his head tipped in

the wind as if he caught her scent. They were far apart but his stance changed, shifted from easygoing to on guard. As if she was the enemy. Lord, how she regretted that they'd come to that.

Sherry tucked her tiny red revolver into her leather waist harness and pivoted toward her vehicle. Maybe, just maybe she could get away...

"Sorry, babe," Shane's voice carried on the ocean breeze, halting her, "but you're not the winner of the five-hundred-thousand dollar lottery."

She waited for him to draw nearer before answering to give herself a chance to regain some kind of mental edge. "What?"

"Five-hundred thousand dollars. The military's life insurance. We're at war so they upped the amount."

How dare he? She felt like throwing up. But these days it seemed they dared say almost anything to hurt each other. That simultaneously saddened and angered her.

Her fingers itched to slap him and damn him, he didn't even flinch as her hand headed toward his face. As if he knew he deserved it. That alone stopped her mid-swing. Her arm fell back to her side.

She settled for, "You bastard."

"You really could come up with something original and less worn-out." He sounded as weary as she felt with the fighting.

She sagged back against the palm tree, rough bark biting into her hands as she gripped to keep from reaching out to touch him and reassure herself he hadn't died over that ocean. "We're past even being civil to each other? Can't we try for the children?"

"Sorry." He slumped back against a tree across from her, his helmet dangling from his hand. "It's been a crap day."

"How's the crew? Who's on the gurney?"

"Everyone's okay. Stones has some burns on his hands, but we think he'll be fine. We caught a little fire in the plane, put it out. Nothing catastrophic in the big scheme of things. A little in-flight emergency."

Nothing catastrophic?

Fire in the plane?

Horrifying images filled her mind of how close they must have come to dying out over the ocean, of how close she'd come to standing by this banana tree waiting forever… Her stomach jolted up again lickety-split. The horizon bobbled.

"Sherry? Where are the kids?"

His voice helped steady the earth under her feet again. "In one of the underground bunkers because of the sirens. I heard there was a threat out there."

"Damn straight. That's why they have bunkers here. Where *you* should be. What if I'd gotten my ass shot off out there and then something happened to you, too?"

He'd thrown that argument at her no less than a

hundred times to coerce her into staying in the U.S. permanently rather than working overseas as a teacher for NGO groups intermittently. She couldn't seem to make him understand that their life together didn't have to fit the same mold as most people he knew. They could follow a different path. Different didn't mean bad or wrong.

Since he'd used his same argument, she gave him her same answer. "Keisha would win the half-million-dollar lottery and our children."

"All that because you're too stubborn to go in the bunker, too? I get that you have to save the world. But those kids count on you."

"And they don't count on you?" What made his calling different from hers, damn it? She wanted to shout as loud as the cackling monkey shrieking in the trees. "I'll put down my gun when you put down yours, Slugger."

She held up her hand for him to stay quiet. Let the birds and monkeys have center stage when it came to decibels. "Don't bother answering that. We both know you should have married a different kind of woman. That's why you're here with those papers in your flight bag."

His brown eyes held hers until she lost track, their hands stuck to the damn palm trees rather than plastering all over each other as they would have in the past. And yet she suddenly became aware of their feet just inches apart in undergrowth. His black combat boots smashed down grass and pine straw, with her dusty brown boots close enough it made her think of their feet tucked together in bed on a cold night when he warmed her ever chilly toes for her while they spooned against each other.

"Shane?" Her voice wobbled.

He cleared his throat and straightened. "We don't have time for this now. I have to go to debrief."

She shook her head. "There you go again. Start a discussion, hook me in, then cut me off as if I'm inconveniencing you by speaking too much. I really hate it when you do that."

"Ah, a nice, non-antagonistic 'I' statement rather than an aggressive 'you' statement. Our marriage counselor would be proud."

"Go to hell." She rechecked her gun in her waist harness and strode away into the jungle toward her rusty Jeep, pretty much failing Marriage Counseling 101 for today.

"You always have to have the last word." His wry voice echoed after her.

Last word? She didn't give a spit about who had the last word. She would have been cool with stopping and talking and figuring out this problem. Or maybe even just indulging in a no-holds-barred, thank-God-you're-alive kiss. But she had to keep walking into the dense jungle toward the Bondo covered vehicle because if she turned around...

Shane would see her tears.

CHAPTER TWO

"GENTLEMEN, YOU'D BEST stay close to the air base where no one can see you."

An order from a three star general. Not something Shane heard every day, but this hadn't been an ordinary day by a long stretch. The scent of musty military tent hung heavy in the tropical heat as Shane shifted in his seat on his bench. Second row back with the rest of his crew. A select contingent from the air base had been gathered into this make-shift command center—so near Sherry's village it was all Shane could do to keep his butt planted on the metal seat.

What was the Director of Operations for the Joint Chiefs of Staff doing here on this tiny Caribbean Island?

Only way to find out—let the imposing guy get on with the brief.

"The island is crawling with reporters and photographers from the village trying to get the scoop on who blasted the pirate ship." General Hank Renshaw dominated the room with more than just his height, his salt-and-pepper buzz cut just missing the tent rafters.

Shane had seen the General on television before and couldn't help but think again no wonder he'd flown larger airplanes. Folding that oversized frame into fighter planes would have been a cramped challenge.

Postal's hand shot into the air and held until he got the wave to speak. "Sir, how did they hear this fast?"

"It was on the Drudge Report before you landed. Now it's all over the Internet."

"No shit?" Rodeo muttered from beside him.

"No shit. We have tried to keep your names out of the press." He paused, a half smile digging into one side of his craggy face. "I realize we're in the Caribbean and the base does share the beach with the village. If you go there, make damn sure you're not in uniform. And definitely no talking."

Shane raised his hand. "Sir, what's the press's spin?"

"Good question, Sergeant. Base public relations has already issued an official statement and we have every reason to believe dissemination will stay accurate through the press. No sympathetic drawing of a buccaneer free spirit. This was a terrorist attack." Renshaw paced, his hand clutching his Black-Berry. "We sent out one of the first reports to Captain Greco's wife."

The seasoned bomber pilot glanced down at the BlackBerry in his grip, frowning. His thumb twitched. What was he holding back? Generals didn't show stress. Something big had to be shaking down.

Renshaw shoved the BlackBerry back in its case, then put his hands behind his waist, boots braced and continued his briefing, "No reason not to give her the scoop. She's a damn good photojournalist with solid contacts. But we need to keep the lid on why we've been flying planes in here for the past month."

Ah. Finally. The reason for General Renshaw's presence.

"Intelligence indicates today's incident wasn't coincidental." He scanned the room of two dozen Air Force personnel. "We have reason to believe a new terrorist cell is settling in on one of these tiny islands. And *that* part the press does not know."

A cold ball of dread settled in Shane's gut as heavy as the musty smell of the military tent, as heavy as his determination to get his family the hell out of here. God, how close they'd been to terrorist thugs all this time and he hadn't had a clue.

He'd thought drug runners were their only concern. He should have known better. Drug runners and terrorists were tight these days.

Somewhere through the fog of the hellish images in his mind he heard Postal speaking again.

"General, what's the latest on Stones?"

"A local nurse from the NGO camp—" General Renshaw glanced at his BlackBerry again, scrolling through to check his notes "—finished her assessment and declared him stable enough to fly back to the States later tonight or first thing tomorrow. The healing will be painful as hell. But he's alive."

The General relaxed his stance, a smile creasing his craggy face. "Gentlemen, you did well today." He nodded. "Go get some chow and hit the rack. You've earned your sleep."

They filed out of their seats and toward the door.

"O'Riley," the General called out, halting Shane in his dusty tracks.

Shane pivoted and pulled to attention. "Sir?"

"At ease." The General waved him over to a corner, pulling out his BlackBerry. Yeah, this guy was addicted to the thing—more like a "Crack"-Berry, he'd heard it called for workaholics like General Renshaw. "It's come to my attention that your family is currently living here."

"Yes, sir, my wife works with an NGO. They're pulling a short stint here bringing immunizations and family services." Sherry's crew provided day care, while she taught workshops on topics ranging from domestic violence to job training. She and her crew even oversaw online programs for obtaining high school-like degrees. Anything to help an overtaxed family.

Her three-week intensive program on life development skills culminated in leaving behind a computer for a local clinic. The computer also enabled her to stay in touch, sending updated flyers on nutrition, brain-building activities and all-around child nurturing.

Damn, all their marital problems aside, he was proud of her.

General Renshaw's thumb massaged his CrackBerry. "I realize staying here at the air base would put an unnatural hardship on you after all the regular separations military families suffer. I have three children of my own. They may be grown, but I remember how difficult those separations could be. How old are your girls?"

"Six and eight, sir," he answered, impressed that the General remembered he had daughters. The man cared about his people, no question. But such attention to detail was beyond rare.

"Cute ages. Very cute. Time flies by though." He holstered his CrackBerry again. "Feel free to visit them whenever you're not working, but make sure you change to civilian clothes and keep your head low. No chatting with reporters. Obviously what happened today is common knowledge. But about the terrorist cell developing? That's need-to-know only information for now."

"Understood, sir." He could see his wife. He just couldn't talk to her. Still at least he *could* see his family with the consent, because actually nothing would have kept him out of that village tonight. "Thank you, General."

"No problem, Sergeant."

Now he simply had to deliver divorce papers and figure out how to get his wife to leave the island without breaking the bonds of secrecy of his job. A piece of cake, right?

Damn.

Dealing with Captain Jack Sparrow had been easier than figuring out how to make his wife do anything she didn't want to do.

"DADDY'S HOME! DADDY'S HOME! Daddy's home from work!" Cara squealed from the surf, pointing into the distance past all the other swimmers and late day sunbathers from their camp.

Sherry tensed as the waves crashed over her and Malaika—Mally as Shane dubbed her early on. Mally squirmed in her mother's arms to get down as she chanted, "Daddy, Daddy, Daddy…"

Sure enough, Sherry could see her soon-to-be ex-husband stepping from the jungle looking no less hunky in his low riding black cargo shorts and white T-shirt than he had in his flight suit. The late afternoon sun shone on his golden hair, showered clean now, soot long gone.

All the other people around her faded away and too easily she recalled the first time she'd seen

Shane at a squadron baseball game. She'd tagged along with a military neighbor intent on bolstering Sherry's spirits on the six-month anniversary of her divorce.

And Shane strode up to the plate to bat. He'd made a triple. *Thwack*. God, he'd been so handsome, hot—damn near gorgeous—she couldn't help but stare in appreciation. When he'd come up to her wanting an introduction, she'd thought no way. A guy who looked that perfect had to be stuck on himself.

He'd been persistent.

Very persistent—in charming her daughters.

Two weeks later, they'd begun dating. Two months later, they'd married.

Why, why, why couldn't she control herself around him? She wasn't normally an impulsive woman. Looking at him now, however, she could already feel her defenses lowering...

Sherry squeezed her eyes closed. Still the setting sun shimmered through in an orangey glow, much the way Shane eased under her skin regardless of all the ways she told herself she couldn't be the stay-at-home Betty Crocker he wanted.

She really wasn't ready for another confrontation with him. Not yet. How convenient that her daughters were eager for Daddy-time.

"Go ahead, girls." She walked them both to the shoreline, her friend Keisha shadowing her as the water sluiced around their feet, dragging gritty sand away with each receding wave.

He called to them both from the beach, "Cara, Mally…"

"Daddy!" the girls squealed in that perfect unison way that Shane had often said made him feel like he could conquer kingdoms.

He opened his arms with just the right timing to stroke their heads as they launched at him. A girl clutched each calf and "riding" a foot while he walked across the beach toward an oversized rock away from everyone else. Palms shadowed the scenario, so sweet, so heart tugging.

They'd played this routine out dozens of times over the years, their spindly arms locked tight as they took their long awaited trip on Dad's foot. Then he would extend each arm and both girls would reach up, grab hold and swing free in an acrobatic move that used to scare the crap out of Sherry. Cara and Mally swung up and around until he had each child on one hip with her arms around his neck.

"How's my best girl?" his voice drifted on the salty wind.

"I'm good." Cara answered.

"No!" Mally shook her head, beads in her braids clinking. "*I'm* good."

"Nuh-uh," Cara insisted, ever the confident older sister. "He means *me*."

And there they went on like always as he

brushed a kiss on both their heads while Sherry backed from the too enticing family ritual she would be losing. He was a good father, without question, and she was glad for her girls, but she couldn't let that cloud her thinking when it came to the painful disaster their marriage had become.

Distance. She needed distance desperately. She backed deeper and deeper until the water sucked her in again, warming around her waist. Waves slapping her shoulders, briefly enveloping her head and momentarily blinding her with sea spray.

Keisha drew up alongside her, her willowy friend paddling gently as she sat on a surfboard. "So he just shows up here to talk to you."

"To deliver divorce papers." Sherry kept her voice low even though the rest in their group would know soon enough. Her eyes lingered on the trio as Shane dropped to sit on the rock, the girls at his feet playing in the sand and chattering, no doubt in a nonstop litany of catch-up details.

"Papers like that out of the blue?" Keisha shook her head, her short hair shaking free of a few droplets of water. Her fearless friend slid from the surfboard to stand next to her. Keisha always made the most of wherever they went. She'd even gone on a wildlife search for a Komodo dragon in Indonesia and taken up archery in South Africa. Her surfing lessons in the Caribbean seemed positively tame in comparison. "Girl, that's harsh."

"I knew they were coming. I should have told you, but you know things have been rough."

"I remember you had a trial separation last year, but you got back together."

"More than one separation. Even a stint in marital counseling. It's just really hard to admit we…" Failed. Lost all those beautiful dreams. She blinked fast and told herself the salt spray stung her eyes. "I just expected a FedEx package, not the manly kind of package."

With long sympathetic exhale, Keisha stroked her damp, short bobbed hair behind her ears. "What do you say after you get the girls off to sleep we find ourselves a bottle of wine—"

"Tequila." Straight up.

"Oh, yeah. Better yet. We'll toast our independence."

"Apparently I'm the most independent woman on the planet since I'll soon have two ex-husbands to my credit." She plowed her hands through a wave.

"You'll have two *idiot* exes to your credit. If they're not man enough to stand next to a strong woman like you, then screw them."

"Not anymore." She couldn't stop the retort as sexual frustration reared its ugly head.

"Oh yeah. Right." Keisha thumped the heel of her hand to her head. "I got a little into the moment. Flashbacks to an idiot or three in my own past."

"Well, you are definitely a strong woman."

"Thanks." She shrugged her shoulders twice, then a third time.

"Still tense from the alert siren earlier?"

"A little. Nothing to worry about though." Keisha brushed aside the concern as always. They were two of a kind—too darn independent women both working themselves into the ground. "Did your guy give you any hints as to what's going on with the siren and all?"

"He hasn't said." Sherry sidestepped a local family, mother and father swinging their son between them into the waves. Envy pinched without warning. She stepped back alongside Keisha. "I assumed some drug runners out in the bay and a shoot-out."

"Where are drug runners *not* a problem in the world?" Her dark eyes pierced right through Sherry. "Are you sure you're okay?"

Sherry avoided her gaze. "What do you mean?"

"I hear that his plane was more than a little shot up, pouring smoke, scary looking."

"I'm used to it after five years as a military wife." She skimmed her fingers along the frothing waters around her. No giving herself away by punching the waves this time. Keep it light, easy. Focus on the warm sun soothing her shoulders. Try like crazy not to let the sound of her children's laughter and low rumbling bass of laughter on the wind stab her heart.

Keisha stalled Sherry's restless fingers, forcing her to make eye contact while she squeezed her hand gently. "Nobody with a soul could get used to heart-stopping moments like that."

Sherry allowed herself to accept the comfort for a moment, let it soothe the ache that had squeezed her stomach and pushed up to her throat all afternoon long. Too much comfort though, and she would start thinking like a wife again. Dangerous.

She dug her feet into the sand and backed away, letting the lukewarm water draw her deeper so the sweet image of him sliding down to sit with the girls and build sandcastles would grow smaller. "The gunner you treated, Stones, he's really going to be all right?"

"Don't worry, my friend. He's going to be okay. He won't have a career as a hand model, but he should be fine." Keisha squinted into the horizon, her surfboard floating under her arms. "So there's really nothing going on around here, nothing any worse than normal?"

What was she digging for? Keisha obviously wanted to know something and Sherry was too deep in her own fog of pain to figure out what her friend wanted to know. She tried to sift through the day and figure out what she'd missed, but came up blank. She truly was a flipping mess. "Not that he's told me yet."

"Well, it looks like you'll get the chance to ask

him more in depth because here he comes now. And if the expression on his face as he's checking you out in the bathing suit is any indication, you can Mata Hari just about anything you want from that man."

Sherry jerked to look toward the shore and holy cow yes, Shane was on his way toward the shore's edge. The girls skipped alongside him, each holding a hand as he walked a slow-hipped pace so they could keep up. His shirt was gone, his shoes too as he wore only a pair of black cargo shorts.

Great. How was she going to manage reasonable conversation around this man any better than she ever had? Cargo shorts or flight suit—she couldn't even let herself think about the "nothing at all" image of him—her brain always did short-circuit around the too perfectly hot Shane O'Riley.

SEEING SHERRY IN A bathing suit was taking a serious toll on his sanity on a day that had been beyond bizarre.

Pirates.

Terrorists.

Now his wife showing up as enticing as any mermaid siren.

There had to be something to the whole Caribbean islands voodoo stuff, because his world had gone off-kilter. Reasonable didn't even enter his brain. Water streamed down her body.

Sure she wore a conservative bathing suit, two piece, blue, the top more like a tank shirt that met the bottom of the suit and still…even after five years of marriage just the sight of her twisted him inside out faster than the turns of this crazy ass day.

And there wouldn't be the traditional welcome home after the kids fell asleep, the kind where he and Sherry raced for the bedroom to relieve the pressure building inside both of them.

Hell, even without that, he found himself clinging to just the family part.

Would this be the last time they were all together? The last family welcome home with his kids? Would she let him have access to the girls—his *daughters,* damn all legalities—after the divorce? How would he handle it if suddenly their disinterested other dad demanded his fair share of holidays?

His jaw clenched. Neither of them would want a scene in front of Cara and Mally—or the personnel she worked with, for that matter. Interesting how he'd barely noticed the people around him, a smattering of NGO employees and people from the village. These people probably knew more about her right now than he did.

He really would rather deal with pirate terrorists than wade through the mess of his personal life.

Sherry finished emerging from the water like the siren she'd always been. He vaguely registered that her friend trailed her. A good thing, though, Keisha's presence along with the girls would keep things more civil for everyone.

"Hi, Shane." She stopped beside him. Not touching. No kiss hello. Of course not. But her eyes lingered on his throat, on the black cord that held his wedding ring, where he put it when he flew since they didn't wear rings in flight. Her face softened. "If you want to join us for supper, then maybe you can help me tuck the girls into bed—if you want to."

He did. And he wanted to take it as a good sign that she included him in this routine of theirs, more than he'd expected given the bitterness of their last argument. Of course she loved the girls and would want what worked best for them. He hoped. But he'd seen too many divorces around the squadron go messy in a heartbeat to get comfortable.

The girls chattered on while he and Sherry said nothing.

Keisha waved from the beach—with a surfboard? He never knew what to expect from her. He really needed to warn her and Rodeo that they were both on the same island. And he would. Soon. When he didn't have his own problems staring him in the face. "Hey, Keisha, cool surfboard."

"Hello, hotshot." Her smile was tight. No question whose side she was on.

She slung a backpack over her shoulder and

hitched her surfboard more securely under her arm before turning to Sherry. "Want me to stick around? Or take the girls?"

Sherry shook her hear. "You can go on ahead. We're okay. Really. But thanks."

"If you're certain." Keisha turned toward him and shot him another one of those eat-shit-and-die looks.

Damn. The temperature dropped a good twenty degrees.

As her footsteps faded, silence wrapped around him and his wife. Well, not a real quiet because the kids gabbed on and there were still people on the beach, but the two of them didn't speak a word to each other. Just stood and stared and waited for the other to offer something up.

Had it always been that way before the fights shut them down? No talk. Just cohabitating in the same space until it was time to have sex? If so no wonder they'd fallen apart. No substance to bolster the marriage.

"Daddy?" Cara asked, her voice as melodious as always. "I want a story before bed."

"Do you have a present for us?" Mally bounced on her toes, thumbing free the wedgie on her Dora the Explorer bathing suit.

"How long are you gonna stay this time?" Cara asked with wide eyes, standing still and solemn, growing up too fast as she stood, slim and tall in her first two-piece bathing suit.

"Can we go home?"

He wanted to say yes to everything, but he'd never lied to them and he wouldn't start now. He settled for, "A bedtime story for sure. Two. You each get to pick one."

"Yippee!"

Still nothing from Sherry as she stood in her bathing suit with a sarong. Heaven help him. Celibacy stunk.

"We've said enough." Too much. "We'll be eating dinner in about two hours, if you want to join us then."

Sounded like an eternity. "Thanks. I have some business back with the crew, then I'll be there."

"We'll be waiting."

He watched the three of them walk away, the trio that had once been his world. An image of the first time he'd seen them at a squadron baseball game came to mind. She'd been there with a neighbor, cheering on the woman's husband. Her friend had been cheering *Sherry* on for ditching her loser ex-husband and encouraging her to get out of the apartment.

Meeting her, he'd known she worked for an NGO. He'd admired her work overseas, but thought it to be more of a once a year variety.

Yeah, he'd been deluding himself. He'd let testosterone fog his brain because he'd wanted her too damn much. Furthermore, he simply hadn't realized the toll their dual travel schedules would take on the family.

Nope.

Shane had taken one look at her and those cute kids and seen the home and family he'd been looking for all his life.

Or so he'd thought.

He scrubbed his hand over his jaw. He should shave before he saw her again…

Damn it, all. There went his pulse again. Time to cool off.

He climbed a low rocky overhang and dove into the water. The water swallowed him in a tepid pool, clear, a school of fish parting in a frantic dash. The perfect way to unwind after a hellish day.

He broke clear of the water, the sun overhead beating down on the small group of other sunbathers, mostly from the base, a hundred feet away. He soaked in the warm healing waters, his body feeling battered from the ravages of real combat. Backstroking, he allowed himself a moment to study the other group, the shore with a mini picnic area. Apparently this was a camp favorite. The main gravel road into the jungle looked well-traveled, with two smaller dirt paths still well beaten down.

But quiet.

Sherry had taken the girls down the dusty trail to the right. Alone. His intellect told him the terrorist camp was firmly rooted on one of the other islands. The General would have told them if the camp had been here. They didn't want the grief of blasting up an NGO camp. The U.S.A. would rain hell on their head.

Except those same terrorists had made a ballsy attack on a Caribbean cruise ship.

Even now he eyed a speedboat in the distance with different perspective. How did he know it wasn't a cohort of their earlier encounter with the Jack Sparrow wannabe? The General had mentioned a terrorist camp setting up on one of the other islands, but nothing stopped those same terrorists from operating off this island, as well.

Right now, his family was too vulnerable to attack, Sherry out there on her own with two small children to protect. He could be a few minutes late meeting up with crew. He had more important business to tend to first. Shane plowed through the water toward the shore.

Toward Sherry and his daughters.

CHAPTER THREE

S<small>OMEONE WAS FOLLOWING HER.</small>

Sherry could feel it. She'd been around edgy places long enough to have cultivated that itchy sensation of someone dogging her heels. Person or beast, however, she wasn't sure. Somebody or something dangerous even?

How damn dumb she'd been to run from Shane. But God, she'd walked this path on her own hundreds of times. Animals stayed clear because of all the traffic. Yes, she always had to be somewhat on alert in other parts of the world, but her NGO had security. Today's siren and Shane's near brush must have her feeling fidgety.

What sucky timing too. Alone, with only her one small gun tucked in her bag to protect her two small kids. She weighed her options. She didn't feel comfortable whipping the weapon out in front of the girls—scary and dangerous to do just because of a "feeling."

Better to plow ahead faster. She hitched Mally higher on her hip and clutched Cara's hand.

Leaning, she angled close to her daughter to shush her latest made-up tune that might drift on the wind and alert someone of their presence. "Sweetheart, let's play the quiet game, okay? Daddy's going to join us soon and we'll get to talk lots and lots then, but for now—"

"Mommy needs some peace and quiet?"

Single parenting most of the time had its stressing moments and apparently she hadn't done as well as she'd hoped at hiding that from her children. She brushed a hand over her daughter's head. No lying to kids. Their innocence saw through.

"Yeah, sweetie," Sherry whispered, "Mommies need peace and quiet sometimes. Shhhhhh…"

Sherry pressed her finger to her lips.

The girls mimicked her gesture.

Guilt sucked as she thought of all the things she'd wanted to give her girls when she'd taken on the precious responsibility of parenting them. Here she was, two broken marriages later, wandering the world, hearing threats around every banana tree.

She was doing her best to keep her kids safe. And Shane was coming soon, hopefully very soon. Why oh why hadn't she let him come right away? Because of her stupid, stupid need for space to gather her defenses.

Her children should have come first.

Suppressed memories from her childhood rose to the surface. Her mother had always turned those moments into games. They were just playing hide-and-seek. Or a grown-up tag. Nothing to worry about. Parents always kept their children safe.

And her mother and father had kept her safe even if there had been a few hair-raising moments that left her with vague, unfocused nightmares. Somehow, though, they'd managed to explain away the deaths of others in the camps. A favored babysitter. A neighbor in charge of immunization distribution.

Why had she not thought of these experiences before and put them into an adult's frame of references? Because she'd never faced a moment near an airfield with an alarm blaring and Shane's condemning face staring down at her.

However, she'd never deliberately taken her children to dangerous locales. Ever. She'd been careful of their safety. They may not have had Cartoon Network 24/7, but they were safe. They learned things about the world other children merely viewed on the news.

Her girls had an appreciation for the simple things of life. And hey, she treated them to cartoons on her satellite TV and DVD player. She couldn't deny them when she couldn't resist indulging in her obsession for taped catch-up sessions of her secret indulgence—her favorite soap opera.

Damn it, she hated how he made her second-guess herself and ohmigod, her mind was rambling in fear.

Leaves rustled behind her. Muscles bunched in

her arms. It was probably just someone else from the camp.

She hoped.

Her gun was in her bag and she longed to reach for it, but feared a shoot-out with her daughters too vulnerable around her. Most likely it really was a local villager or workmate.

Mally buried her face deeper into her mother's neck with a tiny shudder and muffled squeak. "Too tight, Mommy."

Sherry dropped a kiss on her head. "Sorry sweetheart."

Ever-musical Cara hummed a nursery rhyme lowly from her side, the quiet time game slipping away, a sure sign of her nervous glomming on to her mother's tension. The branches parted. Sherry slid her children behind her in a flash. She jammed her hand into her purse, her hand closing her gun—

Shane blasted through. In just his flip-flops and shorts, hair wet, he joined her.

Sherry couldn't swallow the scream. The breath she'd been holding had to go somewhere. Only half recognizing her own husband, she kept stumbling back, pressing her body closer to the girls'.

Her fingers stayed clenched around the butt of the revolver, safety still in place. Her hand shook until Shane had her by her shoulders, gripping her, rocking her. "Shh, honey. Calm down. It's me. It's me. You're okay."

Sherry gasped for breath even as she felt the girls relax behind her, both reaching around for their dad. She hated that she'd scared them for nothing, but doggone it, better safe than sorry.

Her fingers slowly unclenched from the gun and slid from her purse. "Scared the sh—" she glanced at the girls and exhaled, swallowed the curse and continued "—the *spit* out of me."

"Shh. I'm just being careful. Let's not frighten the girls." He held up a hand and—whoa he looked hot all wet like that with his cargo shorts clinging to his slim hips. "We'll get them back to the camp."

She forced humid air in and out of her deprived lungs, the scent of flowers and mulchy leaves filling her overwrought senses. Her eyes lingering on his wedding band on the black leather string around his neck. "And everything's okay, with the crew and the flight?"

He cupped the back of her head and held her eyes. "There *is* need to be careful, but not panic."

His slow, logical tones reminding her she really had made a mountain out of a molehill here. She'd let all his old arguments work her into a frenzy for nothing. "It's only a mile more to camp. We'll make it before dark."

"I'll walk you there, then head back to base to check in with the crew."

"Oh." The reality of his other obligations crashed over her. "I forgot all about that. Sorry."

He waved away her concern. "Are we still on for supper?"

She hated that he had to ask, but that's how things were and she needed to accept it. "Yes. We'll see you then."

"Good. Good."

A simple word, then the things they needed to talk about weren't meant for the children's ears. And all too soon those words—words that would end something that had once been beautifully promising—would be out there. She knew they had to end it. They were good at goodbyes.

If only her fingers didn't itch to crawl over that bare chest of his for one more steamy welcome home.

DEREK "RODEO" WASHINGTON knew when his butt was toast.

Today was apparently one of those days.

He eyed his old childhood pal and crewdog buddy Shane sitting on the cot next to him in their tent. They'd finished with business, meeting up after the session with the General for a smaller debrief of their own where they'd decompressed about the whole pirate ship thing.

Derek knew he should thank Shane for the inside scoop about Keisha Jones being on the island, but his brain was still on stun.

"Keisha?" Derek kept his voice low so the others wouldn't overhear. "Keisha Jones is *here?*"

"I've said yes three times now," Shane answered with unwavering patience as he buttoned up a short sleeved striped cotton shirt. "She and Sherry have both worked for the same NGO off and on for as long as I've known them. It's not out of the realm of possibilities they would work the same camp on occasion."

"Right. Right." He massaged his empty ring finger and thought of the woman who he suspected had been eyeing that very spot four and half years ago to make sure he was free for a fling. "I should have considered it."

"Apparently she was the nurse who took care of Stones." Shane tucked his shirt into khaki shorts.

"Damn. Just damn." It wasn't every day a man had to face his worst mistake square on, especially this close on the heels of nearly getting his ass shot out of the sky.

He'd been a fool back then, convinced his heart was stuck forever on a woman who'd dumped him the year before, a woman who'd gone on to marry some lame ass dude who didn't treat her right. Derek had been feeling low, and Shane had tried to help him move on by introducing him to Keisha. He'd figured he needed a fling, too numb from the rejection to see she'd wanted more.

The attraction had been there, no question. He'd thought they could at least enjoy a steamy hot affair…until in one flash of a weak moment during sex he'd goofed. Big time. Worst time.

When he'd called out the wrong woman's name.

Keisha had bucked him off in under ten seconds flat—bare butt on cold tile.

He'd made the mistake of telling the story during a drunken maudlin moment in an Officer's Club bar—and his call sign name "Rodeo" had been born.

Now everyone in the fucking Air Force knew. Damned if he would let them humiliate *her,* too. Not only did he have to stay away, but he had to keep them away from her. "She's here."

No longer a question.

"Yeah, dude."

"Good thing I have to keep my ass firmly planted on this air base. I'm not going anywhere near that camp."

"That scared of one willowy wisp of a woman, are you?"

"I value my life."

"You know we're allowed access to the beach—commonly owned by the base and the camp." Shane scrubbed his fingers through his short blond hair until the wet strands spiked. "Maybe you could just swing by there and take this chance to apologize."

"You don't think I already tried? Don't women talk?"

Shane dropped to sit on the cot, fishing underneath for his leather flip-flops. "Sherry said Keisha's pretty closed mouthed on this one."

That took Derek back a moment. He'd been worrying about the woman for years and she didn't even mention him to her best friend? Maybe it was too painful. Yeah. That had to be it. "Well, I'm not saying I deserve forgiving, but I tried apologizing. She damn near took my head off pitching the vase of flowers. Woman's crazy mad. I know when to cut my losses and keep my distance."

"Yipee-o-ki-a, cowboy."

Rodeo scowled. "Not a word where she can hear you."

"You think she's got the place bugged." He grinned.

"I'm talking about me." Derek thumped his chest. It was bad enough having people poke fun at him. He wouldn't have anyone look crossways at Keisha over something that wasn't her fault. "It's not respectful when she might, you know, hear."

"Oh, so you're a *gentleman* as well as a gourmet chef."

"I think you may be picking on me." Just because he'd hung out in his grandma's kitchen and developed a liking for cooking didn't mean anything. Plenty of manly men were great chefs. He seemed to recall many a day Shane had wandered across the apartment complex hall into Derek's place to hang with him and his grandma. Shane had ended up spending many an hour sitting at that table with a baseball in his hand while Derek and his grandma cooked.

Derek also remembered sounds of the fights echoing through the apartment wall. Those same shouting matches that had chased the kid into Derek's grandma's kitchen. The defensive expressions on Shane's face back when they'd been boys in the hills of Kentucky. The refusal to accept consolation. No discussion.

He could feel the wisdom of that now.

"Who me? Pick on you?" Shane palmed his chest in mock horror. "You think I'm the kind of guy to jab a buddy when he's down? I believe my feelings are hurt."

"I would feel bad about that but I'm too busy hiding out like the coward that I am when it comes to that woman."

"So you admit it." A full-out grin split the guy's Brad Pitt mug.

"Hell, yeah. I swear, if there had been a knife handy for that woman then, I'd be singing soprano now, if you get what I mean."

"Can't say that I blame her."

"That's why I'm hiding. If this were her fault, I'd take her on in a heartbeat. But I screwed up and she won't accept my apology. Nothing left for me to do except stay clear of her." Still, he wondered if she looked as hot as she had four years ago, lithe body, her braids falling all around him as he...

Damn it. There had to be something about leaving the moment unfinished that plagued him so.

Call him egotistical, but he wanted to soothe her *and* her feelings. He was a man after all.

"Fair enough. Damn shame you can't hang out at the beach and unwind."

"Sand *with* water—but no camels and exploding cars, you mean." For now.

"Yeah, I hear yah."

Derek wondered if Shane had tried the flowers. Probably that and more. Seemed silly to think about suggesting such a superficial fix for a huge problem. Not to mention he felt like a bum for whining over his problem when Shane had bigger problems. He should offer to help with those kids or something. "Screw worrying about me and something that happened years ago. You take care of yourself, pal. All right?"

Shane stayed quiet and pushed to his feet with a nod.

"Good luck." Derek called after his bud, a paltry offering. He'd been privy to enough four-beer discussions to know.

Women. They just weren't worth the pain.

He sagged back on the very comfy pillow he'd brought along from home, deep and feather filled, calling his name for some serious, much-deserved sleep.

Not even his stalwart grandma could pry his butt out of this tent.

"I'M SORRY IT COULDN'T BE, a better welcome home."

Sherry's soft words surprised Shane as they tucked their daughters in for the night in her camp tent, Spartan for the most part but with sweet hints of home. Two of Cara's spelling tests were taped to the tent walls along with caboodles of Malaika's artwork, jungle prints and birds for the most part. Damn good for a six-year-old, if you asked him.

He recognized the two well-traveled beanbag chairs—pink and purple—in the corner. The reading center. A stack of books between the furniture confirmed his memory. The girls had painted their names over their seats on the canvas.

And Sherry's satellite TV/DVD player perched on the small table to use for the girls' home schooling videos and sometimes for plain old movie entertainment.

He pulled his thoughts together and focused on the moment. "I didn't expect posters and such. This is good."

Damn good, just the four of them.

"Okay. Just so we're on the same page." She started to brush her hand along his arm—then her hand halted, hovering in midair between them in like an awkward aborted aerial maneuver. The moment finally eased and she turned away to sit on Cara's bedside, the room growing oddly silent. "Please don't stop singing just because I'm here."

Strange he hadn't even realized his daughter had been singing lowly. He'd been apart from them too much lately with all the rotations in and out of the Middle East. Taking his post beside Mally, patting her back while she finished those last moments of drifting off, he listened to Sherry talking with Cara.

"I'll hum along if you teach me the tune," his wife-for-now said. "Where did you hear that song?"

"I made it up." Cara bunched the sheet under her chin, her silky black hair fanning over the pillow-case.

He knew she loved to sing, but when had she started singing her own material? The thought kicked at his heart. The kids were changing too fast while he was away. "You make up your own tunes?"

"She sure does," Sherry answered. "She's been doing it for about a year now. But you know what? I don't think that's one of yours. Musicians are artists, just like Mally is an artist. When I look at a bunch of pictures, I can tell which one Mally drew in a heartbeat."

Cara scrunched her nose. "That's 'cause she always draws trees and families. Duh."

"Cara…. Is it your song?"

Her forehead scrunched as much as her nose, guilt stamped all over her face. "Sorry."

"I accept your apology, but I want to know why you lied."

Cara glanced at Shane with wide, tear-filled eyes. Her silky black hair brushed her shoulders, still damp from her bath, dampening the neck of her cotton nightgown.

"Daddy's not going to get you out of this one." Sherry looked to him for support.

He realized he didn't have a choice even as those glistening dark eyes bored a hole in his heart. He cleared his throat and put on his best "Dad" voice. "Where did you hear the song?"

"On the other side of the island." She rushed to add, "but I didn't leave Mally alone for a second. I promise. I kept her with me the whole time. We just played in the sand and 'splored a little. When we're at home you let us play in the neighborhood as long as we don't cross a street. We never crossed a street."

His gut did a total nosedive as Sherry paled beside him. It was all he could do not to bark that wild boars didn't cross the street either, but losing his temper like his mother on her bourbon wouldn't fix anything here.

First, he needed to right his stomach.

They tromped completely across an island? Alone? All out fear gripped his heart in a cold fist tighter than anything he'd felt this afternoon. He couldn't even find words to express his frustration, no small part of which he wanted to direct at Sherry and ask her where she had been. And remind her he'd been begging her not to haul their kids around the world.

None of which would help his hopes of an amicable divorce discussion.

"Cara, stop." Sherry held up a shaking hand. "You know you broke the rules of staying near the camp, so don't try to talk your way out of this. Right now I'm too scared of what could have happened to you two, I'm too upset to discipline you. I love you, but we will talk and there will be punishment. Do you understand?"

Big fat tears leaked from the corners of Cara's eyes. She trembled until the three of them launched into a hug so tight it damn well could have collapsed the whole tent around them.

Thank God the children were all right but what-ifs scrolled through Shane's head all the same. He could see the same scenarios mirrored in his wife's eyes.

A knock on the front tent pole jerked them from the intense moment. Shane looked around to see Keisha poke her head through.

"Hello, uh," she stuttered, blinking in obvious surprise, "I can come back."

Sherry shot to her feet, smoothing her shorts and double tank tops. "No, your timing's perfect. Shane and I need to talk now more than ever.

Thanks for offering to watch the girls. You're a life-saver."

"They're no trouble." Keisha swung her back-pack onto a table in the corner alongside Sherry's portable DVD player, apparently unaware of how squirrelly her two charges could be.

Yet since they were already in bed for the night, Shane decided they could be trusted to sit tight for now.

"Thank you for the help, Keisha. It's nice to see you again." He cupped her shoulder on his way past.

"No thanks needed," she answered with a re-serve that made it clear with yet another reminder. Her loyalty still lay firmly with Sherry, and he was in an icy cold enemy camp.

Derek was wise to stay in his bunk.

Shane closed the tent flap behind him.

Three long strides later he walked beside Sherry in the dark on the outskirts of the tent camp. Finally they could have "the talk." The divorce papers still waited in his flight bag but he couldn't see signing them on some rock. They were an unconventional couple, sure, but that was pushing things even for them.

He pressed a hand to her back and guided her around a flickering light pole on his way toward a small clearing by the camp's parking lot. He figured they could sit in one of the open topped Jeeps for their talk, safe and near the children. "Damn, it's a scary business bringing up kids. They're changing so fast. I wish I could have been around more to help you."

"I know you can't help the deployments, Shane. We both did the best we could. It's just…" She stared up at him with those cornflower blue eyes full of regret, except they'd both learned two trial separations ago, regret didn't equate with a solution.

Stopping by a rusty old Jeep, he held out a hand to help her step up. She eyed him for a long moment while the night beasties cawed and hummed in the jungle. Finally, she fit her hand in his and leapt up into the vehicle. He circled around and took the seat by her and sank inside with a heavy sigh.

It had been a helluva long day.

If he had his druthers, he would just sit here with his wife and stare at the stars while pretending the world hadn't collapsed in on them in some kind of cosmic rapid decompression.

Sherry shuffled next to him. "What's going on here, Shane? First the alarms to go to the bunker. Then your emergency landing with your plane all shot up. You can't convince me this is just some little training op." She jabbed him in the chest with a finger, her finger hooking ever so briefly on the ring wore around his neck yet not on his finger. "And don't you dare tell me need to know only. This involves our children on a major level, so I damn well need to know."

"*Our* children," he said, relieved at her wording.

"I wasn't sure you would think of them that way after the split."

"Oh Shane, you have to know those girls love you as much as any father from birth. You're more their father than Clint with his obligatory cards and occasional guilt visits now that he's totally obsessed with starting his new foundation. I know that."

Her ex worked in a "Doctors Without Borders" program and now headed his own group. Admirable. His daughters had reason to be proud, except they didn't even really know him beyond some vague uncle-like figure who refused to give up legal custody. Shane had discussed adopting them more than once… Certainly he loved them as much as any father.

He gripped the steering wheel, his thumb working absently along the notches in the leather to keep himself grounded. He needed to pace. But more than that, he needed to keep his tone non-confrontational. This was too important. "It's the legalities that put me on edge here, babe. I would fight to the death for them, but I'm not sure how far that fight would take me."

"You will be a part of Cara and Mally's lives. I promise." Those pretty blue eyes of hers seemed as honest and true blue as always.

He had no reason to doubt her. At least they always had honesty between them.

How much of a part of the girls' lives, he still

wanted to ask, but figured it was best not to press her now. Take it a step at a time and keep things as civil as possible.

Besides, he had another battle to win with her. Getting her to leave the island and her work here altogether. "You're correct in thinking today's incident wasn't a simple sort. I can't tell you everything—"

Her head thumped back against her seat.

He tapped her lips. "Hold your protest. I *can* tell you enough to satisfy your curiosity."

She shoved away his hand. "It's not some idle curiosity. It's a deep and important need to know for my family's safety."

"Fair enough." His hand fell back to rest against his knee. "It's fair to say these days that no one in the world is safe from the threat of terrorism. It's like a damn hydra. We chop off one head and it grows another in an unexpected place."

He'd gone damn far for her and he hoped she appreciated that.

"Who shot at you?"

He went with what the General had given the okay on, the part already hitting the news. Thank goodness there had been time for him to talk to her before she got to her portable television. "A cigarette boat full of terrorists tried to overtake a cruise ship, and we stopped them."

Her jaw dropped. Good old-fashioned dropped. Closed, then opened a couple of times before she finally spoke. "You make it sound simple, but ohmigod, these are the sorts of images that gave me nightmares the past five years. Are you okay?"

"I'm here. The crew's alive and the plane's in one piece. The guys who shot at us are gone. That makes for a good day."

"That's not what I meant. How can you just shake that off?" She gritted her teeth. "Oh, hell, never mind, forget I brought it up. We're just going to argue. What about these terrorists? Where are they operating out of? What's going on…"

He saw the realization dawn as he stayed quiet the longer she babbled.

"Damn," she whispered. "You can't tell me, can you?"

"I wish like hell I could tell you, but please trust me when I say you need to take the girls and go back to the States." He put everything he had into the words.

A sigh deflated her. "Well then, it's time for me to pack up my canteen and take my girls on home."

That easy? She was ready to go? And it hadn't escaped his notice that this time she'd said *my* girls. "That's it, Sherry? You're ready to leave?"

"Hell, yes. I like my head attached to my shoulders, Slugger." Her breathing went heavy, ragged, her hands fisting on her thighs. Did she even know she was pounding against her knees as she spoke?

"And no way am I letting one of those bastards get a hold of one of my children. I'm outta here. I'm the kind to educate and clean up. I'll leave the fighting to folks like you."

Talk about a hollow victory. Sherry and the girls would be on the first flight out in the morning, his time with them too short. He turned toward her.

The solitude of the moment wrapped around him, striking him with its rarity. With their hectic travel schedules, time together was scarce enough and they'd had children from the start.

He couldn't see shortchanging the kids, but he wondered if maybe somehow they'd shortchanged each other. "Keisha's a good friend to watch Cara and Mally while we talk."

"She is. The girls are worn-out enough, though, I think they'll stay asleep. Keisha can use the time to study."

"Study?"

"She's working to get her certification as a physician's assistant."

"That's great, really great." He shifted in his seat, really hating to add more fuel to an already combustive situation. "I should tell you something so you can give her a heads-up. Derek's here."

"You're kidding? How? I knew you'd been hoping he would cross train over to the CV-22…but…" She pressed the heel of her hand to her forehead and squeezed her eyes shut for a moment. "I mean, God, why didn't I see him get off the plane? I guess I was preoccupied looking for you…"

A bittersweet smile tugged at her lips and his heart before she continued, "That's just…crummy bad luck for them both at the end of a really crummy day."

"Yeah, pretty much."

He'd thought Keisha and Derek would be such a good match when he and Sherry had paired them up on a blind date. Derek's mom was a military nurse, Keisha an NGO nurse. Seemed like she would be the type of woman he'd grown up to respect and just the sort to help him get over the woman who'd dumped him.

Yeah, he hadn't spent a lot of time with his mom since she'd been in Vietnam, his Army father dead. Derek had actually lived most of his childhood with his grandma.

All a moot point since the Keisha-Derek thing had not gone well thanks to the one-word slipup.

"He's a copilot now, and it's great crewing with an old friend. I should have prepared you for the eventuality that their paths would cross again since we introduced them in the first place." No one would be looking to hire Sherry and him as matchmakers, not after the infamous debacle between Derek and Keisha. "I'm sorry if his being here is uncomfortable for her, but it really was just dumb bad luck. He only joined the crew last week."

"No worries. I'll warn her when I get back to the tent and she'll avoid him like the plague."

"The feeling's mutual. He doesn't want to do anything to upset her."

She turned to face him with a wry smile. "Too **bad** things aren't that simple for us."

"Remember the times we couldn't wait to see each other? When these months, weeks, even a handful of days apart were hell?"

"Of course I remember, but what good does it serve to hash through that now? You want me to be a happy homemaker wearing an apron in our white picket fence domicile so we can make the most out of all your free time."

"Hmm, if you were only wearing the apron…"

"Quit it." A smile flickered along her lips like the off-and-on light above them struggling to shine. "You're not going to distract me with sex."

"But you're tempted." His ego couldn't resist pushing.

The smile faltered away. "Chemistry has never been a problem with us, and it's unfair of you to use it against me now when we're both hurting."

"So what if I want my wife and kids home when I land. Is that a crime? I understand you have a career too, but there are options that won't take you to godforsaken wastelands that make it damn near impossible for us to see each other."

"Oh, you can save the world in desolate places, but I'm supposed to ignore my own calling to serve." The tension seeped back into her voice and shoulders. "I have done my best to work my schedule around yours, and it seems like I get precious little reciprocal help from you on that one."

"Take it down a notch." He patted the air. "I'm in the military. I don't get choices."

"And you give me none as well. Don't you see?" She batted at a persistent bug buzzing with extra force, the air crackling between them. "This is a circular argument? You're a strong man. You need a more passive woman. I can't be that for you."

"You make it sound like I want you to be a doormat."

"You said it." She faced him square on, her eyes not so flowery sweet at all right now, more like the hottest of blue flames. "Not me."

And like always he couldn't resist touching that flame regardless of how it licked at his skin. His hands curved around her shoulders and she didn't pull away—or move forward. Simply held him with the heat.

"God, Sherry…" He wanted to kiss her, ached to gather her up close and hard against him. The desire hadn't left no matter what other problems they'd gone through, probably why they'd managed to hold on this long.

He held himself stone motionless. He didn't really have a choice, not with those papers waiting to be signed. They'd gone too far, hurt each other too much. To backtrack would only bring them to the same place all over again.

Her hand finally drifted up to break the tense stillness between them. She slid her hand into the neckline of his shirt, hooking a finger on thin black rope that held his wedding ring and kept it there for a heated second before pulling away. "This whole day has set me on edge, Shane. I hate how I freaked in the jungle, but it really brought things into perspective, how vulnerable the girls and I are out here." She clenched her fists on her knees, inhaled deep in that way he knew meant she was gearing up to say something tough, really tough.

Her throat moved in a long swallow. "Will you please stay in the tent with us tonight?"

He blinked, certain he couldn't have heard her right. But her words exploded in his head with little after bursts that seemed to grow louder and louder until he could have sworn…

Shit. Realization hit him as fast as the widening of his wife's eyes. Those explosions were real.

Sherry's camp—where their daughters slept—was under attack.

CHAPTER FOUR

THE EXPLOSION ROCKED the ground so hard, Keisha fumbled with the book in her hands until it thudded onto the canvas floor. Her brain and survival instincts kicked in a second later.

The camp was under attack.

And she was responsible for the two precious children ripped from their slumber. Two little ones now shrieking in their beds.

"It's okay. You're okay." Keisha kept her voice low, soothing, even as she surreptitiously patted her 9mm in her waist holster, careful to keep the safety on around the children, but prepped to defend them if so called. She held out her arms. "Come here, Cara. Mally, you too. I need you to both be big brave girls."

She gathered their sweet skinny bodies close. Small. Vulnerable in their innocent scent of baby shampoo, with their bare feet and silky Dora the Explorer nightgowns.

Keisha guided them to the ground just as another explosion rattled the tent poles of their frail shelter.

"Girls, we need to stay low for a while." She

rolled all three of them under Cara's cot. "I'm going to take care of you, though. Your mama and your daddy will too when they get here. There's also a whole camp of soldiers outside watching over us."

She couldn't even let herself ponder overlong how vulnerable Sherry and Shane might be walking around out there in the open. Gunfire sputtered and she did her damnedest to stifle a flinch. She'd been there in the aftermath of the Iraqi war when volunteers were being shot at and snatched off the streets. Her coworkers had labeled her "nerves of steel nurse."

Why was she quaking now?

Because she'd only had herself to worry about. Heart tugging connections made a person damn vulnerable.

Cara hugged her sister. "I guess it's time for the quiet game again today?"

Thank goodness for perceptive children. "That's a wonderful idea and I promise treats when we're all done. Great treats."

Mally squirmed in her sister's tight grip. "Aunt Keisha, you always say too much sugar will rot our teeth."

Aunt Keisha. Her heart pinched again at how these girls loved her so much she'd become a surrogate family member. "Today's an exception—"

"Shhhhh." Cara shushed. "The game."

Right. Outdone by an eight-year-old.

The awesome weight of responsibility for keeping these two little girls safe squeezed around her in bands tighter, firmer, almost as suffocating as any all-over ace bandages.

She needed to reach deep for the woman inside her who'd excitedly toured the Amazon River and held a boa constrictor.

Explosions continued to whistle and burst outside, rattling the beams overhead, shaking loose dirt and a stray bolt. But so far their tent held firm. Best as she could tell from the noise, the attack stayed well to the right of them, over near the headquarters.

Where were Shane and Sherry? Would they dig in where they were? She doubted that. She imagined they were fighting to get back to their children, scared to death for their daughters.

But some things even a persistent parent couldn't help. Were they cut off from coming back?

Heaven forbid something had actually happened to them. She couldn't let her mind travel that horrific path. Not now. Such tragic possibilities could too easily radiate from her and stir the girls into hysteria. She had to keep steady for her young charges.

The tent rustled, near the front, the entrance flap.

Holy crapola. Her heart ka-thumped harder than when a zebra had charged her way during a safari. She hoped it was just Shane and Sherry, but still...

Her hand inched up to her waist where she kept her gun. She hated the thoughts of bloodshed in front of the girls. Such images could never be erased from their delicate memories. However staying alive came first.

"Mama?" Mally gasped.

"Shh," Keisha whispered. "We have to be sure it's the good guys. Okay? You have to be very, very quiet and very, very brave. No more talking now until I tell you."

The flap opened.

Lights flared in the background. Explosions. Mortars whistling. Gunfire sparking. A large man stepped into the opening, eclipsing the camp. A man a good two or three inches taller than Shane and a body more ripped with muscles than the lean father of the girls.

Who stood between them and escape?

Her heart thudded so loud she feared he could hear even fifteen feet away. She tried to make out his clothes, his features, anything. But with no lights inside and his body blocking the blazes outside... She couldn't discern anything other than that he seemed to be searching the tent.

He said something, but a staccato burst of gunfire muted his words.

She squinted. How odd to pray for another explosion that might leech enough light through the canvas for her to determine if she would have to shoot a man to death and destroy the innocence of two young girls.

A whistle sounded overhead. Oh God. Her wish

granted. A mortar. All her muscles tensed as she prayed it would land ineffectively in the middle of some trash dump.

"Shit," the man growled, low and gravelly, from the entrance. "Incoming!"

An *American* accent.

Keisha exhaled long. Hard. Gratefully.

The man, whoever he was, hit the ground, covering his head with both hands. He landed on the canvas floor right beside her. If he turned his head the least bit to the left, she would see his face.

The explosion rattled the ground again—along with her teeth. The battle inched closer this time. The girls screeched. She couldn't blame them for breaking their silence. She wanted to scream right along with them.

The man jolted at the sound of the girls' cries.

A brief peace settled in the camp, no more explosions or bullets. Temporary, surely, but a blessedly welcome moment to regroup.

Keisha hugged the kids closer and called out to the man, peeking around the edges of the quilt straggling off the edge of the cot.

She pulled a wobbly smile. "Uh, hello. I guess you were looking for us?"

Still flat on his belly, the man finally faced her full on.

No. No. No, her brain exploded with recognition of *the* man.

The *last* man she wanted to see, much less have rescue her. Because no way in hell did she ever want to be beholden to Derek "Rodeo" Washington.

The heartless son of a bitch who'd called her by the wrong name during the best sex of her life.

"KEISHA?" DEREK'S BRAIN went on stun. His eyes told him who he saw under the cot with her lithe body curled protectively around the two small children. "Keisha Jones, is that you?"

"*Now* you decide to get my name right?" Her eyes narrowed.

No forgiveness there.

Gunfire resumed outside. Rather poetic actually since theirs had been an ending full of fireworks.

A blast rattled the tent poles and reminded him of more important priorities. "This isn't the time or place for past agendas. Pass me Cara. We're under orders to evacuate to the camp."

She inched from under the cot, staying low. "What about Shane and Sherry?"

"Mama and Daddy?" Cara asked, her clingy younger sister apparently silenced with fear.

"They'll meet us at the plane, kiddo." He hoped. But this wasn't the time or place to lose time arguing. The weight of responsibility for his friends' family settled solidly on his shoulders. "Don't worry. We won't leave without them."

Keisha eased to her feet keeping the low crouch

and he realized she'd cut her hair. Her long beaded braids were gone, replaced by a short bob around her ears. What a strange time to notice hairstyles but this woman had always grabbed him right by the libido.

Definitely dangerous at this particular moment with the acrid smell of battle almost overriding the familiar scent of *her*.

He would ponder her chic new haircut and old perfume later.

Tucking Cara protectively against his chest, he urged Keisha toward the door, palm flat on her back. Her regal spine steely even in the middle of this fiery hell, years after he'd last touched her, somehow felt oddly familiar.

Double damn.

"Run," he shouted to her. To himself.

Mally squirmed, damn near climbing up Keisha's shoulder until she threatened to teeter and fall over. "My doll!" she screamed. "I want my doll... It's under the bed. Cara's got hers. I want mine."

Derek's hand shot up to palm her head and steady the child before she toppled herself and Keisha. "Hang on there, poppet. I'll get it. You're going to give Keisha bruises all over if you keep that up."

He bolted back to the cot and sure enough, a well-loved rag doll poked from under the haphazard covers trailing off the edge. He dropped the doll into Mally's outthrust hands and made solid, intent eye contact with Keisha for the first time in over four years. "Stick close to me."

As if it were "pack up time" he saw Cara grab some leather pouch from the table. He vaguely registered it as a DVD player. A DVD player for crying out loud! He needed to get them out of here before they started packing trunks.

At the tent entrance, he slapped the canvas flap open—to mayhem. The pungent burning smell doubled. Half the camp lights still worked, half shattered making visibility spotty in the night. People ran left and right and he wanted to shout orders, reminding them airplanes and Jeeps were straight ahead, but he would have to leave that to security personnel.

Gunfire still spat in the distance but the big explosions seemed to have waned. Could the enemy cache be depleted for now? God, he hoped so.

He saw a body on the ground ahead in the distance. Nearly in synch, he and Keisha pressed the girls' faces into their shoulders to shield their too young eyes from the death and destruction.

Whimpers sounded from the tiny child in his arms, but he couldn't deal with that now. He heard Keisha offering huffing words of encouragement as she darted from side to side making zigzagging progress toward the CV-22.

He scavenged for a reassurance of, "It's gonna be okay, kiddo."

Those words damn near choked him on the way

up and out. He really hated offering up platitudes when he couldn't be sure. His mother had been full of the rosy pictures before his father's deployments, then before her own deployments, as well. He preferred the barebones truth the way his grandma dished it up.

An ominous whistle sounded overhead. Shit. He looped his arm around Keisha and dropped them to the ground beside a Jeep. "Incoming."

Apparently the bad guys had found more mortars up their sleeves after all. Shit.

He covered Keisha and the girls as best he could, rolling them under the vehicle. Her body pressed against him for the first time in over four years— not in any kind of sexual way. Certainly not, since they had children in their care and could well get their heads blown off at any second.

Still he couldn't help absorbing differences in her beyond the simple cutting of her hair. She'd lost weight, lost some of her softness to be replaced with a lithe athleticism. He wondered how she'd gained it. In a gym? Running?

Who was her workout partner?

The explosion eased. Noise in the camp faded. A brief reprieve. He rolled back out and bolted to his feet, offering her a hand up while keeping Cara secure with his other arm.

His eyes locked on the open back hatch of the CV-22. God, how he hoped Shane and Sherry were already there waiting for them. His combat boots chewed up the last few feet of dusty runway between him and the humming aircraft, the engines already cranked and ready.

If his buddy hadn't made it here yet, how long could they wait? He didn't even want to think about abandoning them to an area under attack—likely from a terrorist group, the group General Renshaw had discussed, the same group attached to the pirates. Thoughts of seeing his friends' faces on the news as hostages...

He shuddered. Cara's arms tightened around his neck as if somehow this sweet little kid sensed his dire thoughts.

Derek waved up the back load ramp. "Inside. Strap both the girls in. We'll be leaving soon."

He couldn't ignore the low cries from the two kids, sadly sweet, barefoot in their PJs as they both clutched their matching dolls and asked for their parents. He cupped each face in turn. "I'm going to look for them. I promise. They wanted you to stay with Keisha, though, okay? This is what your mama and daddy want you to do."

With a final pat on each head, he turned to Keisha, only to find her eyes so surprisingly intent on him it took him back a step for an instant before he forced himself to continue with the critical business at hand. "I have to head up front and check with the crew. I can call in for intel.

Command post may have info, so we won't be running around blind."

"So you're flying these now."

She knew? Or she'd guessed? Too interesting to pass up.

Derek allowed himself a great big ole grin. "You talk about me to Sherry?"

"Your ego would like that."

Sure he liked the ego stroke of that a little too much considering this woman was from that deep in his past.

Damn. He was so busted.

"I need to go up front," he repeated.

Derek made tracks for the cockpit and his flight controls. The reliability of his world as a pilot. No worries about probing questions from a hot woman from his past.

Just the minor inconvenience of possibly getting blasted out of the sky.

PANIC POPPED THROUGH SHERRY with each snap of a bullet pocking the ground at her feet. Through sheer maternal will, she powered her muscles harder, faster, with one objective in mind.

Secure her children's safety.

Shane's powerful body loped alongside her and it dawned on her she likely held him back. "Go on ahead to the girls," she gasped through the stabbing pain in her side. "I'll catch up once you find them."

"We stay together." His clipped tone brokered no argument. He looped an arm around her waist, molding her close to his side as they ran.

"Damn it, Shane," she puffed. "Run. I'll keep you in sight. I promise."

"I know."

"Run. For the girls."

"I am."

"Then let go."

"Not a fucking chance."

He rarely used harsher curse words so she knew he meant what he'd said. He wasn't risking the two of them being separated. Her arguing was only stealing valuable air from their oxygen starved lungs.

Well, *her* oxygen starved lungs. Her athletic husband barely seemed winded. Still, somehow her feet picked up traction in the dusty, dark camp as they wound their way around tents and frantic evacuees. They were in this together *and* they would get the children, because Shane refused to consider any other option.

He was always right.

The ground beneath her feet shook. Ohmigod. Not just gunshots. Mortars.

Her husband launched against her, flattened her against a tree. Leaves and bananas rained down around them. A crack sounded above.

"Shane! Up there!"

"Got it." He hauled them both out of the way just as the tree split in two and fell to the ground.

He gripped Sherry's arm and took off again at a flat-out run again deeper into the camp, pausing to dodge around a… "Oh, no," the utterance tore from her as she saw the dead body sprawled on the ground. Someone she'd worked with, not a close friend but still a familiar face from the immunization staff, a precious life gone.

She lifted up a quick prayer for him as she forced her feet to keep moving until her corner of the compound came into view and she looked…

Where her tent should have been.

"No!" she shrieked. Her brain refused to process the devastation in front of her.

A collapsed structure. One corner scorched.

She clutched Shane's arm. Clutched her gut with her other arm over the hollow agony burning inside of her. Cara and Mally didn't have to have come from her body to be born from any deeper within her heart.

Sherry staggered forward, falling to her knees and clawing at the tent. Her body racked with gasping breaths. No sobbing. That would be like admitting her children had…

She refused to even think the word.

Sherry screamed the girls' names over and over again as she clawed at the remains of their temporary home of the past two weeks. "Cara? Mally?" She paused. "Keisha?"

In some dim portion of her brain, she heard Shane behind her, his voice hoarse, but she couldn't process his words. Her mind stayed locked on digging through the rubble to find her babies. A hint of a purple beanbag chair had her leaping forward.

Shane's hands banded around her waist. "Sherry, babe. Hold on a moment and let me try."

She blinked through the horrified haze as he plopped her on her butt. Another mortar exploded nearby. Her hands shot up over her head reflexively as she ducked in instinct.

Shane didn't even hesitate for the impending danger, thank heavens. What would she do without his help? Although then her heart rate stumbled over itself as she thought of his broad back making too easy a target. He flapped the fabric up in a whoosh of air, his teeth gritted as she prayed, hard, harder than the muscles bunching in his arms.

Huffing in gasps of acrid, war-tainted air, she scoured the fleeing masses around her, shouting questions to the people familiar and not, begging for word of her girls but no one knew anything. Still she clung to the hope that maybe, just maybe she would luck out and catch a glimpse of Keisha and the girls, alive, waiting for help. The loudspeaker blared evacuation instructions that almost managed to overwhelm the sound of airplane engines.

Airplanes. Ohmigod. They really were leaving—and soon.

Shane pivoted away from the mess of her tent
and dropped to one knee beside her. "Sherry,
they're not here."

Hope was so seductive. "Are you certain?"

"Yes." He said it with such surety she knew there
was no mistake.

If only that could guarantee their safety. "All
right. Let's get moving then."

He flipped his palm up for her to take and it
amazed her how quickly she began taking his hand
with ease again in a few short hours. Seconds later,
they were in the middle of the press of evacuating
bodies. Shane seemed to know his way, however,
even if he hadn't shared his destination with her.

The girls?

She truly believed he would have their interests
at heart. It wasn't often she let someone else take
the lead this way. It felt odd though, following. But
it also felt strangely—a relief.

The crowd began to thin as they neared the
earthen airstrip. Four aircraft lined the sandy
runway. He nodded toward the CV-22. "I'm almost
certain Keisha is already here. Derek is like a
brother to me. Once the attack started he would
have gone to the tent to check on the girls."

"Do you think?" That scenario sounded heart-
rendingly perfect.

"Yes, I do." He gripped her shoulders. "And if they're not there, then they're on their way and I'll go back to help them."

"With me—"

"Alone. This is where you load up."

"What?"

"Time to strap in. You've reached the evacuation point and you're wasting my time, lady."

He really expected her to just sit here and *wait* for someone to find her children? If so, the man had a serious screw loose in that handsome head of his.

"Damn it, Shane."

"Move it."

Forget the screw loose. He was too rock-headed.

Her lone ranger hubby had simply never thought to include her in the decision process. Simply issued the order and expected her to follow as if she were mindless. Yet another reason they'd broken up. She needed to be treated as an equal, not like a small child to be ordered about as though she didn't have any reasoning abilities.

She bit her bottom lip. Might as well check inside the plane first. They could be inside. And if they weren't? Then she would wait for Shane to leave before she searched on her own.

Purpose set, she trudged ahead, with Shane behind her.

Her feet carried her the last few yards to the

CV-22 and smoke from the last explosion cleared enough for her to see inside and find… Thank God.

Her daughters, smudged with dirt on their night-gowns but safely buckled in seats on either side of her best friend.

Sherry struggled not to fall to her knees right then and there. She had her daughters safe and sound, ready to return to the States.

How sad she would soon lose her husband.

CHAPTER FIVE

HIS WIFE AND KIDS WERE SAFE.

Shane settled deeper in the familiar comfort of his flight engineer's seat up front in the CV-22 and cursed the damned terrorists that had attacked the NGO camp. An NGO camp for crying out loud. A philanthropic group of do-gooders who wanted nothing more than to pass out vaccines and run a few classes on how to give your kid a better life.

What the hell happened to the time honored rules of engagement? Governments had disagreements. When diplomacy failed, warriors battled it out.

But this terrorist shit…

Fighting a ghostly enemy that didn't value human life, dignity… He couldn't wrap his brain around it. All he could do was put one boot in front of the other, day after day as the fanatic hydra sprouted more heads.

For today at least, he and his people had gotten all who wanted to leave out with only a few minor injuries. Those with wounds had been loaded onto the CV-22 along with Stones for Keisha to tend on their way back to the good old U.S. of A.

At least now they were in American airspace where he could breathe easier. They'd scrambled the crew together, and grabbed their flight suits, helmets and the rest of their flight gear with seconds to spare.

"Vegas?"

Hearing his call sign echo through his headset pulled him back to the present and his job—where he should be.

"Roger, Postal?" he answered his aircraft commander, Bobby "Postal" Ruznick, a wild-eyed, edgy fella who could milk maneuvers out of an airplane that never ceased to amaze Shane.

"I notice your family's all on the roster in back." No missing the interest in his voice. Postal was also a fun-loving gossip.

"Yes, sir, when they evacuated they ran here. Once the call came to leave, there wasn't time to shuffle them to another aircraft." Families weren't supposed to fly with their spouse on the crew— something about not having a whole family on board if something went to hell. "Frankly, I have to confess, with all that smaller arms fire filling the sky, you two are the ones I trusted most to get them out of there in one piece."

The moment stretched with how close they'd all come to losing everything—twice—in less than twenty-four hours. This new strain of terrorists weren't messing around.

He'd meant what he said though. Risk taking Postal and steady perfectionist Rodeo made a synchronistic match flying an airplane.

Rodeo keyed up his interphone mike. "Well, shit, Shane. You're going all sensitive on us. With all the love flowing here, next thing you know, Postal will start crying. You know how emotional he gets when we have crew movie night."

"Just because Gracie hauled my ass to the movie outing for the kids in the squadron, and I got a bit choked up when the Little Mermaid lost her voice…" He thumped his chest. "Damn near killed me when she couldn't sing. Of course Gracie's always working on making this wild man get in touch with his 'tender side.'"

Laughter rumbled through the headsets—a much needed release after the twenty-four hours they had. But Postal didn't seem to mind the ribbing a bit, apparently happily secure in his relationship with Gracie as well the sensitivity she wanted to tap.

Rodeo thumbed the mike key. "Honestly, those kid movies are tearjerkers. No shame in that." He paused. "How many hoops are you going to have to jump through before your fiancée sets the big date?"

"Gracie's a shrink. Very practical—needs all the

proper steps followed. We'll get there," he answered without the least waver in his voice. "I may be a jump feet first into the fire kind of guy, but getting this right is important enough to wait if that's what she needs from me."

And didn't that stab Shane clean through? If he and Sherry had taken more time to talk through a life plan before emotions ran too hot and high, might they have avoided this painful hell?

Perhaps then he would have a different call sign than Vegas. He and Sherry had loved each other from the start but there had been trouble fast, arguments, differing life plans. After the first trial separation, he'd gotten shit-faced drunk in a Las Vegas casino. Not too difficult since he rarely drank.

He'd woken up the next morning in the parking lot with no shirt and tassels on his nipples. His crewmates told him he'd given them all one helluva show when he'd danced on the table in nothing but his boxer shorts and the golden tassels.

Now every time he heard his call sign, he remembered how damn bad he and Sherry could hurt each other.

"Vegas? You with us, Sarge?"

His hands fell to rest in his lap. "Yeah. I'm with ya." The plane was flying fine. He'd checked and rechecked engine health and he had a backup flight engineer in the rear of the plane. He was free to stretch his legs if he wanted—take a break and get his head together. "Except if y'all don't mind, I'm going to check on my kids."

Postal winked. "Go for it, dude. But I'd be careful if I were you."

Shane's gut bunched. "What do you mean?"

"I saw your wife had her mini-DVD player out to entertain the kids. No telling what kid flick she's got playing now. Seems like they always kill off one of the parents and then I'm reaching for the tissues…"

Postal met his gaze dead on, holding, no sappy talk between guys, especially with a plane full of witnesses. That was as close as they would come to saying, *Hang tough. Don't let her trounce your heart again, dude.*

"I'll keep my eyes averted from the DVD players. No Kleenex needed, but thanks for the heads-up." Shane unstrapped and thumped Postal on the arm once in gratitude for the support.

Standing in the bulkhead, bracing for balance, he peered into the belly of the plane, taking in the all too touching tableau of his wife and daughters cuddled together, girls sleeping, resting on either side of their mother. Sherry cradled the DVD player, watching, tears streaking from her eyes over whatever she was viewing.

What an odd time to realize she never cried around him.

Beyond those tears of the moment, a deeper exhaustion stamped itself across her face. He burned to take some of that burden from her, but knew she wouldn't let him.

Her biggest flaw. She didn't know how to ask for help and he didn't know what to do for her.

She'd chosen a hard as hell life path for herself—saving the world, super mom, wife. Well, wife-for-now. He admired her. He just couldn't figure out how to live with her or give her what she needed.

He also couldn't seem to stay away from her.

Shane found his boots hauling his sorry butt down the center of the cargo hold, thud, thud, thudding with a metallic echo as he walked past Keisha tending wounded passengers. He nodded in her direction without pausing.

Finally, he reached his family, braced a hand on the cargo hold and allowed himself the luxury of just staring at them while the kids slept and Sherry stayed engrossed in whatever she was watching. He and Sherry had even discussed growing their family someday, when things slowed down. They would have a baby, maybe adopt a little boy as well.

Derek's grandma had been such a strong influence in his life, more a parent to him than either of his, he didn't need a blood connection to make someone feel like a family member. Derek and he had a brother bond no one could break.

Why couldn't either of them figure out how to build a family of their own?

Sherry stirred, jolting him out of the past as she snapped her DVD player closed.

Her eyes met his, all warm blue and weepy. She rushed to grab her tissues and swipe at her eyes, plastering a wobbly smile on her face.

The seat by Cara was empty and too easily he could drop down to sit with them. That was his right still, after all. But it would hurt damn bad when he stood up again.

So he kept his hand planted on the cool metal of the side of the plane and stayed standing where he could bolt back up front with the pilots. "Whatcha watching?"

Sherry cricked her neck from side to side. "I have a friend back in the States who sends me my favorite soap opera."

"You watch a soap opera?"

Her cheeks pinked. "Yeah. You have a problem with that, Sergeant Fan of Pro Wrestling?"

He held up both hands in surrender. "No problem at all." He lowered his hands and couldn't risk asking. "So why the tears?"

"Blair just found out that Brandon is really alive, well, he's really his twin brother Blade who's a better man than Brandon who…" She shook her head. "It's complicated and sappy and I'm totally addicted."

"Blade and Blair, huh? We could be a soap opera couple—Shane and Sherry."

Her cheeks went from pink to deep rose.

He couldn't stop a chuckle. "You've had that thought before."

She swatted his chest. "Stop teasing me. I may have entertained the notion when I met you."

Interesting.

And did she realize that she hadn't moved her hand from resting over his heart. Their eyes met, held. Her fingers curled, then unfurled. His muscles contracted in response to the caress.

She snitched her hand away. "I probably should have taken a nap like the girls, but now that everything has calmed down, I can't seem to unwind."

"That's understandable. These are unusual circumstances." How long had it been since they'd all slept? It had to be two in the morning. He nodded to the girls and gestured to the cargo hold. "This flight tonight is a once in a lifetime experience."

"What do you mean?"

"They usually don't let aviators fly their families around." Trivial chitchat, but even though he couldn't bring himself to sit with them, he didn't want to leave either. "There's some rule about it, but given the mayhem and the crisis… Like I said, these are unusual circumstances."

Her cheeks puffed with an exhale. "I'm glad to hear that. I would hate for this to be your normal workday."

A surprised burst of laughter rolled free. "Pirate ships? Not normal."

Camp catching mortar fire, well, that one had happened before, but he didn't want to overburden her at an already stressful time. At least they'd all left the NGO camp together.

As if she read his thoughts in one of those seamless marital moments, her eyes narrowed tightly on him while the plane hummed lowly in the background. "I already guessed that you were going to try and make me leave while you stayed behind."

He stayed silent. No need stoking her anger. He'd done the best he could in a hellish situation. After finding the tent remains empty of his family—thank God—the plane had been the next logical option. Not a chance would he have let Sherry walk away from there once he had her within the security of the airfield. And no way would he have left the island without his daughters.

But a wise man knew when to keep his yap shut.

"If the girls hadn't been in the plane." She cocked her head to the side, her blue eyes positively ice chips. "You would have gone so far as to force me inside and strap me down, wouldn't you?"

He knew his wife when she went cold like that, she meant business. Might as well pony up the truth. He'd won anyway and the kids were blessedly okay. He shrugged.

"I'm not upset at the decision, just mad as hell

that you didn't include me in the process. I guess I can still be fool enough to trust you."

Ouch. "You were right to trust me. I was keeping you safe and taking care of the girls."

"You could have told me. Maybe I would have agreed to your plan."

"Would you have gone?"

That shut her right up, but it was okay with him actually because he knew she was thinking. One thing they could always trust. They were honest with each other and right now she was weighing her answer to be fair.

She shrugged. "I don't know."

"Fair enough." He owed her equal honesty in return. "There wasn't time for discussion and I didn't want to slow things down by carrying you over my shoulder if I didn't have to."

A smile plucked at her lips. "Betty Crocker would have liked that."

He let himself enjoy the rare moment of humor between them, the rest of the people on the plane fading for now. "There you go taunting me with that apron image again. You're a wicked woman, Sherry O'Riley."

She rolled her eyes, gesturing a hand to her grimy jeans and sweat stained T-shirt. "Yeah right. That's me."

Once upon a beginning they'd laughed together

often. But the moment faded and their broken dreams, fights, resentments returned.

Except now he couldn't help but think muddy jeans and a stained T-shirt did nothing to hide her loveliness, her honey blond hair pulled back in a straggly ponytail that just made him want to sweep the stray strands back and caress her weary face. Sherry had a natural beauty that didn't need makeup or high-end clothes.

Shane broke eye contact and glanced over her shoulder a few seats behind her where Keisha stitched a cut over a soldier's eyebrow. He noticed Derek hadn't so much as glanced to the back of the plane since takeoff.

Of course if Derek did make an appearance, daredevil Keisha would probably take up parachuting as fast as they could all say *Komodo Dragon*. "I guess we don't have to worry about the two of them running into each other anymore after today."

Sherry gathered her sleeping daughters closer. "We owe them both more than we can repay for getting the girls here safely."

"Yeah." He really needed to talk to his buddy privately and see how that meeting had shaken down. They'd likely both been so preoccupied with protecting the girls and running for their lives, there wouldn't have been a spare second to discuss "rodeo" moments…but still, the face-to-face encounter couldn't have been pleasant. "I need to get back up front to the crew compartment."

Her features pulled tight with stress. "Are we out of danger now?"

They were never out of danger these days, but that answer didn't serve anyone any good. "It appears so, but I'll breathe easier once I have the three of you on U.S. soil again."

Except once they landed, there would be no avoiding the divorce papers. And they would be Stateside at Hurlburt Field—and that much closer to the courthouse for filing for an end to their marriage.

ALL HIS LIFE HE'D PLANNED to be the good guy in the white hat, save the day and win the girl.

However somehow he'd screwed his life up so badly there was no denying the truth. He'd stepped over to the black hat side and there was nothing he could do but pray he got through it without losing face—or worse yet, his life.

Right now, nobody would guess what churned in his mind as he mingled with his Air Force compadres on the flight line at Hurlburt Field while everyone unloaded from the harrowing evacuation from the Caribbean island. Thank goodness everyone was stateside again and he could move forward with his mission. He could get through this, damn it. He squashed down the pain and made his way toward base operations, wanting the hell out of these too bright halogen lights slicing through the night.

Now that they were back, they would take a break from flying and start their top secret D.I.T. Course—Directives in Terrorism Course. The class in counterintelligence and counterterrorism techniques where he would steal secrets and buy his life back. Finally, he could get this hellish nightmare past him once and for all.

He only had to become a turncoat. A *traitor.*

An icy shudder racked through him in spite of the stifling Florida heat steaming up from the tarmac. A traitor.

He'd done a dumb ass thing and gotten in over his head, no question. Never in any corner of his mind would he have expected himself to be a person who would even contemplate treason, much less actually commit it. Even worse, he'd never expected to betray his Air Force crew members.

But he was scared shitless.

These people who'd trapped him knew ways of tricking a person he'd never considered, and he'd been trained to be on the lookout for such things. He tried to console himself with the fact that he would only be passing along scant data. He would do his best to keep it as benign as possible, nearly outdated. However he was dancing close to the edge and these people cut off heads.

Damn it all, this should have been a low-key

time, taking a class, catching some rays on the beach. Most everyone Stateside. Life resuming a semi-normal pace. They would begin training ops, some flying.

But primarily the D.I.T. Course.

There were also representatives from everywhere from Great Britain to France to the Ukraine to Rubistan… The fifty-person class left plenty of room to have foreign friends as students and speakers. And sometime during the class someone from the outside would make contact. He didn't know when. He simply had to live his life waiting with his heart pounding its way out of his body.

He blinked back the sting in his eyes giving the stars an extra twinkle. Regardless of how simple they vowed this should be, he would be lucky to make it through alive. He didn't trust his connections. Once he gave them the information they demanded, he would have to get out of the military regardless or they would demand more and more from him. He wouldn't be able to simply resign or they would kill him. He would have to do something worthy of being discharged.

He'd started a list of possibilities right away. Top two? Dishonorable discharge by going AWOL. Except that would likely be transparent to the people pressuring him.

Which left only one option that he could see.

He would have to stage an accident. He would

have to maim himself in such a way he would be medically discharged. Nausea roiled at the thought of the inevitable pain. Surely though it couldn't be worse than what he felt inside right now.

And it was nothing in comparison to the agony these people would inflict on him if he didn't do what they wanted. He had to accept the reality of his situation.

He entered the Base Operations building with none of the normal feeling of homecoming. Just a sense of dread for what waited in the next two weeks.

He'd fucked up. He'd made himself vulnerable and now he'd been compromised by the enemy. This was the only way he could see to stay out of jail—or out of the sights of a firing squad.

CHAPTER SIX

"KEISHA!"

Marching across the tarmac toward the base operations building at Hurlburt Field, Keisha wondered how she could have done such an amazing job at erasing that bourbon smooth masculine voice from her memory, and now, she recognized him with just one word. Four flipping years. He should be nothing more than an unpleasant blip on her emotional radar.

Or wait. She needed a better analogy, because yeah, she wanted to get this just right. He was nothing more than a *splat*—an obnoxious bug splattered against her windshield and cleaned away at the nearest car wash.

Of course he had helped save the girls' lives. She owed him a thanks for that. She slowed her steps, her body taking that adrenaline let-down moment to remind her just how exhausted she was. She'd been awake for what felt like a century. Tended more patients than she could count. Briefed their cases to the physicians here.

She wouldn't mind curling up to sleep on the concrete if people would promise to step over her.

Pivoting, she faced Derek Washington. He didn't look tired at all, damn him. In fact he appeared lean and fit and sexy in his flight suit, that same sexy bod that had lured her into his bed, but with four more years of maturity and muscle.

This would be the fastest "thank you" on record. "Thanks for your help back there in the camp. I would have had my hands full getting both girls out on my own."

His eyebrows made a mad dash for his hairline in shock.

She huffed. "What?"

"I didn't expect you to admit you needed my assistance."

"I'm not an idiot." *Uh, hello? Make that a fast thanks. Remember?* "Thank you again. I'm glad you weren't hurt sticking your neck out for us. Nice seeing you again. You take care now. Bye-bye."

Fanning her fingers in a farewell wave, she spun away striding past a couple of the other crew members. Oh yeah. She was on her game. She'd shown Derek. With an extra swish to her walk she hadn't expected to find in her tired body she strutted right on toward the base operations center again.

Sherry and Shane were ahead of her, each carrying a limply sleeping child, the halogen lights illuminating the sweet scene. She didn't want to interrupt their rare family moment so she slowed her pace a step or two. Sure Sherry said they were headed for divorce, but as far as Keisha was concerned, she hadn't seen any ink on those contracts yet. She would be giving them both space and toss in some free babysitting if she could figure out how to sneak it past without them realizing her agenda… All important stuff to put on her to-do list.

But for now, she wanted to savor her victorious moment in getting the one up on the first non-life threatening moment of today's reunion with her "most mortifying incident."

"Keisha," he called again.

He expected her to keep right on turning around?

Except it would seem odd if she didn't but…. She walked and thought and, well, swished for her own ego's sake. Then lucky for her, Derek pulled up alongside her so she didn't have to make a decision.

She did, however, stay silent and waited for him to talk rather than accidentally wading into dangerous waters when maybe he only wanted to tell her something like she had toilet tissue stuck to her shoe. "Yes?"

"How are you going to get home? Unless you plan to ride with Shane and Sherry in his four-seat Jeep."

Oh.

Shit.

There hadn't been time to grab her backpack when they'd evacuated. She had no keys to her car. She looked ahead and saw no signs of Sherry and Shane. Keisha's head flopped back and she stared up at the stars, the late night moon full and damn but she could swear it was mocking her with a smirk.

The larger cargo plane with the rest of the NGO workers wouldn't be landing for another couple of hours. Everyone else on this plane had either been sent to a hospital or had already sprinted out while she tended the wounded. They'd been lucky to lose only the one casualty, although even that loss of life left her soul weary. Damn it, they'd all been through enough for one day.

She could call one of those services but it would take hours. Hopelessness washed over her bushed body.

Where was the spirit of the woman who'd gone snowboarding in the Andes? "I'll call a friend."

"I'm sure she'll be overjoyed at the 3:00 a.m. wake up." He loomed over her by a good five inches, a rarity for her that caused her to stand tall and go on the defensive.

"Or *he*."

That stalled Derek's long strides for a pace and a half. "My apologies for the assumption. You're right. Any fella would be more than happy to wake up to a call from you."

Ah, man. He was being nice now. From the tone of his voice it sounded flat out genuine too. Not the B.S. kind of flattery. Pure, good guy stuff.

"There's no guy right now." Why had she admitted that? She should have just risked the wrath of her next-door neighbor and let this whole conversation with Derek end now. They were at the base operations building anyway.

"Keisha." His warm chocolate eyes almost lulled her weary body to sleep as surely as the melodic tones of his voice. "We all almost died tonight, the crew members, too. I think in light of that, we can set everything else aside for the short time it would take me to drive you home. What do you say?"

She looked around her at the rapidly dispersing crowd, civilians and military, all fleeing like birds from the shoreline when a dog came yapping along. She liked that image because it made her comfortable to think of Derek as a dog after how he'd hurt her.

Okay, that image firmly planted in her mind, she was safe enough from temptation to climb in a car with him.

"I say, yes and thank you very much for the ride." Her lips curled in a wicked smile. "Hope you don't mind, though. My home is about an hour away, in Pensacola."

HOME.

As much as she loved to travel, Sherry had to admit, home looked amazing tonight. Not much of a home, actually.

She stared through the windshield of the car at the tiny place she and the girls had only rented a short while ago in Navarre, a beach town halfway between Hurlburt Field and Pensacola. Shane cruised his Jeep to a stop in front of an aqua colored condo, part of a fourplex, each unit a different color in standard bold Florida style.

Shane slid the vehicle into park. "You've moved again."

Who'd have thought her totally drained body would have enough energy to go on the defensive? "The unit has a heated pool and it's near the beach and the zoo. Of course the girls have seen most of the animals up close for real and outside of cages, but still, they enjoy it."

The engine idled in the driveway, both children asleep in the back, Mally even snoring slightly in her exhaustion.

Shane shut off the car and pocketed the key. "The girls have been moved around a lot with military life."

Why was he doing this to both of them now? "Yeah, well, when we split last year, we had to give up the house on base."

"That was a tough one, coming back and all your things were gone."

Damn it, she was all for assuming half the blame, but she wouldn't take the culpability for everything. "Shane, that was the way you wanted it.

You told me it would be easier if I packed up and left before you got back. You said you couldn't bear to watch me and the girls drive away."

"I know." His mouth curved into a bittersweet smile in the moonlight. "Then I found out there wasn't an easy way."

"So we tried again." And bombed.

"I like this place, the neighborhood." He gestured to all the bikes, basketball hoops and swingsets. "Lots of kids for the girls to play with."

She couldn't help but ask, "Is that a dig at my homeschooling?"

"No. Absolutely not. You know I support you in that a hundred percent." Whenever he was in town he even pitched in with some of the lessons. It was her traveling he objected to.

"Okay, sorry to get my back up." They'd fought so often lately it seemed to become a habit to go on the defensive. How many times had they misread each other's intent because their natural inclination was to assume the worst?

On nights like tonight, it was difficult to argue with his reasoning about her keeping the girls in the U.S. all the time even as much as she tried to tell herself this whole thing had been a fluke. Good God, they lived in a place where many people vacationed. They could have just as easily have been there with the girls for Easter break or some other holiday.

He reached across the seat and toyed with a loose lock of her hair. "We're both exhausted." He stroked the strand behind her ear. "Let's unload the kids, then I'll hit the road and find a room back on base."

"You don't have an apartment?"

"My deployments have been nearly back-to-back. It was cheaper to crash with friends or get a temporary room at Hurlburt."

No home at all? He'd spent time with the children over the past year, but she'd never realized he didn't have an apartment to take them back to. They'd always logged the day playing—water parks or mini-golf or an amusement park a few hours away.

The urge to invite him to stay burned strong, just on the sofa of course. They couldn't share a bed without the risk of more happening and if more happened…

Her heart hurt even thinking about it. They'd made the decision to go through with this divorce. After so many reconciliations only to have her soul torn apart by yet another breakup, she was done. They were done.

Come to think of it, even the sofa could be dangerous.

She opened her Jeep door and reached for the back where Mally snored away. Scooching forward the front seat, she unlatched the back seat belt and scooped up her limp daughter.

Her limp, damp and too warm daughter.

Alarms went off in her head. "Shane, I think Mally has a fever."

He peered at her over the Jeep's black bikini-top. "Are you sure she's not just sweaty from being curled up asleep?"

She skimmed her hands over her little girl's forehead and then her belly. "Possibly, but I really don't think so. How's Cara seem?"

Shane ducked inside and came back up, Cara secured to his chest, her head lolling on his shoulder. "She's cool as a cucumber."

A pinch of relief took the edge off her worry. At least both her girls weren't coming down with something.

Yet.

Shane hitched Cara higher and made tracks toward the door. "Let's get them both inside and check with a thermometer."

She nodded and followed him up the curving paver stones walkway until they reached her salmon pink door. "The extra key's under the third stone."

"Got it." Shane knelt, securing Cara with one hand and flipping the circular decorative walkway rock with the other. He plucked the key from the dirt and dusted it off on his flight suit before inserting it into the front door. "Do you have an alarm system?"

"Yes. Don't worry. I'll get the code." She shot past him, her youngest child clutched to her chest. Was it her imagination or was Mally growing hotter?

By the kitchen door, Sherry stopped at the code box and punched in the numbers—their anniversary. Damn it, she needed to change the numbers.

Her mind shifting to mega-mommy-mode, she took Mally to her little bed where she could rest and rushed to the bathroom medicine cabinet. Seconds later she pressed the thermometer band across her daughter's forehead and watched the reading rise to...

103.6 degrees.

"Shane," her voice wobbled even as she popped open the bottle of children's Tylenol she'd brought with her just in case.

He rushed from across the hall, from Cara's room—easy to guess the girl's room since they had their names on the doors in the wooden letters, pink on Cara's, purple on Mally's. "The verdict?"

"One hundred and three point six." She slid a hand under Mally's head and lifted ever so slightly. "Come on, sugar. You need to wake up for just a second and chew these."

"Nuh-uh." Her tired and grumpy daughter rolled

away, burrowing under her Dora the Explorer linens. "Wanna sleep."

"I know, I know. And you can very soon. As soon as you do what I asked."

Mally curled up in a ball and shoved her face under her pillow.

Shane sat on the other side of the bed. "Let me give it a try." He scooped up the fractious groggy one and put her in his lap before holding out his hand for the pills. "Mally?"

Their daughter peeked up. "What, Daddy?"

"I'm sleepy, too." He stretched in an over-wide yawn that went on and on as he patted his gaping mouth.

Sure enough, Mally yawned too and "pop, pop," Shane rested the chewable tablets on her little tongue. Mally snapped her mouth shut with a woozy grin and chewed before snuggling back to droop against him.

Sherry shook her head. "That's cheating."

"It worked."

"You're lucky she didn't bite your fingers."

"I was willing to take the risk." He stared around the room decorated with Dora accessories and a beanbag chair reading center in the corner like at the tent. Except here she'd added a purple netting to surround the beanbag chair. "What do we do now?"

"Wait for her fever to go down some before I go to sleep." Sherry swung her legs up onto the bed beside Mally. "Then I'll set an alarm to make sure we don't sleep through giving her more medicine."

Shane dropped onto the purple beanbag chair. How he managed to pull that off and still look mega-hot, she would never know. "Sherry, you have to know I'm not leaving, right? I can't leave you here without a car, not with a sick kid. And honestly, I don't want to leave my sick child. I'll sleep on the sofa, but—"

"Stop. Of course you can stay." She was wiped out and quite frankly didn't trust herself not to drift off if she didn't have some relief. "We can take turns checking on her. I appreciate the help. When it comes to her welfare, I want what's best."

"That's it?" He crossed his long legs in front of him. "No fight?"

"I know we argue a lot, but I'm not that unreasonable. Come on, Shane. I'm too tired to fight with you." She waved him toward the hall. "Go shower or something. You can have the sofa. You can even have the master bedroom if you want. I'm going to stay in here on the trundle."

He simply stared at her without budging from his purple throne. She knew that stubborn look. He was going macho on her.

She formed a T with her hands. "Truce. Compromise. I'll shower and change first. But you sleep first. Deal?"

Narrowed eyes, not certain if she believed him

or not. But Mally was set for the moment and a shower sounded heavenly... "Sure, babe. Deal."

She shoved to her feet and padded down the hall to her bedroom. And okay, she jumped under the shower to make sure she didn't expose her daughter to any extra germs. None of this had anything to do with looking fresher for her husband.

Her almost ex-husband.

No letting her mind wander to times of sharing showers with Shane. Definitely no wondering if he was listening to the shower and wondering about her naked inside.

Surely he was too tired for that.

She patted herself dry and changed into her most modest pair of sleep pants and a Navarre Beach T-shirt.

"Sherry," Shane's voice reached to her from across the hall with an unmistakable urgency. "Call 9-1-1. Mally's having convulsions."

CHAPTER SEVEN

SHANE HAD FACED DEATH more times than he could remember and sure, it always shook him. But nothing had rocked him harder than seeing his little girl go into convulsions.

Even having the security of the Emergency Room around them now didn't lessen the fear in his gut since they still didn't have a diagnosis. He paced in the exam room while Sherry sat beside Mally lying limply on the bed.

The wait for the EMTs had been interminable even though the ambulance had arrived before her convulsions ended. He and Sherry had sat on either side of her bed, damn near helpless, the phone clutched to his ear while the operator tried to give instructions and maintain calm. Basically: keep Mally from hurting herself by rolling off the bed or hitting her head.

Sherry had used her cell to call Keisha in case her nurse friend could arrive sooner than the EMTs. Keisha—and oddly enough, Derek—had pulled into the driveway just as the emergency technicians loaded the gurney with Mally strapped on into the ambulance. Mally's convulsions had stopped by then, leaving her flaccid. Awake but nonresponsive.

The whole thing had lasted less than ten minutes. Ten minutes of hell.

Sherry had ridden to the Emergency Room in the ambulance. He'd followed in the car with Derek—who'd insisted he'd better drive. Keisha had stayed with Cara in case she got sick as well.

Thank God for friends.

Now, pacing in the ER exam room with Sherry sitting next to their still droopy child, Shane had to move or every bone in his body would rattle. His teeth would chatter. He might well punch a wall and break a few of his rattling bones. Instead he forced steady breaths in and out, air laden with antiseptic hospital stench.

The pediatrician would be back in soon. Meanwhile, a nurse monitored Mally's vitals quietly from the corner. Nothing seemed like enough because they didn't have conclusive answers.

The doctors were fairly certain it was just what they called a "febrile seizure"—a fever seizure. Sometimes a regular flu bug caused a fever to spike too high, too fast for the body to handle so the brain shuts down non-mandatory functions—a seizure ensues until the temperature lowers.

However, if Mally didn't perk up soon, they

would do a spinal tap to rule out more serious ailments—like meningitis.

Damn. The world narrowed to this room and their sick child.

Sherry held Mally's tiny hand and stroked the top again and again, as if afraid of touching any other part and risking hurting her since they had no idea what was wrong. "She's had all of her immunizations. I'm hyper-vigilant about that because of the places we travel. Neither of the girls has missed a well-baby checkup, or an annual checkup now that they're older. I have Keisha look them over anytime I think there might be the least little possibility of a sniffle."

The elderly nurse looked up from the chart, a tiny teddy bear pinned to her white cardigan. "Sweetie, nobody said this is your fault."

"I'm her mother. I can't help but wonder if I missed something." Sherry shifted her attention to him, dark shadows staining weary half-moons beneath her eyes. "Look how sick she is and just yesterday afternoon I had her outside playing in the ocean."

Could it already be morning? Grit stung his eyes more than the alcohol scent hanging in the air, but yeah, the sun was probably about ready to make its way to the Florida horizon.

He stopped on the other side of the exam gurney. "And just yesterday afternoon she played with endless energy and no signs of fever. I was with her there. Are you going to blame me, too?"

Sherry scraped her hand over her ponytail still damp from her shower. So much had happened in such a short time. "Don't play word games with me right now. I'm too tired and scared."

"No games. Just the truth. Children get sick, babe. This is not your fault or mine, but we do have to deal with it."

The nurse nodded in sage agreement from her corner before taking Mally's temperature again. The numbers flashed on the screen *one hundred and one*. Still ill, but not frighteningly high. "You got the Tylenol in her and helped bring the fever down. You got her here quickly. You did all the right things."

Thank goodness Keisha was at the house with Cara. Keisha had promised to give Cara a physical and make sure she hadn't picked up whatever bug her sister had stumbled upon.

Shane reached to cover his wife's hand with his own over their kid's. "That means conserve our energy—not waste it by casting blame. Okay?"

"All right." She nodded with a quivering chin. "I'll try."

Mally's head lolled to the left on her pillow toward Sherry, the paper beneath her crackling. Her tiny mouth worked with mumbling sounds. Everyone in the room stopped breathing, stopped moving even as they waited.

Garbled sounds stuttered out, but Mally's lashes fluttered just a little. God, he hoped this bit of rousing was as big a hopeful sign as he needed it to be.

The moment of inaction snapped and the nurse hurried to check vitals. Sherry nailed the call button with her thumb repeatedly, shouting into the speaker for the doctor, tears filling her eyes for the first time since this nightmare had started, even if she held back those tears from falling. His wife never let tears loose except for her television shows when she thought no one was looking.

Mally's arm flopped over toward him, grappling for his hand just as the door swung wide with a doctor and another nurse.

"Mama? Daddy?"

Sherry's watery eyes met his over the exam table with such relief and beauty that Shane found himself groping behind for a chair. Had to be adrenaline letdown and relief over Mally's rousing.

Not a driving need to comfort Sherry, to be by her side no matter what, not an irresistible draw he'd never felt to any other woman.

DEREK HAD DONE HIS BEST to be polite to Keisha earlier.

Sitting in the ER waiting room cradling his fourth cup of crappy coffee, he replayed the car ride with her and wondered what he could have done differently to make the thing go more civilly. He'd offered the woman a lift home, for Pete's sake. Of course there really hadn't been a choice unless she wanted to call a cab.

So he'd offered her the comfort of his SUV when he was dog tired and the whole time Keisha had done nothing but ignore him, staring out the window. She couldn't even be fucking polite. Damn childish, in his opinion. He couldn't imagine what he'd seen in her in the first place, beyond the sexual. And he liked to think he was the kind of guy who slept with a woman he liked, as well as wanted.

Their drive down highway 98 to Pensacola had been eerily abandoned, no beach traffic, the hour late and dark, the view intermittent with patches of beach and subdivisions with palm trees down the median while the string of tiny towns slept.

Then the panicked call had come about little Mally.

Hell. That made everything else seem petty in comparison. He'd only just passed Sherry's place in Navarre, so they'd pulled a U-turn and rushed back to the O'Riley condo. Keisha had stayed to watch Cara in case she took sick too, and he'd driven Shane over.

Hours ago. He glanced up at the industrial clock on the wall. What was taking so long? That couldn't be good. Derek finished off his lousy hospital coffee from the machine in the corner.

He had been parked in the ER waiting room

couch for at least a couple of hours—drifted off a little in spite of the java jolts of caffeine. Damn, what a long and strange as hell day and a half starting with pirates, add in the hottest woman from his past...

The click of an exam room door jarred him from a dream of long braids and even longer legs. He scrubbed his hand over his face to swipe away the sleep. Heaven forbid any lingering images might be mirrored in his eyes.

Shane strode toward him.

Derek bolted upright, prepping himself to support his friend through the worst if need be. "How's Mally?"

He crushed the cup in his hand, a hint light-headed from holding his breath. Hell. But then that little moppet—his goddaughter—meant a lot to him, kind of like a surrogate kid since he planned to wait a while before having any of his own. Derek had been surprised when they'd asked him to stand up for the kid. He'd assumed she'd been baptized during Sherry's first marriage, but she said there really hadn't been time. Her first husband had left soon after baby Mally's adoption.

And then at the baptism he'd met Keisha...

He shook off the past and forced himself to breathe before he passed out and made himself a big old hindrance to everyone rather than a help. "So? The doc's verdict?"

"They think she's going to be fine. The mix of Tylenol and Motrin seems to be controlling the fever." Shane sagged to sit beside him. "The doctor believes she picked up some bacteria, maybe from a strange food or something left out too long. Who knows given all the things they come into contact with on the island. He's prescribed her a heavy dose of antibiotics, but she should be past the contagious stage."

Not the worst, but still… "Sounds like scary shit to me."

"Scary shit pretty much sums it up." He exhaled, scrubbing a hand over his eyes then his head looking so worn-out Derek wondered if his buddy might nod off like the elderly man two seats down sitting beside his nurse's aid. Shane's hand fell to his lap and he blinked, clearer. "Mally's perked up though, so they're going to let us leave. Sherry's finishing the discharge paperwork. We should be going in about twenty more minutes."

Derek shook his head, those dreams still lingering, taunting. "Times like this make me glad I'm not a parent yet."

Shane shook off his exhaustion long enough to pin Derek with a piercing stare. "Speaking of your lack of attachments, what are you doing hanging out with Keisha Jones in the middle of the night again?" Shane hooked a foot over his knee and lounged back. He might be running on fumes but it appeared he could still play guardian angel for his wife's friend. "Last time you yanked her around may have been an accident, but if you do it again, I'm going to be honor bound to hurt you, dude, all officer/enlisted stuff aside."

Derek stared at his hands clasped between his knees weighing his words carefully—a sad state between friends who'd always laid it all out there, no-holds-barred. "She needed a ride home, and the O'Riley gang had already loaded up and pulled out."

"That had to be awkward for you both."

Derek snorted and lounged back in the vinyl covered chair— Did they make this furniture so damn uncomfortable with the express purpose of giving a person a bad back to drum up business? "Not awkward at all since she promptly turned her head toward the window and pretended to sleep until the phone rang with your S.O.S. call." He took in his friend's dog-tired face. They'd been through tough times, heavy combat, but he'd never seen Shane this worn down. "You and Sherry need to get some sleep. Is there anything I can do to help out?"

"Thanks, but you've been up as long as I have. We both started this day at the same time."

"I don't have kids to look after today. I'll rack all afternoon, no problem." He couldn't help but think of how difficult it had been for his parents to juggle their dual military careers with parenthood, the price they'd all paid in rarely seeing each other. Whole family outings were virtually nonexistent. No. He figured he would wait until after retirement for the family gig. "I'll be all rested up for the start of the D.I.T. class, but what about you?"

A half smile dug into his face while a nurse's cart rattled down the hall. "I'll be like any other father in there. How many do you think walked the floors with a colicky kid or dealt with a child's nightmares? Comes with the territory."

"You're making single sound good—" Derek stopped short, realizing what he'd said, given his friend's marital troubles. "I'm sorry, dude. I wasn't thinking. Actually, I was wondering if you had any advice for how I could make Keisha talk to me again."

Shane's eyes went wide with shock while the hospital's PA system paged a doctor to the maternity ward. "You don't actually want to get back together based on seeing her again just once?"

"Hell, no," the words fell out fast and sure. Real sure. He thought so, anyway. "Now that I'm living here and I'm a friend of the family she and I are going to see each other. Makes sense it would be better if things weren't…so tense between us."

"Fair enough." Shane shrugged as the entrance door swooshed to admit a couple, one cradling his arm carefully as they headed for the sign in desk. "Why not try some flowers?"

"What do you take me for? A dunce? I went that route right away—a dozen red roses delivered the morning after, well, you know." Shit. His face felt hot. "She threw them at me. Good thing I ducked and the vase shattered against the wall instead of my head. I thought I told you that."

Shane's face twitched with a stifled grin, the traitor. "Why not try again? More time has passed. Feelings aren't as intense."

Hmm. He didn't know if he agreed with that. Things surely felt mighty damned intense for him. He allowed himself a quick "what if" moment, as in, *what if they'd just met?* And actually...

He would send her flowers for real, not for forgiveness. She was a hot, fascinating woman he hadn't even begun to understand.

Except even the whole "rodeo" incident aside, when he looked at his parents' mess of a marriage and Shane's falling apart relationship, he should know better than to go after someone too like himself.

So he would send "I'm sorry" flowers. As much as he might wish otherwise, he definitely wouldn't be sending Keisha any "Hey there, baby" roses.

SHERRY HITCHED HER BABY girl Mally higher on her hip. Of course her six-year-old could walk just fine and she was a bit heavy to carry. But after the health scare they'd had the day before, Sherry felt the need to hold on to her youngest daughter that much tighter as she walked out of the Hurlburt Field Medical Group clinic. Cara shuffled along silently beside her, sucker in her mouth.

Sure the emergency room doctor had reassured them Mally likely only had picked up some kind of bacteria—albeit one he'd never seen before. He'd also told her to bring Mally to the pediatric clinic for a follow-up visit the next day.

Even the pediatrician had deemed Mally on the road to recovery. The fever was gone. Whatever mysterious bacteria had caused it had apparently been trampled by their daughter's healthy immune system.

The resiliency of youth never failed to amaze her.

Thankfully, the doc had even taken a quick peek at Cara and she seemed totally fit too. Her sister's bug had left her untouched. Both girls took their lollipops—which kept their chatterbox mouths blessedly occupied and silent for the moment. Sherry appreciated the quiet moment, her heart heavy with hours of hearing about wonderful "Daddy-this" and "Daddy-that." But oh God, he'd been such a rock of support during Mally's seizures. What would she have done without him?

Sherry made her way toward the exit, the door swished open to release a blast of heat from the sweltering Florida summer. She'd made the twenty-minute trek out to base for the doctor appointment, it would be petty not to let the girls say hello. As hard as it was to see him now with their marriage in ashes around her feet, she couldn't deny him the chance to hear the good news about the girls' health as soon as possible.

After she'd loaded up the girls in her minivan and driven over to the squadron, she dialed her cell phone and let Shane know they were outside waiting…if maybe he wanted to join them for a drive-thru meal?

She tried to quell the odd thrill in the pit of her stomach over seeing him. It must simply be a product of all the high drama of the past days leaving her feeling in need of the comfort of his presence. Ah hell. Who was she kidding? No matter how many fights there had been or would be, she'd loved him enough to marry him once. He adored her daughters. She had to face the fact that Shane would always hold a place in her life.

The hard part would be in learning to set the boundaries.

Seconds later, Shane cleared the door and stepped into the parking lot. The man really ought not to be let out during daylight hours. It wasn't fair to adult females the way the sun played with the different colors of gold in his closely shorn hair.

She didn't even let herself think about the way his muscles filled out the flight suit in all the right places. All of that simply wouldn't be wise to her hormones, over-revved from living under the same roof with the man. Taking care of a sick child had kept them both blessedly exhausted.

What would they do now?

She opened the car doors and let the girls run across the lot to meet him.

"Careful," she called as they sprinted.

"Hey there." He held out his arms for both of them to race and jump onto his boot to stand on it for a ride. "How are my girls?"

"All better now, Daddy." Mally garbled through her sucker.

Cara crunched hers, grabbed the stick and answered, "I'm not sick at all and we both got suckers."

"Yeah," her sister interrupted, "We're going to get Kids' Meals with you, right? Right? Huh?"

"That's right." He scruffed a hand over each of their heads, his smile so wide it tore a fresh hole in Sherry's heart.

Even with exhaustion marching across his face and accenting every line earned by thirty-four years of living and fighting wars, his never-failing gentle side with their kids still touched something inside her.

As she stood off to the side, the front door to the brown brick building swished open again—but no Air Force guys swaggered through this time as she'd expected. Instead an older teen in a floral shop uniform came from the squadron and walked toward his white van. A wiry young man—around college age—made his way toward them and there was no mistaking his frazzled air. He clutched a long white box in his hands, a red satin bow holding it closed. Someone was about to get a dozen long stemmed roses, no doubt.

A pinch of envy tweaked her right in the middle of her heart. It had been so long since she and Shane had even tried to romance each other with things like flowers and candy and surprise little tokens left on each others' chest of drawers or pillows.

She couldn't even bring herself to think about the future and the possibility of a romance with anyone else.

The delivery guy paused halfway in his vehicle, then hopped down and approached their car. "Hey, mister," he called to Shane, "I can't seem to get past the security in that place and I'm supposed to make a delivery."

"Yeah, we're locked down tight in there when it comes to receiving packages."

A frisson of fear iced up her spine at just the thought of an enemy trying to sneak in some sort of bomb to harm *her* husband.

"Well, I've gotta deliver my roses or my boss will chew me out. You think they'd have an X-ray or somethin' if they don't want me to open the box."

She thought she remembered Shane telling her

that they did, actually, but there must have been a traffic jam inside or some other distraction.

Or heightened security? The shiver intensified.

Shane eyed him warily. "Who are you looking for?"

"It's kinda complicated actually, because the person who's supposed to get the flowers didn't want them and now I'm supposed to give them to the person who sent them in the first place and I got paid a lot of money to make this happen. So, I need to find…"

The harried delivery boy searched the tag as the building's front door opened to release a gush of personnel in flight suits, BDUs and regular Air Force blues. Service members from other countries mingled throughout, as well. Shane had told her they would give insights on terrorism from their country. Some were here to glean insights of their own.

The crew stuck together as she would expect—Postal, Rodeo, Sandman, Padre and even Stones with his bandaged hands. They must be the others from Shane's D.I.T. class heading out to lunch. Sure some went home, but the bachelors usually made a point to take the foreigners out to show them some good ole American hospitality.

The delivery guy finally fished out the tag from the mangled red bow. "I'm looking for Derek Washington."

Derek broke from the crowd with a wave. "That's me."

Derek? Getting flowers? She hadn't realized he'd been seeing anyone. No wait. They were returned flowers… Ah…a premonition replaced that frisson in a heartbeat.

She felt like she was stuck in the middle of one of those parts of a movie where you just want to squeeze your eyes shut and plug your ears because it was gonna be embarrassing for Derek and there's nothing she could do to stop it.

The crewdogs started smacking him on the back, razzing calls, rising from the crowd, "You dog," "Way to go, dude," "Spill some details, man," and so on while their new squadron commander Liam "Mighty" Quinn watched from the periphery.

The delivery guy strode forward, thrust the long white box into Derek's hands, and judging by her husband's friend's widening eyes, Sherry figured he'd glommed on to the fact that this was not going to play well.

The frazzled college kid inhaled deeply, "Ms. Keisha Jones paid me fifty bucks to tell you to, 'Take your roses and stick 'em. All twelve of 'em, one at a time.' She says she's allergic to the flowers almost as much as she's allergic to you."

Sherry bit her lip. Hard. She understood why Keisha didn't want to have anything to do with the guy, but four years seemed like a long time to hold a grudge. And to be so public about it? Sheesh. It almost spoke of emotions.

Strong emotions.

Ah hell.

Her friend was on the road to heartache and feeling the way she felt right now, Sherry hurt all the more for what Keisha had ahead of her.

Wrapping her arms around her stomach, she stared at Derek holding the box of flowers while Padre smacked him on the back and whistled low, "Burned, sir, even worse than Stones's hands!"

CHAPTER EIGHT

"I CAN'T BELIEVE I burned supper."

Shane reached around Sherry and took the frying pan from her hand, liking the soft feel of her too much. "It doesn't matter, babe. We'll order pizza."

Sherry thumped the stove with her other hand, wriggling more than a little too much against him for his comfort right around the crotch level. She tossed aside the yarn potholder Mally had hooked for a Christmas gift. "How is it that I can cook over an open fire or a kerosene flame burner? But put me in front of a stove and I'm a helpless loser."

"Cut yourself some slac—"

"It's just Hamburger Helper, for heaven's sake." She snatched up the empty box and pitched it into the sink with a hefty ker-thump alongside the purple and green pot holder.

"It's Hamburger Helper at the end of an unbelievably exhausting few days." He stared at her totally wiped out posture and made a decision he knew he would regret but jumped in feetfirst anyhow. He just couldn't watch her in pain and do nothing. He would take the hit and hurt later. Shane rested his hands on her shoulders and started to massage, gently, thumbs working along the tendons up her neck.

Her head lolled forward as her body sagged back. She groaned. "You're not playing fair."

He pressed his cheek against her hair. "Do you want me to stop?"

"Of course I don't." Her sigh expanded her back against him.

He continued to rub along her shoulders and neck, keeping it platonic. Although any patch of her skin turned him on. And of course with her leaning back against him, her sweet bottom nestled right against his crotch. No way could she miss his hard-on pressing against her.

They both stayed still, against each other, and actually things couldn't go much further anyway, not with Mally coloring in her room and Cara singing along with a DVD.

Shane worked persistently along a kink on her right shoulder blade. "Why even bother to cook when you're obviously so tired?"

"Because you eat out all the time when you're TDY."

Her words stilled his hands for a second before he picked up the pace again. She'd cooked for him. The charred black mess in the pan had been for him. He felt an odd kick in his gut. Hell, funny how weird little things could mean more than roses.

Hmm. He would have to remember to tell that one to Derek. Maybe between the two of them—both equally clueless guys—they could wade their way through the maze of women's minds.

But wait. He wanted a divorce. He wanted out of this heartbreaking hell he and Sherry had tortured each other with for the last three years of their five-year marriage.

She sniffled. "We can't go out because Mally really should rest, but I don't want to order pizza."

He couldn't see her face as she stood with her back pressed to his chest, but he knew from experience his tough as nails wife was stifling back tears and that meant pizza would not darken their doorstep. Pizza now equaled defeat. "Okay. We won't order pizza."

He slid his hands from her shoulders and down her back before reaching to turn on the faucet and fill the pan with water, all the while being careful to avoid her eyes. He grabbed the dish soap off the window ledge from beside a jar of seashells and glitter. "Why don't you check on Mally?"

That would give Sherry a face-saving way to swipe away the tears she never showed—and quite frankly, he didn't know what to do with her in one of those weepy moods anyway. Seeing her lose it did something to his gut that made him…uncomfortable.

He would rather scrub a pan.

Shane watched her stride away, spine straight, apparently as determined as ever to be superwoman while walking by a corkboard filled with the post-cards she and the girls sent from around the world to see when they got home. As much as he worried about them, he had to admit his girls were advanced for their age. Sherry had done an amazing job parenting and educating them.

Ten minutes and a clean frying pan later, Sherry entered the kitchen with a smile on her face and—unless he missed his mark—freshly applied makeup. She had the perfect hips for low slung jeans. Her pretty pink T-shirt fit her form and rode up just enough to show off her belly button ring that drove him wild.

What was it about him that wanted a conventional wife and life, yet these unconventional parts of her had him hard in a heartbeat?

He sniffed. Oh yeah. Perfume.

Wait. Oh hell. He wasn't supposed to be noticing stuff like that anymore.

Whose bright idea had it been for him to stay here? He didn't even really remember them deciding anything. They'd sort of fallen into it today. He knew he wouldn't be in her bed. His body would leave a permanent imprint on the sofa, but still, he was here, in their routine.

Smelling Sherry's favorite apple berry scent from Home and Bath Shop. Enjoying her smile.

Before he realized he was talking he found himself saying, "How about I make grilled PB and Js like we used to have when the girls were little?"

An answering smile tugged his face. God, they hadn't had those in so long. He wouldn't want a steady diet of the things, but for a trip down culinary memory lane…

Her smile broadened. "Sounds great."

"We can spread a picnic blanket in the living room."

He wished he could claim to have come up with the idea on his own, but it was one of those meals he'd enjoyed at Derek's grandma's. She could make anything taste gourmet. She'd had the boys help bring her things when she cooked. She'd vowed no man should go into the world unable to feed himself. Derek had spent more time at her side, so his repertoire in the kitchen far outstripped Shane's, but he could hold his own.

He wouldn't starve when he and Sherry split for good. A sobering thought he didn't want right now, not with the promise of at least one more family meal in his future.

A meal that went by all too quickly, filled with laughter. Man, he'd forgotten how good an old fashioned PB and J with apple juice could taste in the right company. All the little things he would miss, like how Sherry cut the sandwiches into four triangles and his wife always missed a bit of grape jelly in the corner of her mouth.

Good memories that all threatened to cut him off at the knees as he tucked the girls in while Sherry cleaned the kitchen. Rituals. Two stories, a hug, prayers, tuck the covers tight for Mally and waft them like a parachute over Cara.

There hadn't been rituals in his family growing up—unless you counted the race to the front of the line for supper to get enough food, then sitting on the couch watching TV with his brother silently while their parents fought in the kitchen. Usually his older brother took most of his food, so Shane would leave for Derek's to eat.

Rituals.

He had to admit the ones Sherry introduced him to had been a helluva lot more fun than the ones he'd grown up with. Her living room might not be all perfectly put together, a stack of boxes still waiting in the corner to be unloaded. But Sherry's own eclectic style shone through with tribal masks on the wall over the television. Hand loomed pillows of giraffes from Africa on the sofa—and an overflowing toy box in another corner.

Suddenly he was worn-out. Dog tired, but in a good way. He'd put in a full day's work with the class on combating terrorism. He'd enjoyed lunch and supper with his wife and kids. This was what he'd wanted.

For a minute, he let himself forget the rest and settle in the moment. He dropped to relax on the sofa—aka his bed—and stuffed the giraffe pillow under his head, propping his feet on the armrest at the other end.

His eyelids closed and he must have drifted off because the sound of Sherry's footsteps next to him startled him ever so slightly. Still he kept his eyes closed to see what she would do.

She sank down into the recliner next to the sofa, silent for a few moments. "That was nice."

Apparently she knew he was awake after all. Well, even spending so much time apart they had been married for five years. "Normal."

And with that one word he could flat out feel her bristle. He didn't even need to open his eyes.

Instead he reached to rest a hand on her knee, or thereabouts where he figured it would be. Bingo. He nailed it, so he squeezed a gentle apology. "Whoa, Sherry, I didn't mean anything by it so back down. I just meant simple pleasures. We could have eaten PB and Js in the middle of the Congo and I would have said the same thing."

"Sorry." Her hand fell to rest on his, apology accepted. "I guess we both have such great big hot buttons that are all too easy to push. That's always been a problem."

He could think of a few mighty hot buttons of hers he'd like to push right now with them touching each other. And just that fast a simple get-together went straight to a sexual encounter in his head without enough warning for his defenses to adjust. He wanted her. Under him, around him, on top of him, beside him, any way he could take her or have her. He always had.

He sat up with a slow roll of his feet to the ground and looked at her. Yep. With the way her pupils were dilating right now he suspected she could read the need steaming through him at the moment. Was she thinking of the neck massage? Of how damn good it felt to touch each other again?

Maybe the same hot passion poured through her veins as well. "You know, we're not divorced yet." He pinned her with his eyes the way he wanted to hold her with his hands. "Why do we have to deny ourselves what we both want?"

The comfort, the release, the mind-blowing pleasure they could find in coming together.

Naked.

Yeah, he liked the idea of Sherry and naked in the same sentence. He liked the idea and Sherry and naked in reality even more. "Well?"

"I seem to recall there were reasons, but right now I'm having trouble remembering what they were."

He clasped her hand firmer and tugged her toward him. She didn't resist. In fact, she swayed toward him until she toppled into his lap with an ease born of years of familiarity.

Their mouths met with the same effortlessness. Sherry breathed a welcoming sigh into him that puffed the flames higher. She tasted of peanut butter, sweet grape jelly and tangy woman. Her adventurous spirit always spilled over into sex, the way she grasped at every inch of him with desperate hands as if committing all of him to memory or torturing him to death. He was never quite sure, but the bottom-line effect served to clench his jaw until it damn well hurt.

His energies had more focus than her frenetic pace. He wanted to savor certain parts because that seemed to carry the promise that there would be a next time to get to the others. For now, he had an obsession with the crook of her neck and her left breast.

He trailed his mouth from her kissed-plump lips down the graceful arch of her neck to that vulnerable spot where her neck met her shoulder and sure enough—she jolted. Yelped ever so slightly, then sighed with her head lolling back.

Yep. Erogenous zones were well worth finding and committing to memory. He sprinkled the spot with gentled brushing kisses for a while. How long he didn't really know, but any man who carried a timepiece into the bedroom deserved to be buckshot in the ass.

Sure enough, she got itchy for more and made her demands known, those frantic wandering hands of hers gripping his shoulders until her fingernails dug in deep with her whimper for *more.*

So he sucked, lightly—no leaving juvenile

marks to embarrass her—keeping her distracted as his hand made a sneak attack under her blouse and into her bra. Advanced move, making it past the bra to cup the sweet, warm weight of her breast and on the first try, but he wasn't messing around anymore.

"Shane, wait, slow down. Please," she gasped against his mouth even as she continued to kiss him. "I think maybe we should think this through a little more."

As much as he hated hearing what she said, her words hammered through his passion fogged brain. This wasn't a game. The rock hard pain in his pants demanded a release he could only find with this woman. His woman, for a while at least until he'd screwed it up because damn it, he couldn't accept her as she was and she couldn't accept the man he had to be.

And just that fast, the passion cooled for him in an icy splash of reality. Taking this further would only hurt her because those papers still had to be signed. They had children to consider, children who might grow hopeful if they caught a whiff of a chance at reconciliation.

Damn, tearing his hands, his mouth, his body away from her took more self restraint than he'd anticipated. Almost more than he possessed.

Breaths ragged, he rested his forehead against hers. "I'm sorry. I didn't mean to rush you."

"I'm an adult, Slugger. I didn't say no."

The idiot within him couldn't help but reply, "Do you want to keep going, just slower?"

A pained laugh tumbled once, twice from her. "Of course I *want* to keep going or you wouldn't be missing two shirt buttons. The question is *should* we keep going? We already know the answer to that."

He kept his head pressed to hers while they shared air if nothing else. "I knew this would be tough, staying here with you. I just had no idea how difficult."

She slid from his lap to sit beside him, but took his hand. Brave lady—with such sad eyes. "Shane, I don't want to turn into some real life soap opera diva with a slew of ex-husbands, broken relationships, unable to keep from tumbling into bed with a man because our names sound beautiful together."

He shook his hand free and took her chin. "That is the silliest damned thing I've ever heard of in my whole life. You're not going to sleep with me tonight because my name starts with the same two letters as yours? Well hell. Call me Alex. My name's Shane Alexander after all. Or call me Slugger. Or hell, call me Zeke for no good reason at all. I don't care. Better yet, *you* choose. Call me anything you want. We are who we are. The name's just a tag. I'm Vegas." Ouch. Not a good example when he thought of how he'd come by that call sign during one of their numerous breakups. "Our call signs are labels slapped on us and often enough changed where we're used to being called any number of different things."

"Now you're being ridiculous." She pulled away from his touch altogether, putting space between them, showing him all too well that he was losing ground fast. "I'm trying to make a point. We came to a difficult decision to end this marriage. None of our reasons have changed. I'm committed to my job and the travel. You're committed to yours. You still have that dictatorial way when you're here of expecting us to fall in line to your way of running the house and I have mine. After the way my parents subjugated my wishes to theirs all my life… I have to be given some breathing room. We are two leaders who can't seem to find a way to compromise."

He couldn't resist sliding his hand up to cup the back of her neck. "Okay. I hear what you're saying. Let's make this simpler, live in the moment. Why don't you think we can be friends with benefits?"

"You have got to be kidding." Her voice rose with each word. "Not without tearing each others' hearts to pieces. And it's really unfair of you to use your knowledge of what turns me on to get me to fall into your arms." Her voice wobbled.

Uh-oh.

He cupped the back of her head and pulled her face to his chest because he feared there were gonna be tears and God help him, he really couldn't handle them. He'd never been able to handle the threat of tears from her.

Another way he'd failed her. Except if he let himself get overwrought with emotions, how the hell was he supposed to do his job?

Damn. He'd never quite thought of it that way before and considering it in that light only made things worse because it signified one more way he'd screwed up—and would continue to if they stayed together. In his line of work, there were times he simply had to focus, clear away everything, including distracting sentiments.

Turning that off and on—workplace/home then home/workplace—was easier said than done.

Today's briefing in the D.I.T. class had included information he should have seen coming but had kicked the props out from under him all the same. The attack on the NGO camp and the terrorists in the cigarette boat out to hit the cruise ship were linked. The new terrorist camp had set up shop smack-dab on Sherry's island.

Of course they were gone now, relocated to God only knew where. No one was a hundred percent clear on why the two attacks were linked. Why not attack the base? Why expose themselves so totally for no gain?

There had to be an emotional component in there somewhere.

Regardless, the moment he'd heard, his head

had damn near exploded to think of his wife and
kids tooling around an island mere miles away from
terrorists. He eyed the couch with its pillow, sheets
and blanket all stacked neatly in the corner. Hell,
as protective as he was feeling now, he would sleep
on a bed of nails before he felt comfortable letting
them out of his sight.

CHAPTER NINE

SHERRY WAS GOING TO LOSE her mind if she had to spend more time with Shane.

But once the girls had heard his crew was playing in the squadron baseball game, there was no stopping them from attending. Of course they wanted to see Daddy play. How could she say no when she knew Daddy was only a day away from packing his gear and moving out for good?

They didn't remember losing their father when they were young and honestly Clint Holloway had been an ass, abandoning them all. This split with Shane, though, would leave a permanent ache on their hearts and already it slashed clear through her own.

But she was good at hiding pain. The throbbing agony of sending Shane to war for the first time—again, and again, then realizing the rotations into the war zone would just keep coming.

Not to mention her husband now flew in a new aircraft, one still in the testing phase, which meant constant in-flight emergencies and heaven only knew what problems.

Yet, they went through all of that, then had smiling welcome home parties with banners and cakes and hot sex. Baseball games and PB and Js. The high and lows, the joy and pain, of this lifestyle were so extreme she felt like a yo-yo on supersonic speed.

Her nerves were frayed clean through.

So here she sat at yet another "restful" baseball game, days after her husband had been shot at by terrorists.

Keisha fidgeted beside her on the metal bleacher, halogen lights flickering off and on, fickle in the almost sunset. "I can't believe you made me come with you. You really owe me big time."

"I needed the moral support. Besides, I can't make you do anything you don't want to do and you know it."

"Okay then. I want to help you with the girls because I can see you're tired, and as much as you deny it, I know you don't want to be alone with Shane." She looped her arms around Cara and Mally on either side of her.

"Maybe." Of course she also wanted to eat a whole bag of jelly beans in one sitting but that didn't make it good for her. "Or maybe you're just a little curious about Derek."

"You're mean, Sherry," she said with a playful swat of a friend at a pillow fight.

"Thanks a lot. I am many things, but mean is not one of them."

"Machiavellian, then."

"That, I will own up to." Sherry watched the game silently for half an inning while her daughters slurped down juice boxes and chomped gummy bears. She smiled and waved at other wives, itchingly aware of the whispers going around among the other women as the ocean roared in the distance at the seaside base.

Are Sherry and Shane together or not?

She should stay home more.

She never shows up for wives' club functions.

I bet she can't even cook Hamburger Helper.

Did you see in the paper she worked in the same camp where terrorists attacked, the same terrorists trying to kill our husbands?

Okay, the last one was pushing it. And nobody had actually ever said any of that to her face. She just felt they were condemning her for being different—which could totally be coming from inside her own fears of letting Shane down.

Reading the news on the Internet about the connection between the attempted attack on the cruise ship and the attack on the camp had gut punched her. Mostly because Shane hadn't bothered to tell her himself. And even more because this time, she did blame herself for placing her girls in harm's way.

Her gaze roved restlessly, a part of her wanting

to leave, hole up and hide. Then her eyes settled on poor Stones hanging out supporting his squadron. He could go to class, even drive, but sports were a definite no, with his hands still in bandages.

Suddenly weary, Sherry leaned back on her palms, her yellow shirt hitching up to show off her new belly button ring. She started to tug the cotton tank top down, then stopped. Who cared if some of the other wives gasped at the daisy? Some sent smiles of support. She knew Shane went crazy over the body jewelry.

Except then she felt like a real dweeb for taunting him after pushing him away. God, she was totally messed up in the head. Sometimes it seemed she didn't know what she wanted, except she felt this perverse need to show him what he was missing because he couldn't compromise.

Real mature. And speaking of making a display. She turned to Keisha. "So what's the deal with the big roses hoopla at the base? You're no more allergic to roses than I am."

"Says who?"

"Says me." She nudged her gold glitter flip-flops against Keisha's leather sandals. "You took a milk bath in rose petals in South America once because some guru told you it would cure your migraine."

"Don't you have better things to do with your time than memorize my life?"

"It was kinda memorable since their bathhouse was public."

Keisha's lips pursed—the outrageous adventurer suddenly all prim. "I wore a bathing suit, which is more than a lot of the people there could say."

Sherry couldn't help but wonder about those flowers. Four years and Keisha still had obvious feelings for a guy she'd seen just a few times. Sure there was an embarrassing event, but there had to be more to it than that. Somehow it became vitally important that she decipher Keisha's reasoning because she didn't want to be four years down the road from a divorce from Shane, still avoiding him, hurting, doing stupid things like throwing gifts back in his face.

She wanted to have a life, and if the answer to doing that could be found in Keisha's situation, then damn it, she would probe a little deeper than normal and hope her friend would just forgive her. "Why did you give Derek back the flowers—and that publicly?"

Keisha crossed her feet at the ankles and actually appeared to be giving it some serious thought, no anger at Sherry in sight, thank goodness. "A bunch of reasons, I imagine. He sent me the roses at work, which brought up questions and therefore embarrassment. Reason number two, he should realize that I would feel like roses are cliché and don't say anything special about *me*. And most importantly, he sent roses right after the big screwup and I made it abundantly clear then that I did not want those roses. Either he was taking the simple way out. Or he must have forgotten—and I do *not* like being forgettable."

"Wow, that's a lot of emotion for someone years in your past who you claim to care nothing about." Sherry stared down at the baseball field full of men and one woman. So many to pick from and yet women always seemed drawn to the guys destined to leave tread marks on their hearts. Except Derek wasn't a bad guy. Neither was Shane. It all had to do with the way folks had paired off. Bad judgment. "I'm sorry I set you up with him."

"It's not your fault. I'm a big girl. I make my own decisions." Her eyes narrowed as she assessed Stones sitting on the end of the bleachers watching the game, obviously miserable over not being able to participate. A slow smile crawled up her face. "Do you mind if I, uh, go check up on my patient for a few minutes?"

Stones and Keisha? Hmm. An interesting combination. They would certainly be the most fearless couple on the planet. "Sure. Feel free. I'm just here so the girls can see Shane anyway."

Keisha's smile made it all the way up to fire her already warm brown eyes. "See you in a bit then."

She started a smooth and speedy scooch along the length of the bleacher until she stopped beside the burly gunner with bandaged hands. Tony "Stones" Scapoli didn't seem in the least upset to see his nurse either. Tony reached up and pulled out the earpiece to his iPod.

Sherry had once asked Shane why the gunner carried the thing around like a permanent appendage.

Her husband had explained that apparently superfluous noise bugged the hell out of Stones. A low rumbling drone of an aircraft? Cool. A normal conversation? No problem. Regular, productive, sane life.

He was all about live and let live.

But then add in a dickwad—Shane's word— bartender who couldn't stop flapping his jaws for a full flipping hour about how he could do a better job at everything from trash pickup to world peace. Stones would be over the bar and in his face in heartbeat, which would make poor old Padre have to break up the fight in one of his "come to Jesus" head buttings.

Slapping on an iPod was easier on the noggin. Gotta love the distracting qualities of the music of Flogging Molly.

Sherry wished her own problems were as easy to avoid as sticking an iPod in her ear. She tried not to stare down the bleacher, but Keisha chose just that moment to throw back her head and laugh at something Stones had said.

"Strrrrrrike three!" the umpire called as Derek swung the bat.

Derek glared up in the stands. Keisha smiled. Stones didn't even miss a beat. With the outrageous need to "poke the bull" he'd always displayed, he slung an arm around Keisha's shoulders and leaned in to whisper something in her ear.

Sherry could hear it only had to do with pizza preferences for after the game. Derek, of course, looked pretty much like he'd caught the baseball upside the head. Interesting. And guaranteed to start sparks all over everywhere if he and Keisha kept this up.

Romance. Everywhere. Just waiting to taunt her.

Couples. Two people together.

Two. Sherry straightened on the steely hard seat.

It takes *two*. To make or break a couple. Something she hadn't thought about in her own life. She'd been busy blaming Shane for parts of their breakup, but she needed to take responsibility for her own faults. Her own defensiveness.

She stared out at the field now that it was time for Shane to step up to the plate. Silence settled after the initial round of cheering as it always did when his turn rolled around. Sandman leaned forward on third base, his arms swinging as he readied to bring home a run. Although ladies-guy Sandman certainly didn't miss the chance to wink at the two women in the front row.

Postal hung out on first with a wild-eyed look, inching off the plate every three seconds which yanked the pitcher's attention away as he threw the ball to the first baseman in hopes of tagging the crazy pilot out. No luck on that one yet.

Shane just waited for his turn to bat, testing the weight and feel of the aluminum in his hands. He didn't ever speak of his history as a pro ball player. Many of the younger airmen around the squadron didn't even know. But anyone around thirty or more knew full well all Shane had sacrificed to defend his country.

As a young high school senior, he'd been recruited by the Cincinnati Reds' triple A team that played at Louisville Slugger Field, eventually moving up to the Reds' major league team.

He'd played right field. Been a helluva batter with stats that were beginning a buzz.

Then in his late twenties, 9-11 hit. He'd finished out his season and enlisted in the Air Force. He'd flown as a gunner in AC-130 gunships until moving over to be a flight engineer in the new CV-22.

Yes, people in the squadron knew about his past, of course, but he always lived a Spartan life. Sherry respected him for that and agreed. She didn't want their girls growing up as spoiled rich kids. The security of a large nest egg was there if they needed it—but only if they needed it.

The pitcher let loose the ball—way wide.

"Ball," the umpire called.

The girls wriggled in their seats, shouting and cheering their dad on. They weren't novices when it came to heckling the pitcher.

The next pitch flew straight over the plate, low and outside where Shane liked them best.

Swish, pop.

Seeing her husband plow that ball over the fence even now, watching the even glide of his run, and most of all, savoring the absolute peace on his face over playing even a low-key game, she wondered how he could have ever given this away.

Not the money. The actual game.

She'd known he missed it. She hadn't known he'd lost a part of himself.

How odd. She realized he scheduled his time around baseball season on TV, caught live games whenever he could. She'd sat at many of his games and thought she was actively watching, but she'd missed such a crucial part of him.

Was this simply more of their being too caught up in child-rearing to look at each other? Somehow she didn't think so. Something was shifting inside her that she didn't quite understand, something foggy and nebulous.

Something important that she feared she could well miss if she didn't stop the whirlwind of her life long enough to pay attention.

He'd always sworn he was living a new dream, equally exciting. He'd vowed he was a lucky bastard to get to have two once-in-a-lifetime careers. She'd always accepted that at face value and believed him.

How different might his life have been if he'd stayed in the spotlight, on the field? Would she have been as attracted to that man? She honestly didn't know.

Shane finished running the bases, bringing in three runs for his team and winning the game. Ending the game.

If only life could be that easy for them.

The crew and others from the D.I.T. class poured from the dugout to rally around and cheer the victory, even the classmates from other countries had joined in—some better players than others. Sherry couldn't help but grin at the force, minus aim, the Ukrainian had put on the ball.

Cara and Mally were already clambering down the bleachers toward Shane to join everyone for the customary pizza party afterward. Her kids knew the routine too well for her to sneak out with them.

They'd told the girls Mommy and Daddy would be living in different houses, but Cara and Mally either didn't believe them or refused to accept it. Every time Shane and Sherry brought it up one of the girls changed the subject, or mentioned how they lived in different houses lots of weeks. How would they make the girls accept that these family routines were coming to an end? How would she handle this? Would Shane simply have a new woman in his life to bring the girls to games?

Too many painful particulars to weed through right now.

Why, oh why, couldn't she be like Keisha and simply discover a sudden allergy to pizza?

HE SLUNG HIS GYM BAG over his shoulder after the game and wished he could enjoy their victory, but nothing would feel right again until he got his life back from those bastards.

Damn, but he'd taken simple pleasures for granted before. A baseball game. His apartment. His wide-screen TV. This was the American dream. Not some mansion on a hill.

A place of his own, his bills met and a few dollars in his pocket to shoot pool with his friends or take out a woman. And he'd risked it all because he had to be a big man.

He strode across the field and into the parking lot on his way to his truck. Only a couple of days into the D.I.T. class and already his contact had notified him anonymously, pressuring him for information about American military plans to combat terrorism on home and foreign soil. Damn it. What should he choose to leak?

Leak. He preferred to think of it in terms like that. Like a leak to the newspaper because the word traitor scoured his insides.

He'd put the guy off by telling him better stuff was on the syllabus for later. They shouldn't take a risk this early for such a small payoff.

The roar in his head was louder than the ocean beating the distant shore. One step in front of the other. He should get a flipping Academy Award for holding everything together, going to work, going to the baseball game—now heading to the pizza joint with the crew like any other normal day.

Except nothing would ever be normal for him again.

He could feel the new commander's eyes on him all the time, even now as he did nothing more than *walk*.

But that was Lt. Col. Liam "Mighty" Quinn— watching. Assessing.

He told himself that was just the new dude getting to know his people. But what if the Mighty Quinn had some sort of freaky weird sense? The longer guys stayed around and dodged that silver bullet the more they had that extra sense about things.

Old Man Mighty Quinn was definitely one to stay clear of for the duration of the class. The man had been chosen as boss of this first CV-22 squadron for a reason. He was damn sharp.

He reached his truck, thumbed the unlock button. Hell, he never used to mess with that before. This was a safe place—or so he'd thought. Now he didn't trust anyone, anywhere.

He slung his bag across the front bench seat.

There were too many eyes on him here. Damn it all, he just wanted this over with so he could get on with his life. The military dream would be over, but at least he would *have* a life, one where he didn't have to look over his shoulder every three seconds.

Startling him from his thoughts, Rodeo strode past, smacking him on the shoulder. "Hey, dude, something wrong with your truck? Do you need a ride to the Pizza Shak?"

"No, thanks, it's all good."

"Okay, see you over there then."

He watched the way Rodeo's eyes trailed Keisha Jones as she loaded up in the O'Riley minivan. No question, Rodeo had a thing for the woman. Too bad life sucked this bad right now there was no time to enjoy watching that one play out.

God only knew when he would feel safe having any kind of a relationship of his own with a woman again. These people dogging him would use anything against him to make him do what they wanted.

So far they hadn't said anything about his sister. Of course Tabitha was only his half sister, with a different last name and they'd grown up in separate homes. Hopefully she'd slipped under their radar. He'd made a point of avoiding Tabitha's calls like the plague lately.

No, he was definitely going to have to stay away

from attachments—family or romantic. He would play it cool, though, so as not to raise alarms. If the situation called for a date, he would bring someone along. Someone new, a one time only sort of thing.

He watched everyone going about their daily routine of getting into cars and driving away, totally oblivious of how easily that security could be taken away from them. Ignorant of the danger that lurked close, soon to steal away some of their safety. How strange to think of seasoned combat veterans as naive, but they were. The lot of them.

Not him. He knew better now.

From here on out, he was definitely a loner. No half sister Tabitha. No long-term girlfriends.

And he would just have to pray for forgiveness when he did the unforgivable.

CHAPTER TEN

PIZZA, POOL AND PARTYING with his family and pals after a game of baseball.

Shane figured he ought to be counting his blessings. It didn't get any better than this—exactly the way he'd dreamed his life when he'd been tromping up the stairs as a kid on his way to escape to the peace and safety of Derek's apartment. This was good. Laughter, the clank of pool balls, the heavy scent of good old-fashioned oregano in the air.

He tipped back his mug of beer, nodding at all the right times as his daughters chattered. Sherry stayed as quiet as he did, sipping her water with lemon.

Sure he had his family with him, like a normal dude. Fifty percent of the time, he came here solo, shot pool with the crew at a local hangout.

Although Stones wasn't playing pool tonight. He was making time with Keisha two booths over which had Derek looking like he wanted to pop Stones between the eyes. And that would bring Padre out to break things up.

Normally that would go badly for Derek before

Padre arrived because Stones had, well, huge stones. A big, burly badass with gonads the size of cannonballs when it came to a fight, regardless of whether his hands were injured or not.

Except right now, thanks to those 'nads, they were all alive and Tony "Stones" Scapoli was living in agonizing pain with bandages on his hands.

God, it was good to see Stones flat out alive. The larger bandages on Tony's left hand reminded them how close they'd all come to exploding in a ball of flames out over the Caribbean Sea. Although apparently the experience hadn't changed Tony's push-the-envelope personality in any earth-shattering way given how he was flirting with Keisha in spite of Derek's scowl. The big hulk of a man kept his hair a hint too long.

He always said, "I'm headin' to the barbershop today, sir."

His jaw in need of a shave which he justified with, "Sorry, sir, it's those Italian genes. I shave twice a day and still can't combat them."

Shane felt a tug on his well-worn Cincinnati Reds T-shirt. He looked down to see Cara staring up at him. "Run that by me again, sugar?"

"You'll be there when I sing? I got the solo in the vacation Bible school program. It's on Friday."

They must have just started today, one of those weeklong afternoon programs. How Sherry crammed it all in, he would never know. "I'll be there."

"Promise?"

"Pinky swear." He hooked his pinky out for her to join with a grin.

The jukebox cranked to life, Jimmy Buffett tunes of course, about ninety percent of what played in this part of the country.

Swaying to the song, Sherry pulled another slice of pepperoni pizza onto her plate. "Why don't you go ahead and play pool with the guys. We're fine here."

"Yeah, right." He lounged back and took another swig off his mug of beer. "Run off and leave you sitting here when we haven't seen each other in weeks. That's the kind of sh—uh, stuff that got us into arguments before."

She swirled cheese on her tongue and swallowed. "Really. Go. Don't you think we've had enough together time?" She pulled a strained smile that echoed the tension building in him. "I'll give the kids a bunch of quarters to play the video games."

She scooped out her coin purse and shoved it into Cara's eager hands. Both girls bolted for the video games before she could blink, each girl singing along with Buffett's tune "Fins" and making a shark fin on top of their heads with a hand.

Shane couldn't suppress the smile. He'd taught them that. Something of himself the girls would carry with them always. A silly little something, but fun. His smile faded as he faced his wife again.

Great, now they were alone with all that tension and he had the sense she wasn't happy with him and he didn't know what the hell he'd done wrong. "Do you want me to get another pitcher of beer?"

"*You* can have the pitcher of beer with your friends. I'll go speak to some of the other wives. No big deal."

She chewed off another gooey bite of pizza and why was that such a turn-on when he was actually pissed off at the way she was ordering him around? He was only trying to do what she'd asked him to do for the past five years—hang out with the family.

"Do you even know any of the other wives?"

Ire stained her neck all the way up to her jaw, a betraying tell of her fair complexion. She leaned forward on her elbows across the paper covered table and whispered, "Are you being a snippy bastard on purpose? I know I don't do the standard wives' club functions, but I'm not a total loser when it comes to supporting your career." She plopped her pizza back on the plate and swiped her fingers clean on a napkin. "Aren't things strained enough between us without you deliberately being a jerk?"

Upon reflection, he had pretty much stepped in it with that comment, because, yeah, sometimes he resented the fact that she didn't do the cookie drive gig. Or sometimes when they landed from a deployment, she and the kids weren't there with the welcome home contingent because she was off in another country.

But damn it, she never made much of an attempt to get to know anyone, and then she complained about being lonely when he was gone. So yeah, the pissy comment had slipped out halfway on purpose. "I don't need to try around you. It just works that way for us."

Her jaw tightened. "Go play pool."

He'd been a husband long enough to know that translated into married-ese for *Get the hell out of my face.*

"Fine. If you insist." He slid out of the booth and made his way toward Padre, the most calming dude in the group. Hopefully some of that would rub off on him then he would quit falling victim to the urge to pick fights.

Of course maybe arguing was easier than trying to keep the peace when the whole divorce thing was slowly killing him. Especially on days when he glimpsed the old something fantastic between them. Better to break open old wounds than to ruminate over the ones he couldn't fix.

For now, he would hang with peacemaker Gabe.

Gabe "Padre" Holtz could break up a bar fight faster than anyone in the squadron. He wasn't overly large but carried a confident air that defied argument whenever he grabbed the two combatants by the scruff of the neck for the "come to Jesus" meeting of the minds.

Some thought he must be crazy drunk to wade

into such contentious waters and risk life and limb—not to mention black eyes and fractured bones. Yet he was always stone-cold sober and always the designated driver.

A good guy. A man to trust.

Padre passed him a cue stick. "You in?"

"Yeah, if y'all are ready to rack 'em up for another round."

"Rodeo's out for this round so you can take his place." He slid the chalk down the length of the table to Shane. "He's off sulking in his gin and tonic. Got tired of being teased about the flowers incident."

"It's been pretty harsh for him." Shane chalked the tip of his stick. "I've heard talk about changing his call sign from Rodeo to Rosey."

"Man's gotta learn to lighten up."

"Tough to lighten up when a woman's involved." He knew that firsthand.

"Maybe we could all take a lesson from Sandman." Padre nodded at the local playboy who was busy passing a drink to his latest lady love. "He seems to survive those broken hearts with grace in his search for 'the one.'"

At the next pool table over, Postal broke the set balls, playing with Sandman.

"Maybe," Shane agreed more out of politeness than anything else. He didn't really want to play pool. He didn't know what the hell he wanted—except for the hammering in his head to go away.

Screw pool.

Shane shot a look back over his shoulder to check on Sherry and well hell, she did have women hanging out at her table to chat with. Whether she knew them already or not, he didn't know. Sandman's latest girl-friend joined them, parking herself beside Sherry while the new squadron commander's wife and Postal's wife-to-be both sat across from her. They were sharing a pitcher of margaritas and laughing their asses off about something or another.

He'd been too busy trying to manage Sherry he'd forgotten the woman was so independent, she didn't need him for a damned thing beyond sex. And while he wasn't one to discount the mind blowing benefits of sex, he had to admit...

He wanted more. And Sherry had made it clear she liked her life fine as is.

SHERRY SAT IN THE MIDDLE of her living room floor amidst a mess of crayons and coloring books as scattered as her thoughts and her life. At least the kids were in bed and she had the comfort of her friend Keisha sitting cross-legged beside her, sip-ping a homemade margarita.

They'd left the guys at the pool hall well over two hours ago. A wise choice given how edgy things were between her and Shane.

Sherry jammed the copper crayon in the box beside the thistle one. She swept up the maize and peeled off paper until the color showed again, then sharpened it to a point.

Keisha licked some of the salt from the rim of her frosted glass. "I think you're losing it."

Sherry glanced up, startled—and a little afraid. "What do you mean?"

"That's going to be the most perfect box of crayons in the world and the girls are just going to dump them all over the carpet again in the morning. Why not put the crayons in some kind of plastic tub?" She held up her hands in self-defense to stall Sherry from talking. "I know I'm not a parent, but I'm a little liquored up so I'll step out on a limb here. Sure seems to me you make a lot more work for yourself than you have to in parenting."

"You don't understand."

"Try me." Keisha pulled on the straw, slurping.

Sherry shoved the crayons down fully into the box, evening the rows as if that might somehow order her thoughts. Hah. Yeah right. She tried her best to explain the inexplicable. "These girls were entrusted to me."

"Uh-huh. That's what being a mom means. A kid is entrusted to you, whether they come from another country or from your belly."

"You make it sound simple, but I feel like I owe their parents something, too, this…" She couldn't figure out how to put it into words.

Sherry stared down at a fistful of crayons, colorful, like her house. Each one special and unique.

She'd thought she was showing her girls the world. She'd been careful not to repeat experiences from her childhood. Plenty of people took their children with them to exotic places without a thought for pure pleasure trips. She'd actually had a philanthropic goal in mind.

Never would she have knowingly put the kids in danger and yet she could feel the censure in Shane's gaze throughout their marriage. Betty Crocker wouldn't haul her children into a camp likely to fall under siege.

Sherry thought about her children sleeping safely in their rooms, dear little lives entrusted to her by their birth parents long in the grave. Mally's mother had died of AIDs in the Sudan. Sherry had been reassured by the government that Mally tested negative—not that it would have changed her mind once she saw that precious tiny face. Once she'd looked into Mally's eyes, Sherry's heart had recognized her child. Thank God, though, two tests later, they'd been reassured of Mally's clean bill of health.

Still the convulsions and the bacteria scare had shaken something loose inside her, reminding her of that time in their lives when she'd feared her stomach lining would be lost forever from the worry of waiting for a more official confirmation of her daughter's health. Now, it was up to her to keep these girls safe and healthy and well-adjusted and happy and a million other parental responsibilities compounded by choices she'd made.

Had she screwed up? With her job? The divorces? Hell, the way she stored their arts and crafts?

She looked down at the multicolored crayons again. Had she done the right thing in taking the girls from their original homeland?

Her fingers closed around the crayons. "Keisha, am I being naive, thinking I can meet the needs of my daughters?"

"What do you mean? You're a great mom with a steady income... What am I missing here?"

"I mean the whole transracial adoption issue." Her arms ached with the sweet memory of when she'd held them each for the first time—Cara at fourteen months, tiny Mally at only three months. "What do I know about being an Asian or African-American woman?"

"Ahhh." Keisha set aside her globe glass. "You tell me?"

Sherry rolled the crayons between her palms. "I really want your help but you're not going to make this easy for me, are you?"

Keisha slumped back against the sofa beside a cherry Kool-Aid stain. "You're the one who gave me both those margaritas while only drinking half of one yourself. If you wanted me sharp-witted, you never should have pulled out the blender and gotten us both all maudlin."

"I'm seriously wondering and scared here." She stirred her straw through the green slush in her own drink. "I thought I had something to offer them and I never realized how much I would learn from them. I love my girls so much. I expected…"

Tears built inside and she wanted to let them out. Shane was nowhere in sight and she knew Keisha wouldn't mind, but she'd grown so accustomed to holding them in she couldn't pull the stopper free when she needed to. Maybe she could just turn on her soap opera and get a good cry on. Not likely though and too late even if she did.

Those bottled tears burned like acid through her veins.

She dropped the crayons into the box and sipped at her melting drink for something to do if nothing else.

Keisha took the glass from her and held both hands in hers. "My friend, you're wigging out because you're going to be a single parent of two small girls." She held on tight. "That has nothing to do with race, sweetie."

Oh God, Keisha was right—a relief on the one hand and of course cause for total fear on the other hand because she did have reason to be scared. Very shortly, she would be on her own.

Had she freaked before, after her first divorce and married Shane on the rebound? What an awful, awful disservice that would have been to him. She didn't think so. She *had* married Shane quickly after meeting him—but she had been divorced for about a year.

Keisha released her hands with a final squeeze before she grabbed the blender to refill her glass. "Was it that bad, the fight you had with Shane that brought all of this on?"

"How did you know? Never mind. No need to answer. I never have been good at hiding my emotions."

"Are you still in one piece?"

"It wasn't the worst fight we've ever had, or even particularly long. He just made a snippy comment that hurt my feelings and instead of telling him he hurt me, I snapped back."

"So why are you cleaning like a fiend instead of telling him you're sorry and explaining?"

"Because we can't live together. Even if I felt like making myself vulnerable that way, he wants me to be someone I can't no matter how hard I try. I want him to be someone he can't." She jammed crayons into the box faster and faster—burnt sienna, sea green, violet, salmon until she broke turquoise blue and a tear leaked from the corner of her eye. "Haven't we hurt each other long enough? What's out there to give me hope? I can't stop thinking this is my fault. I'm a two time loser, for crying out loud. This is my second divorce."

Keisha took the crayon box from Sherry's white knuckled grip. "Your first husband slept with anything with boobs. That's not your fault other than the fact you had the poor judgment to pick an amoral skunk who couldn't keep his dick in his pants."

"Then what went wrong this time?" Sherry held up a hand, then started gathering the coloring books into a stack. "Never mind. Forget I asked. I don't really expect you to answer that."

"I wish I could say for certain because you and Shane are two of the nicest people I have ever met." She finished the last of her margarita and hugged her knees. "Best I can tell you're both so busy saving the world you don't have any time left for each other."

Standing, Sherry made her way over to the corner bookshelves filled with children's books, toys, arts and crafts. She stored the crayons and coloring books. She skimmed her hand over a row of dolls, each one collected from a different country. "All I wanted to do was teach them to be giving people who see the world with open hearts. Is that so wrong of me?"

Keisha pushed to her feet, scooping up the cups and the blender. "Things would certainly be easier if you and Shane had different jobs, but you're both good people. It's tough to fault you for that."

Sherry leaned against the wall by the shelves and studied each of the dolls, a couple of them even boys. She and Shane had discussed adopting a boy as well as trying for a child of their own. They'd never used birth control during their sporadic times together until she'd started to think perhaps she was infertile, and adopting more...

Now their time had passed for that. For a little boy with his baseball and bat, learning from Shane. Losing dreams stirred more of that bottled acid in her veins.

Keisha returned from the kitchen. "Sweetie, do you mind if I crash on your sofa? I've had one too many to drive and you can't leave the kids."

Holy crapola. The sofa. Shane's "bed," even if he wasn't home yet. Was he coming back or had their fight sent him off for the night? She didn't know and she really didn't want to discuss her and Shane's sleeping arrangements with Keisha.

She settled for a, "Sure, whatever," and figured she would cross the Shane-bridge if he walked through the door. A change of subject would really feel good right about now. "So what's the scoop with you and Stones?"

"Tony? He's a funny guy." Keisha picked up her glass and the empty blender and started toward the kitchen area.

"A really nice guy, too." Sherry followed with her glass and opened the dishwasher. "I sure would hate to see you use him to make somebody else jealous."

"Are you insinuating I have lingering feelings for Derek Washington?"

"Who? Me? I heard tell you're allergic to the guy." She put the glasses and the blender in the dishwasher rack next to the frying pan. Dishwasher full, she added soap.

"Very funny." Keisha lifted the door and clicked it closed with a hip bump.

"If just seems to me that if seeing him still bothers you this much after over four years—"

"Stop right there," she said with a hand wave and snap. "It was the most mortifying moment of my life. It's bad enough that, uh—abrupt end with me has been immortalized in his call sign. But what are the odds that we would end up living in the same place, for crying out loud?"

"Well, your jobs were influenced by the good friends who set you up in the first place. Or chalk it up to the whole notion of six degrees of separation. Whatever. But here you are and you have to deal with it. And by dealing with it, if you make this huge scene…"

She sagged against the counter in defeat—or self-realization and snatched up the purple and green pot holder, another of the kids' hooked yarn artwork. "I'm the one drawing attention to myself."

"Pretty much." Sherry wished she could shed as much light on her own man-problems as easily. "Besides, honestly, he's the bad guy in the story, not you."

Keisha fanned herself with the pot holder. "Yeah, right, I'm such an amazing woman in the sack a guy can't remember who he's with."

"*His* problem, Keisha. *His*." She took the pot holder from Keisha and clicked on the ceiling fan. "You probably don't want to hear this, but it's been over four years since the big event, so I'm going to tiptoe out on the limb here."

"You'd better be careful 'cause I could cut that limb right off."

"Fair enough. I'll be on the watch for you and your mighty hatchet." Her eyes gravitated to the wedding photo across the room back in the living area. Shane and Sherry in Ireland with the girls, becoming a family on a hillside. It had been so romantic, tartan plaids and bagpipe music. "A lot changes in four years. And honestly, Derek really is a pretty decent guy."

"A decent guy who called me by the wrong name in the sack."

"O-kay." Her friend had strong feelings when it came to this guy. Interesting. "I can feel that limb giving way under me so I'll grab hold of the tree and shimmy back down to the ground where I can stand firmly beside my friend again. My mouth is sealed on the subject of Rodeo."

"Good! Good. Because I don't carry around bulky hatchets," her fearless friend declared even though she did have an eclectic collection of historic weapons mounted in a case on her wall. "I'm pretty much a chainsaw kind of chick."

"And that's why I like having you on my side."

"You know the part that sucks the most?" Keisha pursed her mouth in a pout that came mighty darn close to resembling the girls' in a snit.

"What?"

"Nobody remembers *her* name."

"Her who?"

"The woman who dumped him," Keisha's voice rose. "The woman who ripped his heart out to the point he couldn't get her name out of his mind. Nobody remembers her name."

Ouch. That really stung. "But you do."

"Kimberly."

"I'm sorry. Truly. But the fact that you still remember—"

"Chainsaw's a coming, my friend."

The sound of the front door turning stopped all chitchat short. They both jolted away from the counter just as Shane walked through the front door. Keisha pinned her with interested, you've-been-holding-out-on-me eyes.

Oh. Yeah. She had failed to mention his living here, but now wasn't the time to go into that.

Shane came through alone and she could see in his eyes he hadn't been drinking anything more than the one beer he'd had while they were there. Looking deeper in his eyes, she found something more…

"Shane? What's wrong?"

He strode across the room with heavy steps, no niceties or howdies. "Sherry, why's the base security sticker missing from your minivan?"

CHAPTER ELEVEN

KEISHA GRIPPED THE DOOR of Derek's SUV like a lifeline as the lights whipped by in the night, a little fuzzier than normal, a testament to all those margaritas she'd consumed tonight. Of course that was why she was stuck accepting a ride from him. Once Shane had shown up all tense and stressed about the base security sticker it had been obvious she needed to clear out. Except she was too tipsy to drive and there hadn't been any prying him from his wife's or kids' sides.

So here she was. Stuck in Derek's car again.

"You really didn't have to take me home," Keisha felt compelled to say to Derek for like the forty-first time. She could have hung out in the O'Riley house like a fifth wheel.

"Yep, that's right. I didn't have to. *If*…I was a jerk with no manners."

"So this is about manners. Okay. Cool." She loosened her hold on the door. That made sense—even if it stung her pride a smidge which was totally stupid because she didn't want anything to do with this man.

Damn it, why did he have to look so hot, though?

The glow of the dashboard lights illuminated him in those black jeans and white polo shirt that clung to his muscular chest a little too well for her peace of mind. Sometimes in her deepest dreams, that aborted encounter between them tormented her. Maybe if they'd been able to finish she would have been able to slot the memory away as something… nice.

Nice? Hah. *Nice* was a mamby pamby word for the steam that smoked off of them that night.

Keisha tore her eyes off Derek—off temptation personified—and stared back out the window at the passing lights and palm trees. "What do you think's up with Sherry's missing base sticker?"

He held the steering wheel loosely in his hands and shrugged while staring ahead at the long stretch of beach highway. "Could be nothing."

"You don't sound so certain." The intricacies of military life sometimes mystified as well as fascinated her. She'd steered clear of military men for the most part since they were too much like her; reckless thrill seekers. Too combustible a pairing in her opinion.

She dated discriminately and usually more the engineer types in the NGO groups. Her parents had been opposites like that, a professor father and a scaffold billboard painter mother. They were loving and living out their happily ever after.

Derek shot a quick glance in her direction with narrowed, assessing eyes before answering. "There have been problems with terrorists peeling them off cars, then using them to get on base."

Terrorists? Holy crap. She'd never thought about military dependants being targeted in such a basic way. "But don't you have to have an ID card to get on base?"

"Yes."

Her mind followed the natural path. "Which they probably forged."

"Shit happens," he said dismissively, his jaw clenched in contradiction. "But the places of highest levels of security still require identification far more complex than just a car sticker and an ID card. So while this raises a red flag, it's not something to get totally wiggy about."

"What will happen next?"

"They'll report it to the OSI—the Office of Special Investigation—and let them take it from there." He turned off the highway into her beachside neighborhood. "Hopefully they can lift some fingerprints from the car's windshield, but it's a long shot given all the people who go in and out of the car—not to mention they recently had the minivan in the shop for mechanical work. But the cops will also check for security camera footage in the area. With luck, they'll uncover something useful, but it's unlikely we'll get to hear what those results are."

"Ah. The whole need-to-know basis." She'd heard Sherry complain about that often enough. Seeing her condo in the distance, Keisha shuffled to find her purse and came up instead with a... small box? "What's this?"

She held it up to the dash lights, a red bow gleaming on the candy container. She glanced over at Derek in time to see him shoot her a wry smile.

"Those are the Godivas that I wasn't going to give you tonight at the baseball game."

She couldn't help but laugh as she remembered one of the things she'd been attracted to about him in the first place—his sense of humor. She winked at him. "Good. Because I'm a—"

"Allergic." He winked back. "Yeah. That's why I didn't give them to you."

"Oh. Sorry to have underestimated you."

He snorted. "You didn't underestimate a damn thing and you know it. I've been working my ass off to get back in your good graces and those chocolates didn't come cheap, lady." He jabbed his finger toward the candy. "Sandman swore women go crazy for Godivas."

"You were asking your crew for advice on how to win me over?" Hadn't she been talked about enough around his workplace?

"No. The crew talks about women. Period."

She relaxed her defenses a bit. "He's the expert on females?"

"Not the expert, per se." He turned into her parking lot and drove along the row of terra-cotta apartments. "He's just the crew player. "That's the reason they call him Sandman."

"I'm not following." She settled into the conversation, better than talking about the real elephant in the car—the attraction between the two of them. "Is it some kind of sex on the beach reference?"

"Decent guess, but no." He pulled into a spot out near her bottom floor number and put the car into park, engine idling. "The Sandman comes at night and the sand is still in your eye in the morning…"

"Ah, okay." She eyed the candy box just waiting to be claimed as waves crashed to the shore just beyond the stretch of apartment buildings. "Does he have a real name? I don't think I've actually ever heard it."

"Hayden Reed."

"And he's a player?"

Derek draped his wrist over the steering wheel and cocked his head in her direction, the strong lines of his jaw stirring a warmth in her belly. "I guess that's not necessarily a fair label. It's more like he never saw a woman he didn't love. And most of them loved him right back."

"Sounds like a prince." She dropped the chocolates like they were a snake.

Derek's hand slid from the steering wheel to toy with the red bow on the candy box—dangerously close to her thigh. "It would be easy to dismiss him as heartless, but he really throws himself into each relationship as if he wanted each one to last. His longest liaison was with a military wife separated from her borderline abusive husband. Hayden had helped her with restraining orders."

"That's awful."

"Not that all his relationships were so traumatic. Once he hooked up with a stripper that ended with him finding her a chorus line gig on an NGO tour."

Keisha couldn't stop her eyes from widening or her mind from racing as she wondered about when their last NGO tour had integrated a stopover to see an "entertain the troops" performance, had it included the ex-stripper?

"Hayden told me once his own dad walked, so after seeing his mom struggle, he couldn't help but sympathize with a woman in need."

"I guess I could see how that would make him more appealing to women, in spite of his bed hopping ways."

"Which starts the Godiva cycle all over again."

She plucked the bow, her fingers a scant millimeter away from his. "So who are they for? Kimberly?"

"Who?"

She hit him. She wasn't proud of it. But she hauled off and smacked his hand that had been playing with the bow.

"Ouch." Derek shook his hand. "That freaking

stings. If I'd done that to you, the cops would be arresting me for assault and battery."

"Sorry. You're right, of course." She winced all the more because he truly was right. She shouldn't have resorted to violence. "But still. You really don't remember who Kimberly is?"

He frowned, blinked for a few minutes then his face cleared, then, "Oh. Yeah. Kimberly."

"Uh-huh. *Kimberly.*" The idiot male. She wondered if she pelted him with chocolates would that be considered violent? That could get out her bottled aggression without breaking any moral codes. "Kimberly is a rather memorable name as far as I'm concerned."

Finally he just reached out and touched her. He gripped her shoulder and held her eyes with his. "Hell, Keisha, that was over four years ago."

But he remembered *her* name. Interesting and rather ego soothing.

Except her name had given him his immortalized call sign. Not so ego soothing. She shrugged off his hand—and yet the heat of his touch lingered, doggone it. "I thought she really trounced your heart."

"She did. Way back then. That doesn't mean I was going to marry her or anything." He held out both hands as if he wanted to reach for her again but kept the boundaries, waiting for her okay this time. "Her dumping me turned out for the best."

Keisha couldn't decide whether to cheer or stomp her foot in frustration. This Kimberly was nothing to him and yet the whole incident had been such a defining moment for her for so long. She let the information sink in and settle around for a while before finally asking, "Where is she now?"

He gripped the steering wheel, but his gaze held her as firmly as any touch. "I honestly don't know and I don't care."

The best ego balm of all.

Her fingers crawled across the bow to grip the box of Godivas. Dang, she really did like the things. A lot. But she couldn't take them now without totally caving. And it wasn't like she really even knew the guy. After watching Sherry's heartbreaks, she'd learned not to leap recklessly into a heavy relationship.

A heart was a fragile thing, even for a Komodo dragon chaser.

The silence stretched until finally he left the car without a word to open her door and silently walk her to her front stoop. The seashore air drifting up from the waves a hundred yards away sobered her up fast. She wouldn't be asking him inside, although it was tough to resist the temptation to—

He ducked his head and brushed a kiss across her mouth. "Shhhh. Don't start a fight. This has been nice."

There was that word nice again, except this time

it sure seemed to carry a lot more weight. She let herself hold on to the lingering feel of his brief but potent kiss. "That was nice too."

"Nice?" he questioned, apparently not as impressed with the word as she had been. "Only nice?"

He dipped his head again.

His mouth slanted over hers and she couldn't help but wonder how he felt so familiar after so long? Then she opened to welcome him back as his tongue teased a hello once, twice, then boldly stroking a warm sweep that sent her already shaky senses swimming. She gripped his shoulders for balance and for fun, because oh my, scaling those muscles could be classified as a mountain climber's dream.

Too soon it was over.

His broad hand stroked over the side of her face. "Good night. Sleep well."

That was it? He was leaving now? But wait. That was a good thing because no way could she invite him in for more. Duh. She gasped in deep gulps of salty sea air to clear her head of the margarita buzz mixed with the heady potency of his kiss.

She rocked back on her heels. Tipsy. Must be the tipsy feeling from the margaritas exaggerating her reaction because she tingled all over.

Still, she had to know one thing before he left. "May I ask just one thing?"

A smile played with his kissed-damp mouth. "You're going to anyway, so go ahead."

She smoothed flat the collar of his polo shirt. "Who's really going to get the Godivas now?"

His bright smile rivaled the crescent moon. "My grandma."

And he was gone before she could shake off shock. He certainly slayed her with that one. She swayed on her feet.

No more alcohol anywhere near Derek Washington. She'd let him get close too fast once and wouldn't be repeating that mistake.

He posed a far more dangerous threat than any Komodo dragon.

SHANE STEERED THE MINIVAN through the base, his gut roiling with dissatisfaction that he couldn't have done more to address the possible threat directed at his family.

It had been a long morning for him and Sherry talking to the OSI. At least the girls had been occupied with their morning at a downtown aquarium in a small group outing with other homeschooled children. After that they would go to their afternoon of vacation Bible school.

He and Sherry had actually managed to have lunch alone together, something he'd never before realized was a rarity. Why hadn't he made a point to do that more often? Even if it was just a burger together. They hadn't talked about anything earth-shattering. Perhaps that had been the whole point.

They spent very little time simply hanging out together catching their breath from the manic pace of their lives.

He'd been busy with work—everyone in the military was, given the deployment pace. Even at home he naturally eased into a pattern of eating lunch with his crew. It was more relaxed, no worrying about who said what that started them on a downward spiral to a fight.

He *hated* to fight.

And really, what did he have to offer her? His smart sexy wife? He had a high school diploma and some money tucked away from his baseball years, but she would just as soon sleep in a tent.

She had two upper level degrees and spoke four languages to his two. The best thing, sometimes he thought the only thing, he could give her was a stable home, and a safe one…when he was there to take care of them.

Yeah, he was a stand-up guy. He wanted to be there for her, and the one thing he could give her, she could already give herself. Had to, because he was gone all the time.

How bad did that suck?

All of which was moot now. No time to ponder. Life had gone back on supersonic speed since it was time to get the girls. He reminded himself that the whole missing sticker incident could have been purely random. Whoever had taken the sticker likely had been randomly targeting military cars. There was still the possibility that the damn thing had just fallen off the windshield.

Yeah right.

And pigs were gonna fly out of his ears.

As he wound his way around the barricades set up on his way out the gate, he was reminded of all the heightened security at military installations since 9-11. No more driving straight up to a gate. Now they had to make a serpentine path around an obstacle course with the threat of spikes to pop tires ever present. All gate guards were heavily armed now. And ID checks were no longer random.

He'd watched all those changes implemented as he'd joined up right after 9-11.

The world had changed—and the military had changed right along with the rest of the world.

Clear of the gate and back into the town, he drove on, aware of Sherry silent beside him. Luckily the girls had an activity scheduled for the day. Sherry schooled year-round since they had such irregular days off for travel and she liked to make the most of wherever they were. So days to herself were rare.

He admired the way she juggled so much. She was a super woman, no question.

Why then, couldn't they manage a relationship?

And no question, they were in relationship hell right now. God, he hated the silent treatment.

Since he and Sherry had exchanged words at

the pizza place, she'd gone all cool on him. The missing sticker had jolted her for a moment, and then she'd gone stoic on him. He could understand that. They'd faced worse—real life and death moments.

But the missing sticker incident still bothered him. Must be because the D.I.T. class had him thinking more about the ever-present insidious threat of terrorism. It freaked him out a little how many updates there were to the class. But it went back to that hydra metaphor General Renshaw had discussed back in the Caribbean. Every time they got rid of one terrorist cell, another head popped up, different, morphing, adapting. Which meant the US military had to adapt their combatant skills as well.

Days like this bothered him most though. Because some people focused so much on the possibility of big hits, they often ignored the likelihood of smaller strikes.

Sure the decal could have fallen off, but he didn't believe in counting on coincidence. Not when lives were at stake. And the thought that someone with evil intent had come this close to his family made his head ready to fucking explode on top of everything else that was going on in their world. But he tamped it all down. Now wasn't the time to lose. He had to be there for them, in control. In charge.

But this most certainly wasn't the best time for

Sherry to roll out her silent treatment, not when he was already coiled tight.

As much as he hated confrontations, he had to go ahead and take care of an important detail. "I'm not getting a room on base. I'm staying with you and the girls, and you might as well get used to it."

"Excuse me?" She turned to face him, all snooty as if he'd suggested a trip to the moon.

He wasn't in the mood for niceties. "I'm very uncomfortable with the idea of the three of you alone, not after somebody possibly targeted your car."

He knew that was stretching it, but he still couldn't shake the feeling something wasn't right. He needed to be near his family and he'd learned long ago in battle to trust his instincts.

"*If* someone took the sticker, they almost certainly don't even know who the car belonged to."

"*If* and *almost*. Not good enough when it comes to the safety of my family."

She stared at him through three streetlights before finally saying, "Who are you?"

Huh? "What do you mean?"

"Shane, talk to me. Don't be an ass issuing orders like this. It's almost like you're deliberately picking a fight and that's not like you at all. If anything, you're the king of avoiding fights. You usually opt for another round of battling terrorists rather than having it out with your wife," she said with a wry smile. "So calm down. We can have a discussion."

He didn't know what the hell she was talking about and even if he could wade through it all, none of it would be germane to the point at hand. "We *can* discuss this, but we'll come to the same conclusion so why waste time?"

"Because I have a *mind.* Because perhaps I might have insights. Because I deserve to know details in this situation that have nothing to do with classified matters, damn it." She crossed her arms over her chest and huffed, a sign she was trying to regain control. And damn it, the way her arms plumped her breasts wreaked serious havoc with his concentration. "I admire the fact that you can be decisive quickly and accurately in battle, but this isn't battle. Or rather it shouldn't be."

Screw control and concentration. "I'm scared shitless that somebody who could have terrorist ties touched my family," he blurted. "Hell yeah, it was just the car. But it was my family's car and my wife and my daughters were only a few yards away. That makes me fucking mad."

Her mouth dropped open. Closed. Open. Then words poured free, "You're cursing."

"Oh, uh." His neck heated and he scratched along the embarrassing show of emotions. "What does my language choice have to do with the price of eggs in Boston?"

She reached to brush aside his hand covering his neck where the telltale blush had heated. "You only curse when you're really upset."

"I curse plenty." Shit, just catch him in battle and he cursed like a fucking sailor.

Did she know she'd linked her fingers with his on the armrest between them?

"Around the guys maybe, Shane, but hardly ever around me or the girls."

"Well...hell."

"Well, hell is right. I didn't realize until now how much this upset you. You could have just told me."

He squeezed her hand. "Communication has never been our strong suit."

Her gaze dropped to their linked hands, then slid to the road as he navigated the noonday traffic. "Do you really think there is cause for alarm over something as simple as a stolen sticker?"

"Normally, no. I'm not even sure now why I've got this...feeling. But I do. And since we are still married there's no reason we can't hang out under the same roof. It's economical if nothing else." Not that they needed to worry about money thanks to his days on the baseball diamond. Damn, things had been simpler then, but he didn't doubt or regret his decision to join the Air Force. Not for a second.

For the first time he wondered if Sherry would have been happier with him as a pro ball player. He would have had time free during the year to join her and the girls. He'd never considered that before— or what it might have been like to join in her type of work. A moot point. They were both committed to their lines of work now.

"Economical?" she echoed him. "Have you accounted for the cost to our mental health?"

Seeing his sexy wife perched in the seat beside him, he had to concede, she had a point. "It's going to be difficult because we can't solve the arguments the good old-fashioned way."

"And that would be?"

"Getting horizontal." His body already throbbed at the mere mention of having her sweet softness beneath him again. "Always worked out the tension between us in the past."

"Or vertical."

"True enough." Sex had always been a reliable connection between them, one he missed like hell. Again he couldn't help but remember that they were still married and still attracted to each other. Why couldn't they act on that?

"Except we didn't work out anything that way. Only stacked the problems on top of each other until the wall grew so high it collapsed on top of us, and the fall hurt so damn bad, Shane, I don't want to go through that again."

So much for his hopes of some farewell sex before the ink dried on the divorce papers. "You're saying if I stay, no sex."

At least her eyes held unmistakable regret. "I'm afraid so. There's no denying that we're attracted to each other but that only messes everything up in my head. We can't go backward or we'll only end up going through this pain all over again."

"The last thing I've ever wanted to do is hurt you." He maneuvered the car through the bumper-to-bumper lunch traffic, stopping and starting at each light. He tried to think of an answer to her last remark and only found that he was tired of discussing this shit.

Well hell, he did curse more when he was upset. He let his foot off the brake and accelerated. "Talk to me about something else. Anything else."

She jolted at his abrupt change of conversational thread and he thought for a moment she would balk and push on for more heavy talk.

Then her arms relaxed onto the rests. "I'm a soap opera addict."

"Okay. I know you watch one—the whole Blair and Blade thing." He grinned. "But you say that like you need a twelve-step program."

She smiled back, then flattened her mouth into a mock serious expression. "Don't joke. I take my shows seriously. It's not just Blade and Blair. I watch lots of soaps when I'm home, but yes, my favorite is 'All My Lives.' So when I'm away, I have friends record the episodes and send them to me."

He thought about her on the plane with her DVD

player, tears in her eyes that she quickly hid. "I know about your DVD player. I thought it was for cartoons and movies for the kids."

"It is. That's how I justified buying the thing. I didn't want the girls to be pop culture dweebs like I was. And when they go to sleep, I watch my soap."

"Pop culture dweebs?"

Her back went stiff in the way that preceded one of her stump speeches. "I truly believe I'm giving them an amazing education in showing them the world, but I still want them to be regular kids when they're riding their bikes at home. I want them to be regular kids who understand all about the latest cartoon characters and catchphrases so they don't feel awkward or out of place."

"Regular."

"Normal kid stuff."

"Normal." He was missing something here, some underlying thread she was subconsciously trying to relate to him if he could just push the right buttons to get there.

"Why are you repeating everything I say?" She snitched her hand away from his.

"Because earlier you said you didn't want them to feel like dweebs like you were." He took her hand back and linked their fingers, his thumb stroking the inside of her wrist. "You wanted them to be regular. Normal. As if you felt…" He left the rest unsaid as the pieces started to come together in his head, but he sensed she needed to say them.

The image pinched at his chest, the image of a young Sherry feeling like a misfit. An adult Sherry making darn sure her girls knew exactly who Dora the Explorer was.

Sherry's hand relaxed in his as she allowed the comfort of his stroking thumb. "My parents were definitely totally granola. We lived like the villagers, all natural. I certainly wasn't neglected or abused in any way. But when it came time to function back home, I always felt awkward. I just didn't have that all-American pop culture ease in my skin that comes so naturally to someone like you."

"Someone like me?"

"Holy cow, Shane, are you that self-unaware?" She pivoted sideways to face him, her eyes blatantly taking in the whole image of him until he felt a bit like a piece of meat, for God's sake. "You're a poster guy for All-American hunk. Blond god handsome, baseball star turned Air Force hero. A fabulous father." A smile played around with her lips. "You could be a character in my soap opera."

Her words that could have been a compliment actually didn't bring him a helluva lot of comfort. And because she thought he was a good dad?

Although that part did give him pause because he'd certainly had his doubts due to his own lack of a role model. He'd always thought of Sherry as the awesome parent, the natural, and seen himself as sloppy seconds.

He had to admit, it felt damn good to hear he wasn't there just for a paycheck and a masculine force field around the house. "Is that why you married me? Because I fit your soap opera ideal?"

She visibly jolted and stopped blinking as if taken aback…then she blinked fast. "No, no, of course not. That's ridiculous."

Except he couldn't deny the niggling sense within him that maybe he'd bought into that same sort of scenario in a different sort—the single mother with two children and how he embraced the simplicity of being her baseball diamond hero in an old-fashioned way, a fella who could knock one out of the park for her. Only to find out she didn't want or need a stand-up kind of guy.

Sherry could take care of herself and her girls just fine. She had dreams and life plans of her own. Her setup for travel and saving the world kept her so on the run she slotted in time for him when she could.

Finally he'd come to realize there was no future for them in that. They couldn't build a relationship on something more like vacations spent together when they'd never experienced day-to-day life with each other.

Then out of left field a thought blindsided him. Did she still struggle to feel "normal"? Was that a part of why she chose to travel so often, placing herself and her girls in a world where she could function? His own deployment schedule often left her alone as well, so he wasn't here with her if she needed help acclimating.

Not that he could see her admitting to any vulnerabilities.

Why had he never considered this before? Probably because he'd never bothered to see deeper into what she needed before. When was the last time he'd actually asked her to talk about something more than the children? Beyond that, they were usually so damn exhausted, he had to be honest that when she started talking about her next assignment he tended to zone her out or cut the conversation short with sex.

Mind-blowing thoughts, now that he considered them. All stuff to consider and talk about later—and they damn well would be talking about it. He needed to get off his ass and stop with the avoidance. Regardless of whether they ended up in divorce court or not, their lives were tied together forever in these two children.

But for now they were coming up on the aquarium. He turned off the road and into the parking lot. He wove through the cars only to find…

A cop car.

With its fucking lights flashing?

The police car squealed to a stop outside the aquarium.

Sherry straightened in her seat.

"Shane." Panic tinged her voice. "What the hell is going on?"

Damned if he knew but it didn't look good. He searched for a positive thought. "There isn't an ambulance. That's good. The children aren't outside, so it isn't something like a bomb threat."

"I can't imagine what it might be…"

Sherry ripped her door open. Shane met her at the front of the car and rushed toward the aquarium entrance. He didn't figure they stood a chance in capturing the cop's attention. Shane opted for racing toward one of the ladies wearing a tag that identified her as an aquarium official.

"Ma'am," Shane called out. "What's wrong here?"

The young woman in an ocean print apron made her way toward them, her face flushed from standing outside in the afternoon heat. "Sir, are you the parents of any of the children on the field trip here today?"

"Yes," Sherry pressed ahead. "Please, tell us what is going on."

"We're asking all the parents to gather in the waiting area," she said with an overstated calm that set off alarms in Shane's head as she pulled out a clipboard and pencil. "What are your names?"

Shane really didn't like the cold feeling icing up his spine. "I'm Tech Sergeant Shane O'Riley and this is my wife Sherry. Our daughters Cara and Mally Holloway are part of the field trip."

The aquarium worker's flushed face blanked of all emotion as quickly as she tucked her clipboard away without bothering to make a single notation. "You'll both need to come with me."

Sherry choked on a gasp and clutched Shane's arm. "Tell us now. Right now. I'm not moving one step until you tell me what's happened to my girls."

"If you'll just step over here where we can meet with the police officer—"

"Now damn it," Shane spoke through gritted teeth, determined to talk to the cop soon enough, but not moving an inch until he heard what the hell had happened. He hooked an arm around Sherry's shoulders, all too aware of his wife wavering on her feet.

The woman glanced over her shoulder as if she could catch the police officer's attention, but the man seemed deeply engrossed in a conversation with two men in suits with badges. Police detectives, perhaps? Oh God, how bad was this?

Finally, the lady looked back, clutched her clipboard and braced his shoulders. "I'm sorry to have to tell you this, but there seems to be a problem with the field trip. At the moment, the teacher and the authorities cannot seem to locate your daughter, your older daughter, Cara."

Sherry slipped out from under Shane's arm with a whimper. He bit back his own hoarse cry of denial and caught her with a second to spare as her knees folded.

CHAPTER TWELVE

URGENCY PUMPING THROUGH HIM, Dimitri Popov gripped the little brat by the arm, dragging her through the deserted feeding room in back of the aquarium. The girl—Cara—hummed softly beside him, irritatingly, but as long as she kept her voice quiet he decided to let her continue. So far she'd kept her promise not to scream in exchange for not being gagged.

The threat of the knife in a face had a way of subduing a child.

Dimitri hauled the kid faster, making his way toward the back exit with purpose. He hated to make so bold a move this early in the mission, but the information this Cara held had caught them unaware.

Yet gratefully so.

Besides, it would be nice to have such a huge ⸱success in an operation for a change. That crew member they had recruited from the base wasn't proving as reliable as they'd hoped in leaking information. He hadn't passed the test they'd set up for him to gauge his loyalty. Dimitri's contacts in the Rubistan underground would not be pleased with the young man.

Dimitri was not pleased. Much money rested on his pulling this whole operation off for them, and never again would he beg on the streets. People in his country understood bone rattling poverty. He made his first kill at twelve. Each time became easier. Two decades later, he didn't even flinch.

He pivoted around a corner, keeping his eyes open for cops as he made his way down the halls painted with images of sea creatures. The place would be surrounded with authorities before much longer. He needed to get out of here with this singing scrap of humanity. Fast.

Strange how this operation was taking more detours than the halls of this place. Had U.S.'s military intelligence made the connection yet between the attack on the NGO camp and the attempt on the cruise ship? The assault on the camp had been an impulsive retaliation by one of their more hotheaded members who'd been enraged by grief over the death of his brother in the cigarette boat.

A reckless, ridiculous move that had threatened their whole operation. The firebrand had died for leading his impulsive raid.

Control. Emotions must be controlled.

A part of what worried him about the sergeant they'd recruited. They didn't actually need the information from the D.I.T. class. Dimitri was already in the class, privy to far more information by serving as a guest instructor—an army captain from Eastern Europe.

Some in his country wondered why he risked his life this way. After all, he had a comfortable existence with his military pay. Now he wanted more than comfort.

After his childhood, he wanted more than "enough" money and he craved complete power.

So yes, he had them all fooled into thinking he was part of the international coalition. Moles were easy enough to plant and Rubistan's underground was eager for new recruits to overthrow their fledgling democracy. Dimitri had been watching and could tell that the sergeant was trying to find a way to wrangle out by feeding them worthless information.

Although how he would evade them in the end, Dimitri wasn't certain. Of course the sergeant didn't realize they knew about little Tabitha. They knew about everything.

Tragic for the sergeant, because now they would have to send a message to that air crewman. Threaten him into line and he really hated to do that this early in the game. But there was no help for it. The flier had access to places they would need later.

They had *many* goals in this mission. Some had been in the works for years. Others had come to light as a surprise bonus quite recently—like this child Cara and the critical information she held from her trek across the Caribbean Island. The little one whimpered but no sympathy flowed through his veins for her. Good girls didn't disobey their parents. In his country she would have been punished soundly.

In his country, she would not have been allowed to run so freely in the first place.

However, she had and now they needed something vital from her. A few more steps and he would be able to slip out of the back exit of the aquarium. The Exit sign glowed even now. Lucky for him he had heard Shane O'Riley talk about his daughters' field trip during class. The man talked about his family all the damn time.

The man made a mistake to let his weakness show like that. Perhaps they should have chosen him as their link by targeting his family in the first place. But Dimitri had sensed a deep loyalty to country in the man, an innate honor. He'd doubted O'Riley could be turned. He almost certainly would have gone straight to the authorities and admitted how he'd been tricked and let the chips fall where they may.

Instead, they were stuck dealing with a scared little boy who acted like such a brave man with big balls. But he crumbled under fear when the real pressure came.

Enough of that. Focus on getting to the Exit. He pushed the bar and—

An alarm blared.

A curse echoed in his mind as loudly as the alarm and the little girl's sudden—and unexpected—screams for help.

"Help! He's not my dad! Kidnapper! Help me!" Cara shrieked, yanking on his hand with the lung capacity of a damn opera singer. "Help!"

He took in the sight in front of him. The back parking lot was full of people. Parents perhaps. Curses again. There was nothing he could do but cut his losses and run. He would pay royally for his mistake. His people did not take well to those who failed, but to be caught would be far worse.

He released little Cara's arm and sprinted into the aquarium again. With luck, he could blend back into the contained crowd. He'd worn a hat, sunglasses and fake mustache in hopes the girl wouldn't be able to ID him if she saw him at any of the D.I.T. gatherings.

He may have failed in capturing the brat today. But he had time, not much, but more. And while he waited for the right opportunity to present itself again, he could focus on the pathetic sergeant who'd been trying to dodge doing his duty to his new master.

SHERRY DODGED THE police officer trying to hold her back into the crowd. Nothing would keep her from her child standing in the back entrance to the aquarium.

"Cara," she cried running across the concrete to gather up her daughter, Cara's thin arms wrapping around her tight, so tight. Her child shook and cried, but she was safe. Sherry squeezed her eyes shut against her own tears pleading for release, except she didn't want to scare her poor terrified child any worse than she already apparently was. "Ohmigod, sweetheart, where have you been? Everyone's been looking for you for over a half hour."

"Well, first I went to the bathroom. I know I'm supposed to ask first but I had to go so bad, and then I got lost trying to find everybody and then—" her voice quivered and her eyes pooled with tears "—Mama, there was this man—"

A man?

Sherry's worst fears smoked through her.

"Ma'am." The chief detective who had been trying to hold her back grasped hold of her arm. "Please, let us do our job and question her first. If you talk to her, you could taint her answers. Please. You have to know how important this is."

Her arms already aching with emptiness even before she released her child, Sherry set Cara down again. "Cara, sweetie, you need to talk to this man and tell him everything that happened while you were missing. All right? You can trust him."

Cara's arms remained vise-gripped to her mother. "You'll stay with me?"

"Of course. I'll be with you the whole time, sweetheart." Nothing would pry her from Cara's side and the detective would simply have to deal with that. She turned to Shane who stood not more than inches away, his face carefully blank but his jaw so tight with tension she knew his fears were every bit as high as hers. "You'll hang on to Mally while I'm with Cara?"

"Absolutely," Shane answered without hesitation. "I'm not letting her out of my sight. I'll be right outside the door waiting for the two of you."

He stepped forward to hook his hand behind Cara's neck to press his cheek against the top of her head. "Love you, baby girl."

She peeked up from Sherry's neck, silky black hair gliding aside for her teary eyes to peek at her father. "Love you more, Daddy."

"Not a chance." His voice cracked.

"Sergeant," the detective warned. "We really need to speak with her, the sooner the better."

Following the detective into the aquarium director's office, Sherry forced herself not to shake and not to cry—the hardest thing she'd ever done. Second only to how difficult it was to keep herself from throwing herself against Shane's chest and soaking up the comfort of the muscular expanse and those strong arms.

FIVE HOURS LATER, Shane checked the locks on the condo for the second time. The sight of the Sheriff's department cruiser circling their block offered a welcome reassurance after a day of pitifully few answers.

Cara hadn't been able to supply them with much of a description of the perverted jerk who'd tried to lure her from the aquarium. A man. Grown-up. With dark hair, a funny mustache, tan and really tall.

Of course to an eight-year-old, any adult seemed really tall.

They were searching security tapes in hopes of coming up with something, but so far images only showed a man with a hat and sunglasses. A man careful to dodge camera angles.

Damn it. He clenched his fists and resisted the urge to punch the wall—which would only wake up the kids and put his hand out of commission and unable to defend them.

He could use a couple of hours in the gym to work off his bottled rage, but Sherry, who was peeking in on the girls for the third time, needed him here. Besides, all his anger aside, nothing would take him away from the three females in this condo right now.

He crossed to the head of the hall and found Sherry staring at their oldest child sleeping. She stood slouched against the doorframe to Cara's room, silently. No telling how long she'd been standing vigil.

"Is she all right?"

"She hasn't wanted to talk about it since spilling everything to the police psychiatrist. Since we got home, other than being a little clingy, it's as if she wants to pretend nothing happened. At least she's able to sleep." Sherry crossed her arms under her breasts, hugging herself tightly. "I don't think I'll ever be able to sleep again."

Screw keeping their distance. He thudded down the tile floor and slid an arm around her shoulders and pulled her toward him. She shrugged away, leaning back against the wall lined with framed children's artwork. "No."

"No?"

"No." She shook her head, blond locks grazing her shoulders. "I'm afraid if I let down that I'll fall apart."

"Nothing wrong with falling apart." He reached for her again, more insistently until she sagged against his chest a weary sigh. "Ah, Sherry baby, this is worth getting crazy upset about, if you ask me."

She shrugged again as he soothed his hands along her back. "It's like the whole world has tipped upside down this week. Those terrorists shooting at your plane. The attack on the camp. Mally getting sick. Now this with Cara. Everything's a disjointed mess. It's all too much for me to hold in my brain."

"Yes, it is." In the past they would have had a solid marriage to support them through a rough time—although everything they'd been through this week went beyond a "rough time." Something about the whole "disjointed" nature of their lives lately hitched in his brain, but he couldn't think overlong on much of anything but the soft sweet feel of her against his chest.

Heat stirred low within him from just the gentle brush of her body against his. Her soft curves, hips and breasts, teased him with memories of bare flesh brushing in a more intimate way. The ever-present need he felt around her fired hotter until he damn near shook from the restraint it took not to press her into a firmer embrace.

She stilled against him.

No way could she miss the hardening length of him against her stomach, her every restless squirm sending a throb through him. He'd been thinking how he needed release from the frustration of the day. Damn, but that fit hand in glove with his notion of how they should be able to enjoy the comfort of sleeping together since they were still married.

"Sherry?" His hand glided lower to cup her hip and rock her ever so lightly against the proof of his aching desire for her. His fingers gripped the gentle give of her sweet flesh. He realized the last time they'd talked she'd said no, but she wasn't moving away.

He didn't like talk much so he kept gliding his hand along her arm, then her back, watching her eyes for any signs of rejection—finding none. If anything, she swayed toward him.

Perhaps on a day like this she needed him every damn bit as much as he needed her. "Sherry, if you want me to leave, say so now.

"Shhh." She slid her hand up the side of his neck and into his hair, her touch so damn familiar. So damn *right*. "I'm afraid if we discuss this too much somehow we'll start fighting again and I'll talk myself out of something I need so damn much."

Even though she asked for silence, still he had to hear her say it. He couldn't take advantage. "What do you need, Sherry? You said you don't want to talk about the why of what we're doing, but we can talk about the how. Tell me."

That kind of talk he could totally get into.

She flattened her body against his, breasts to his chest, hips rocking in a gentle but unmistakable message as she tipped her face to his. "I need you, only, in me, filling me until there's no room left for all the horror." She traced his mouth, grazing her fingernail along his bottom lip with a light abrasion. "But first, I need you to kiss me. I miss being kissed by you, Shane, I miss kisses so much."

Her words of need, her pleading for that sweet intimacy of a simple kiss sent his body throbbing and cut the bands of restraints. She couldn't be any clearer than that. Four months of staying out of each others' bed was about to come to an end.

But first, he would thoroughly kiss his wife.

CHAPTER THIRTEEN

SHERRY COULDN'T LET herself think overlong on the fact that her stint of abstinence was about to come to an end. Thoughts would bring doubts and fears.

Right now, she wanted to feel.

Feel the hard expanse of Shane's muscular chest as they backed down the hall toward her bedroom with his mouth plundering hers with such sweet and total thoroughness. She tried not to let herself think overlong about his wedding ring that hung on a leather string around his neck, rather than resting on his finger where it belonged. She still wore her gold band after all.

And then she couldn't think of anything but the feel of him. Great gracious, she loved to kiss. The connection of their lips, their tongues, the taste and touch tingled through her. She adored the way he cupped her head in total focus on meeting her mouth with his, grazing it over again and again.

Then his easily distractible hands wandered over her body in a delightful precursor of foreplay as they began to lose themselves, their feet tangling in the journey. Her toes curled and she reveled in the fact that her body was every bit as important to him as his was to her.

They crossed the threshold into her bedroom. *Her* bedroom. Even thinking that thought made her a bit sad. It should be *their* bedroom, but they hadn't lived here together.

A distracting thought she refused to allow herself. The furniture was theirs. They'd chosen the big brass bed together. There had been a base-wide yard sale. They'd been setting up house on a shoe-string budget. She'd had little furniture since during her marriage to Clint since they'd spent all their time in tents.

Didn't Shane realize she'd already made a compromise for him in cutting back on travel?

Ooops. Distracting thoughts again.

Focus on the kisses and touches as she tumbled onto that brass bed with Shane—then and now. At first she'd been at a loss as to how to decorate her first home ever. She didn't even have a childhood house for reference. Shane wasn't much help at first with his guy shrugs.

Finally, they'd bought whatever caught their eye—within their budget—and fit it into their base house however it worked out. They'd ended up with two sofas and no recliners in their living room, and a picnic table in their kitchen.

It had all worked out in the end into their home. Some of the pieces they'd kept—like the bed. Oh, the bed, with its piles of pillows and the welcoming floral comforter.

One of the fun things about marriage was the speed and ease with which they could ditch each others' clothes. Pants, shirts and underwear—gone in a flash in a haphazard scatter of drapes hanging on their eclectic furniture.

A symbol of their eclectic lives. Except their lives hadn't worked in the end. Except some parts had. Their parenting. The way they could stand up for causes.

The way they came together, like now.

Ahhh… She arched her back into the sweet pleasure of his mouth on her breast. The jolt shot straight through to the core of her, aching for more. She threw her leg over his and rubbed closer, harder, the friction just enough to frustrate her, make her hurt for more.

"It's been so long," she moaned against his mouth, even as she realized they'd gone longer without in the past when he'd been deployed for war. But with the divorce in the works, every day had been a mark toward forever without him. "Let's go for quick this time. We do slow afterward."

He worked his leg against her in a teasing temptation. "How slow, babe?"

"As long as you can last, Slugger."

"Is that a challenge?"

"For later." She nipped her mouth along his neck, lower until her tongue flicked along his chest beading with perspiration. She continued her tasting, nipping exploration along his collarbone where his wedding ring rested on a black leather chord. "For now I'll challenge you to how fast you can put me out of my misery."

He flipped her to her back and loomed over her, sweaty male and muscle. "Let me make sure I heard you right." His chest heaved. "You want me to see if I can finish you off in record time?"

She wriggled under him. "I don't think it will take much effort."

He nudged his leg between hers with just enough pressure to make her crazy but not enough to give her release. "You've gotta know that in telling me to go fast that's a challenge to make this so leisurely…"

She slid her hand between them and stroked the length of him as slowly as he was tormenting her. "How slow?"

His eyes flickered closed and his throat moved in a long swallow before he looked at her again with sexy, sleepy eyes. "Maybe I can be persuaded otherwise."

"I thought so."

She wrapped her fingers around him, soaking up the familiar feel of him in her hand after four months apart. Savoring the groan of pleasure she wrung from him—which of course sent an answering thrill through her. His hand skimmed up her thigh until his skillful fingers found their target and… What was she thinking?

Who could think? Her body went boneless as she melted into sensation, some part of her brain reminding her to continue moving her hand because he deserved to enjoy this as much as she did. And oh, how she enjoyed.

After the fear and stress of the past days she needed this utter hedonistic moment. Just she and her husband, blotting out the rest of the world because the world had been so very awful for her of late.

She started to mention birth control, but then considered the fact they'd never used any contraception in their five years of marriage. They'd always figured they wanted a big family and would take the kids as they came…but none ever did.

Her body chilled slightly at that disappointment. She'd always told herself it had more to do with their spotty attempts at trying. But five years?

They'd been about to adopt a boy from somewhere…

Heavens, her thoughts were rambling. Was she out to sabotage her own orgasm or what? Men were so flipping lucky. Nothing seemed to derail them on the road to fulfillment.

She corralled her thoughts. Ditch all that had anything to do with something other than sex with Shane, sex complete with a tingling grande finale.

He kissed his way down the length of her to the core of her, ending with the most intimate kiss of all. Her head pressed back into the pillow as her hips arched upward. She'd asked for a speedy release and his skillful mouth and tongue seemed hell-bent on giving her just that, using all the knowledge he had on just what she liked best when he urged her to the edge and...

Shane was over her, filling her, thrusting inside her with the thick hot length just as fulfillment crashed over her with a wave as unexpected and surrounding as any from their shore. Cry after cry pulled from her mouth as he continued to move inside her, wringing aftershocks from her.

The dim light from the bedside lamp illuminated his golden hair, the perspiration dotting his equally golden tan skin. Her eyelids were heavy after the power of all that had pulsed through her, but she couldn't take her gaze from him.

He tensed over her. All those muscles of his bunching into hardened steel as she recognized his own oncoming release. She threw her limp arm over his shoulder and held him with as much strength as she could muster. Arched her back into his final push for completion as he filled her with warmth, then covered her with the weight of him, even warmer.

Her other arm flung over him, her body boneless.

She'd needed the comfort of his body, of the smooth and seamless way they came together, no question. But now she was confronted with the bittersweet ache of wondering if she would ever find anything as perfect again.

THREE HOURS DEEP in the Directives in Terrorism Class for the day, he leaned back in his seat—the hot seat, no question, with guilt burning his gut over what he'd done.

What he had to do.

Listening to all of this was like tying him to a chair in a torture chamber. Everything he heard was a possible land mine of information he would have to give away.

He shifted in the industrial—aka uncomfortable—chair and wished he were anywhere but here. A fruitless wish, but one he allowed himself about three times a day since he'd gotten himself into this god-awful mess.

Other parts were things he wished he'd known or guessed before. He'd already screwed up. He'd already made his mistake.

He forced his attention on today's speaker from the Air Force's OSI—Office of Special Investigation—as the class wrapped up with a few final basics. Special Agent David Reis from Charleston Air Force Base in South Carolina stood in front of the class in his dark suit, crisp walk and talk, speaking on counterintelligence—when you gather intelligence on people who are trying to gather intelligence on you.

Reis paced back and forth in the windowless vault room. "So in a basic overview, the OSI is responsible for counterintelligence as a means of force protection. When you're deployed, how do you figure out who's collecting information on you? Establish a relationship with the local police department—they want you safe, too. They don't need this shit in their backyard. Or at least you hope so."

A low laugh rippled through the room, except for Vegas sitting behind him. But Vegas had been distracted since the start of class, undoubtedly because of the kidnapping attempt on his daughter at the aquarium.

Reis stopped to sit on the edge of one of the desks, the dude still looking as smoothly creased in his black suit as he had at the start of the morning lecture three hours ago. Nothing ruffled these guys. "Build relationships with locals in the shopping place. Get them to know you as a person, build a relationship with you as a person to care about rather than a nameless faceless invader or infidel. You want to be a human to them. Then they'll be more likely to let you know bad crap's going on."

Yeah, he understood that all too well. He tried

to listen to the lecture but couldn't help but see the past replay in his head.

He'd been such an idiot. But damn it, they were slippery in how they lured a person in. All he'd done was go to a club in the capital of Rubistan. He'd just needed to unwind. No big deal. He'd done the same on countless other deployments and TDYs in countries around the world.

This hadn't been routine.

Someone had slipped something in his drink.

The next thing he'd known, he'd woken up on some smelly cot in a cell. His head had felt like an oversized cotton ball. A couple of soldiers from the Rubistan Intelligence Service had been sitting in his room. They'd told him he'd been drugged up on truth serum and he'd spilled government secrets.

Except he didn't need to take their word for it. They'd captured it all on tape.

Then he'd seen the crappy ass little television in the corner. They'd started the player. They'd started his time in hell.

He looked at all the high-tech televisions and equipment for live telecoms and big-screen projections in this instruction room today. Yet back then, he'd been taken down by an out-of-date VCR and tiny TV.

He'd seen himself speaking, selling out his country.

Inconceivable, but he hadn't been able to deny what he saw.

Reis jumped back up again, recapturing his attention. "There's a lot of information on the Internet, gentleman and lady. Take advantage of the source. As a matter of fact, that's a fine way to spend your late nights TDY rather than in some hellhole bar where you'll get into a wealth of trouble and the security cops have to haul your ass out of a foreign prison. Not good for the career, I might add.

Well, that advice came a day late and a dollar short. The cassette player hadn't captured the rest of the night. Racked with the shakes from the drugs, he'd curled up on that cot and cried like a damn baby.

Now all he could do was salvage his life. Bile burned the back of his throat now as it had then. What he would pass along from the D.I.T. class was nothing in comparison to what he'd spilled that day while drugged up.

Nothing.

So why did they want him here? That niggled at him every now and again, but his life was in such turmoil he could do nothing but keep running on the treadmill as fast as he could to stay alive.

He eyed Special Agent Reis with envy as the man wrapped up the talk. "After the break, our guest lecturer Dimitri Popov will be speaking about European counterintelligence activities in Algiers during

Algeria's War with France for Independence." Reis stopped by the door, keying in the cipher lock code. "Take thirty and we'll meet back here."

He wanted the hell out, but his legs wouldn't obey. It was almost as if he'd been drugged all over again as he watched the crew file out. Padre offered support to Vegas and bent his ear talking.

Rodeo stayed planted in his seat, too, jotting down notes in his dayrunner, no doubt still working on romancing his girlfriend. Simple normal stuff.

Normal.

For *him,* he had to accept that nothing would be normal again.

For the rest of his life, he would have to live with the fact that people had likely died in the days that followed because of flight plan information he'd given up while drugged to the gills. He didn't think he would ever be able to forgive himself for that.

The best he could hope for was to get through this alive so he could somehow, one day figure out a way to atone.

CHAPTER FOURTEEN

SHANE LOUNGED IN THE BRASS BED with his wife, watching his all time favorite movie—distraction was mighty welcome these past days—and he wondered where the week had gone? Each night after the kids were tucked in, he and Sherry ended up in bed tangled in the sheets and each other.

No discussion of should they or shouldn't they. No discussion of the divorce they both knew was imminent. They just went into the bedroom and slid under the covers without meeting each others' eyes until it was time for sex.

They were falling into a pattern of sorts, one that couldn't last but the need for each other didn't wane. Supper, then bed. At first he'd deluded himself he was there for Cara's safety. However the police thought they had a lead on the guy who'd attempted to snatch Cara at the aquarium. The pervert was on the sex offender's list, recently released from prison. The police had received a call of him violating his parole by hanging out around school grounds, but hadn't been able to catch him in the act.

The sicko didn't have an alibi for that morning and he bore a resemblance to the fuzzy image on a surveillance camera. Tough to tell though since the man had been wearing a hat and glasses.

Still, Cara's kidnapping seemed to be a random incident and not something personal. Saying it was tougher than believing it. Yet a week had passed without event.

Which meant his time here would draw to a close soon.

He slid his arm under Sherry's shoulders and pulled her snug against him while *Field of Dreams* played out on the television. He wondered if she was trying as hard as he was not to acknowledge that tonight was different. After a week of wild monkey sex, tonight they hadn't made love. They'd gone through all the family rituals, enjoying Cara's solo at vacation Bible school at the end of the week. And oh what a lovely job she'd done, their solemn child coming alive when she sang. Of course after the aquarium scare, Sherry had stayed at the classes as a volunteer snack helper, too scared to drop the girls off.

And nighttime, the simple pleasure of climbing into bed together to watch a movie. Periodically talking about their day, but mostly just soaking up the feel of being together in *their* bed.

He twirled a lock of her silky blond hair while the TV showed the baseball diamond in the middle of the field filling up with all the legends. God, he'd loved this movie since he was a kid.

"How long do you think we can just hang out in the condo and pretend the world doesn't exist?"

"Hmm…" He kept his eyes on the screen where the cars lined up for miles and miles and miles. If only he could simply *build it and they will come*. Back in Grandma Washington's kitchen he'd believed it, believed in dreams. His emotions were a little too raw for one of Sherry's deep discussions so he opted for a flip answer. "Hang out here and remain horizontal all the time. Is that another sex challenge?"

"Not tonight. You've wrung me out, big guy." She rolled to her side and snuggled against him, tracing the pattern on his T-shirt—Cincinnati Reds. "I was just wondering though. Last night. Tonight. The whole week. Seems like a new pattern is forming."

"Do you want one to form?" He closed his hand around hers and lifted it to kiss, mentally ditching her oversized Reds T-shirt. Ah, a fine fantasy image to make real if she let him stay. "A fresh start?"

She stared into his eyes as if searching for something…something she apparently didn't find because she broke contact and rested her head on his shoulder. "I'm not sure what I want long term except for some reason we're falling into bed together again. We need to be together now because the world is tipping. To be honest, I can't bring myself to toss you out."

"Good."

"That's an easy short term answer. Except honestly, the odds are against us since we've done this so many times before." Her fingers fisted in his shirt. "Which means this is going to make things hurt so much worse down the road."

His heart thudded double time under her fist. "You don't pull punches."

She tipped her face up to his. "Do you want me to sugarcoat it?"

He skimmed his hands down her nightshirt, toying with the hem. "Only if we're spreading that sugar on each others' naked bodies."

She giggled, wriggling against him, the cotton of their nightclothes doing little to ease the temptation of her breasts rubbing against his chest.

Her hand slid around to his thigh up to boxer shorts. "Things are good for us when we're here together for the most part. We've built a good home for the girls."

"Yes, we did."

She gave his taut butt a gentle squeeze. "And the sex is great."

"Definitely."

"You're a fun and fascinating man, if only we could live on vacation." She buried her face in his neck and snuggled closer, yanking the froofy quilt over them both. She always had that habit of keeping the air conditioner on subarctic as if to make up for all the times she lived in sweltering temperatures.

He tipped up her chin and graced a kiss across her lips. "Let's get back to those positive things again."

"Good point. We don't dwell on the things that were tough in our childhoods. We just made different choices for ourselves."

"I like to think so." He'd told her that his parents were drinkers, distant types, partiers. He'd never let her know the depth, though, of how far things could go. The dark side of their arguments. There wasn't really any need for her to know since he'd always managed to take care of himself and escape it all anyhow.

Guilt still dogged him over how fast he used to hightail it out of his childhood apartment the minute his parents started arguing. As an adult, he understood he wasn't responsible for their drinking, but as a child he'd thought he should be able to do something.

He had, in fact, done some things. Any time he found a bottle, he'd dumped the contents down the sink.

But when he missed one, he knew the cycle well. First, they would get all sweet and cuddly with him and each other, *We love you, sugar.*

Two to three drinks later, the stumbling and verbal abuse started.

Always verbal. They'd never laid a hand on him. Maybe that's why he'd always found it so difficult to reconcile because it didn't fit in what he saw as a traditional abused child mold.

Oh, they threw things at each other, but never punches.

And he ran. Straight to Derek's for peace and cookies in a place he thought surely came straight out of a Betty Crocker recipe.

We love you, sugar.

I love you, Sherry.

Love that could spin on a dime as people dredged up the most awful barbs to throw at one another and he was just as guilty. *Fuck* it all, this hurt.

Sherry eased her hands up his back, splaying her fingers along the bold planes of his shoulder blades. "Still I'm so sorry that your parents weren't there for you."

He steeled himself not to let the past show through. "I had Derek's grandma and she had more than enough love to spread around for four parents." An image of her in her floral housedress belting out Aretha hits as often as she sang hymns from church.

"You were lucky."

He didn't want to dwell there. "I'm sorry your

folks didn't give you a purple beanbag chair to call your own."

Digging deeper about his own parents made him think more about hers for a change. For the first time he wondered where her parents had actually taken her. He'd never thought to ask about their philanthropic work. Yes, he'd ridden Sherry's back about hauling the children around the world. But for the most part, she'd been conservative about the locales she'd chosen.

He knew before she'd adopted the girls, Sherry had worked some hairier situations. She didn't fit the profile if someone were to meet her for the first time with her glamour girl curves, platinum blond hair and those blue eyes that only had to smile at him once before he was hooked.

But she just scraped her hair back, ditched the makeup and dug right in with everyone else—and still took his breath away.

Had her parents been as careful with their child as she'd been with hers? If not, he knew well what that could have done to her psyche. He'd seen too many children in war torn countries.

He started to ask her, but a light *tap, tap, tap* on their bedroom door stopped him.

"Mommy?" Mally called.

"Daddy?" Cara echoed.

Shane grinned at Sherry. "I guess it's a lucky thing you're wrung out, because I believe alone time is over." He rolled out of bed and pulled on a pair of sweatpants over his boxer shorts. "Just a second, girls."

He headed for the door as Sherry yanked her nightshirt back down over her panties. Shane opened the door and the girls came bounding past to jump on their parents' queen sized brass bed, tunneling under the comforter with garbled chatters of:

"Tell us a story."

"Not tired."

"Can we stay in here?"

"Scoot over."

"Your toes are cold."

Until both girls were settled between their parents with such a perfect rightness Shane felt his eyes sting with the tears he hated seeing in his wife's eyes. Where had they gone wrong? Because they had. He could hear all the past fights between him and his wife echoing in his head, feel them resonating in his heart.

Why won't you listen, Shane?

You don't even know how to fight fair without getting PMS emotional.

You're never here anyway to make a marriage so how would you know?

Nothing I do is good enough for you and the girls.

How can I measure up when apparently you're so damn perfect?

Every word a fresh dagger.

But instead of clenching his jaw, he let his head

sag back into the pillow, Mally's chatter and Cara's humming rolling over him in synch with other echoes of past arguments in his head. And all he could think of was how in the past—the good days—he and Sherry would have reached over the children to hold hands.

DEREK SHOVED BACK his chair, clocking the end of another D.I.T class. Normally he lived for this kind of thing, the deep inner workings of terrorist networks. Before being reassigned here, he'd been battling insurgents who were trying to stop the spread of democracy since the start of war in the Middle East. He'd spent more than his fair share of time in Rubistan.

The hope? Build a democracy there in the same way a democracy and friend had been made of Japan after World War II. A hard as hell challenge, but history making was never easy. The physical and an intellectual challenge charged him up, made him want to be a part of the military for the long haul—the full thirty years.

And then there was this amazing woman strutting through his head throughout the whole lecture. How was he supposed to deal with that?

He should be listening to the lessons in particular since today's lectures were being given by foreign guest speakers—Najim al-Hashi and Dimitri Popov.

Dimitri passed his secret data to their guest OSI

agent, David Reis, then tucked his own briefcase under his arm. "I am most sorry to rush out, gentlemen. I have a luncheon engagement."

Sandman tipped back in his chair. "Is she hot?"

Smiling, Dimitri smoothed his silk European made suit. "She is a sweet little exotic thing."

Padre elbowed Sandman. "Ohhh, sounds like he's been bitten by the bug. Maybe he'll be lured to stay by one of our American beauties."

Dimitri tilted his head to another side. "Bitten by a bug. I am not sure I completely understand what you mean but I believe perhaps the phrase could apply. I am just having trouble finding a way to get time alone with her because her family is so overprotective."

"Ye-ouch." Sandman's chair legs landed all four on the floor. "Well, get moving while you've got your window of opportunity."

"Yes. I will be moving very quickly before all the other men in her life surround her.

Dimitri Popov disappeared through the door, the cipher security lock seal hissing after him.

Stones leaned forward on his elbows, babying his still sore hands even though the bandages were down to minimal, only Band-Aids in a couple of places. "Are you all right, Vegas?"

Shane unpacked the snack lunch he'd brought with him, like the guy always did so he could study during the day and have more family time at night. "I know it's been a week since the incident with

Cara, but I'm not sure how long it will take before we stop checking her seventeen times an hour. I want to wrap them all up and cart them around with me all day long."

"Too bad they can't hang out around here more."

The security for the class was so tight they couldn't even get into the building. Rodeo enjoyed the time with the kiddos, his only occasions with little ones since he didn't have any of his own—or plan to in the near future.

Right?

"This is tough too." Shane tore off a bite of his sandwich. "Given Sherry's independence. The cops thought they had the guy, but they had to let him go for lack of evidence. So I set the alarm system at the condo and she promised to stick close to the house until we're both comfortable again, just until the cops have a chance to investigate things and either pin it on this pervert or find the real guy who did it."

Padre, the eternal peacemaker, slapped Shane on the back. "You know I'm here if you need anything. We all are. You only need to call."

"Thanks. I appreciate that more than you could know, guys." His throat moved in a long swallow that he shook off as if uncomfortable with all the emotion. "So, speaking of independent women, Rodeo, how did it go with the Godivas?"

Rodeo leaned back and kicked the chair beside him. "My granny's enjoying the hell out of them."

"Went that well, huh?"

He liked to give the sweet old lady presents, but he'd just sent her a new DVD player two weeks ago. "It was give them to grandma or have Keisha break out in hives."

Stones folded his arms, his face the world head on look in place. "That woman is 'allergic' to damn near everything."

Rodeo righted the chair he'd displaced. Apparently she wasn't quite so allergic to his kisses. Progress for sure, but damned if he knew what to do next to move things forward to the next level. "She's a tough one to figure out."

A rustle sounded from behind them, another crew gathering their gear for lunch. The pilot stepped forward. "Why not give up? Apparently she's not interested. Let it go and move on. There are plenty of hot women out there." He gave a cocky grin. "The flight suit is a chick magnet."

A series of wadded paper balls hit the cocky pilot in the head until he retreated laughing.

Sandman leaned in. "You've more than done your penance when it comes to Keisha. What more does she expect from you?"

A pound of flesh? A few pints of blood? But he kept those thoughts to himself. "This really isn't a conversation I'm all that comfortable having with you guys."

Sandman's smile went downright gloating. "Ah,

he won't banter the woman's name about. The surefire sign she's the important kind."

Padre nodded repeatedly like a damn bobble-head. "All the more reason why you should be getting help because you're in serious need."

"Something original," Sandman added quickly, getting fired up. "She's not your average woman. I hear tell from Shane here that she's a mountain climber, for God's sake."

A mountain climber? The thought of her lithe body clinging to craggy heights damn near gave him heart failure. "That true?"

Shane nodded. "Don't you know anything about the woman at all?"

Defensiveness slithered up his spine. "I know she went on a Komodo dragon hunt once."

Sandman shook his head. "God, that's spooky shit. I like a woman who squeals at mice and stuff. Gives me the chance to play hero and save the day."

"Yeah," a voice called from the back of the room, the Mighty Quinn stepping forward, "that's gonna play well for you the first time you're TDY and the woman in your life has to fight her own little whiskered beasties," his childhood in Australia peeking out just a hint in his accent. "I've been around about twice as long as most of you. I should know."

There was something to be said for listening to the boss about more than just flying.

Sandman waggled his hands in the air. "Okay, sir. If you say so."

Derek put his fingers between his lips and whistled. "Hello? Thanks for all the insights. Especially from you, sir." He nodded to Quinn. "I know this may come as a surprise to all of you, but I'm not finding any help with this particular woman."

Padre, who'd been mostly silent, stroked his chin. "Originality. Find the gift that speaks to that woman. Godivas and roses are nice. Women like them, but when you tie them up with that something personal…that's when you've got the woman totally on your side."

Shane snorted. "That's all well and good for the dating scene. Except what about us married guys? When do we have the energy to give that kind of thought to romancing each other? Marriage presents its own challenges in just getting through the day. Add children and careers with all the normal problems of life and I'm lucky if I can remember to pick up my boxer shorts, much less remember what kind of candy she prefers."

The Mighty Quinn chuckled from his perch on the edge of the table. "Amen, brother."

"So, sir. What's the answer for the long haul folks?"

"Damned if I know, Sergeant. Damned if I know. I think it's like when the weather goes to dog shit and the instruments are shot and you close your eyes and let your hands fly the plane. You just gotta feel it."

Derek stared at the room full of men who basically hadn't told him a damn thing other than he still had to work his ass off to win this woman over. "So let me get this straight. I've got to figure out the perfect unique gift for a woman and then spend the rest of my life with her flying as if the weather is the worst ever and my entire control panel is busted. Why in hell would anyone want to get married?"

Then an image of Keisha in scruffy khakis and a dirty white shirt flashed through his mind, her long legs, her light-up-a-room smile. Most of all, her take-no-shit attitude that challenged him to be more of a man.

Quinn grinned and pointed to Derek, making him realize he'd been staring off into space for…he didn't have any idea how long.

The commander nodded. "Gentlemen, ask Rodeo. I believe he just figured out the answer."

STARING OUT OVER THE OCEAN, Keisha hugged her knees as she sat in her wooden perch she'd built in the tiny fenced backyard of her corner apartment unit. The bird-watching tree house gave her a sense of solitude when she was stuck back in the claustrophobic States between assignments, so she'd better make the most of this sunset.

Her NGO had a branch office here in Pensacola where she worked. Sherry freelanced paperwork from home when in the States. Neither of them would be returning to the Caribbean village, however. The damage had been too severe. The rebuilding called for larger scale services than they provided. Her heart ached at what the people she'd come to know were now suffering through because of a senseless attack.

After reading over some of the reports faxed to her this afternoon, she needed the peace her tree house afforded her. The ocean at least took away one "world wall" for her as she gazed out through the cut out window at the endless expanse, watching seagulls dive for their dinner. A lot of thinking happened for her in these cedar four walls, fifteen feet off the ground. Lately it seemed most of those thoughts centered around a certain flyboy.

She had to admit the whole being courted thing—while old-fashioned—was fun. Aside from the Godivas and flowers, he'd tried sending her a subscription to the most bizarre safari art magazine ever. Then there had been the tiny porcelain tiger planter with a fern on her front stoop.

He'd even purchased a goat in her name in a third world village. The goat would give milk for a whole family. She'd stood by her mailbox in a puddle of emotions with the certificate clutched to her chest, tears pouring down her face. Had Derek been lurking in the shadows even though he'd lived way over by Hurlburt Field, an hour away?

All of this in only a week. If he was putting on an act, it was a damn good and persistent one.

She sat up in her bird-watching tower—alone. The trapdoor to the ladder closed. The small fan whirred away just below a bald lightbulb she'd mounted at the top of one corner. For now, the light stayed off and she simply enjoyed the sunset.

Not much going on, well except for a sighting of a Bahama mockingbird. Of course that could have a lot to do with the fact that she hadn't bothered to pick up her binoculars. Honestly, the place served as a thinking tower as much as a much a place to add to her diary about new wildlife observations along the beach of swaying sea oats.

Bored, she rolled up the bamboo shades that covered the small twelve-inch windows that rimmed the other three walls of the tree house. She grappled behind for her binoculars to search some of the deserted barrier islands when… From her roost, she saw Derek's SUV pull into the parking lot.

Holy third world goat.

Keisha scrambled back, a stupid thing to do. Darned reflexes.

She had the option of pretending not to be home. Given this place was built in the small back garden of her apartment, chances were he would give up after no one answered the front door.

The ball was in her court. Invite him up or let him walk away. Keep chasing Komodo dragons or wrestle with the stubborn, ornery, exciting man she'd never been able to forget.

She watched him ring the bell, and wring the bell, the decision so close to being made for her. She twisted the binocular strap around her fingers as they lay in her lap, small corner fan doing nothing to ease the heat crawling over her skin.

The great thing about being impulsive was that she made her decisions quickly. She snatched up her cell phone and punched in his numbers and he pivoted on his heel away from the door.

His phone rang and rang. Ohmigod. What if he'd left his cell at home? She started to lift the hatch to shimmy down the ladder and catch him. She would have to sprint to make it to his SUV before him.

He picked up. "Hello?"

"Derek?" Wow, was that breathless voice hers? She so wasn't the breathless type.

"Keisha? How strange. I was just at your place."

"I know." She couldn't stop the great big smile welling inside her. "I can see you."

He was clearly dressed for her, not work, as he stood there in his brown polo and khaki shorts that his muscles filled out quite well. *Thank you very much,* her hormones sighed. Nice, crisp, casual but out to impress. And he held a small gift in his hand.

Oh my. He was getting good at this and she was getting weak.

"Then why didn't you answer the door? It's hot as hell out here, even with the sun going down."

"Your charming manners never fail to win me over." Her smile twitched as she adjusted the speed to high on her fan. She might be daring but she did appreciate some creature comforts.

"Uh, hey, Keisha, do I go or stay?"

Oh shit, he was going to leave if she didn't get her head out of the clouds. "Stay." *Please.* "I'm in the backyard in my tree house. Come watch the sunset with me if you want."

The silence was deafening.

He stood stock-still for a shocked four gushes of the receding tide before tipping his head upward as if searching for trees. He lifted his aviator glasses and set them on top of his military short hair, before his gaze settled on her wooden structure.

Finally, "You have a tree house." He shook his head from side to side, clutching his latest gift offering in his hand, a small box. "Of course *you* have a tree house. I'll be right there."

She didn't know whether to be insulted or complimented by his words. Not that she even had a chance because by the time she yanked the trapdoor open, he was on his way around back. Then, oh yeah, there he stood at the bottom of the ladder. His strong bold face looked up at her before he started taking the rungs, biceps flexing in his polo shirt. *Yum.*

With a final muscle-rippling heft, he swung around to sit in her rectangular structure with Astro-Turf on the floor and a cut out window up high to look out over the ocean. He brought his legs up as well to stretch the length, the small fan a few inches from his boat shoes.

She dropped the trapdoor closed with a resounding commitment that reverberated all the way from her tummy to her toes.

He leaned back on one hand and sat beside her silently. For the longest time neither of them said a word, simply stayed side by side while the sun played hide-and-seek with the moon and stars.

Slowly, the golden moon cast a hazy glow into tree house, the stars splayed out like a fistful of glitter thrown over the sky. She didn't even consider turning on the small bulb in the corner and dimming the perfection overhead.

They must have sat like that for at least forty minutes or more. She'd never met a man who could be still and quiet that way, anyone who could appreciate the beautiful purpose of her perch here.

Curiosity broke her first. "So what do you think of this place?"

"It's an interesting extra to come with the apartment."

Keisha wriggled around, hugging her knees again until she sat beside the heat of his hips. "I built it."

"*You* built it." He couldn't hide the surprise in his voice.

"Buddy, I've built houses in third world countries. I've been a part of disaster relief cleanup after tsunamis and hurricanes." She rested her chin on her hands folded over her knees. Her stomach still jittery, she wasn't ready to meet those piercing brown eyes yet, so she stared though the window at a heron wading on spindly legs with overexaggerated steps. "A bird-watching tower is child's play for me."

He placed the gift by her feet, then gripped her ankle. Torment on two levels. "You did a bang-up job."

Her eyes hitched on the mystery present while her nerves fired to life at his fingers wrapped all the way around her bare ankle. Skin to skin, the memory of the kiss swirling around as if stirred all the more into a whirlwind by her little fan.

"I wanted walls. Privacy is in such short supply when I'm on the road. But when I'm at home there are also so many people, there's a different sort of lack of privacy." She shrugged. "I make the most of creating solitude with this tower."

His pointer finger stroked up and down her calf, her body too accessible in shorts and a T-shirt. "Our crew all bunks together sometimes, but our conditions are somewhat better than yours."

Laughing, she swatted away his hand. "You have HBO and air conditioning. That's a little better than somewhat."

"Are we going to argue?" He palmed his chest. "'Cause if we are, can you give me warning so I can duck before you toss something at my head?"

"You make me sound so harsh." Hey, she'd been angry, damn it. Then she'd been playing, flirting.

"I'm not the one pitching presents."

The past reared its really ugly "Kimberly-Named" head. Keisha flayed the air. "I'm not the one who—"

"Stop." He clasped her hand. "I know what I did. You know what I did. And believe me, I know that it was terrible. Beyond terrible. But can't there come a time when we can let it go?"

"A time to let it go?"

He released her hand, scooped up the small mystery package and pressed it into her palm. "This is the last time I will bother you with a present. Actually, this is the last time I will bother you at all. I've tried everything I can think of to get it right with you and make no mistake, I want to get it right. But I'm not going to trail after you forever."

Derek folded her fingers around the box. "So I hope *this time* I chose correctly."

The last time? He wouldn't be back? No more funky magazines or plants? No more surprises or looking for his face around each corner.

Suddenly the fairly light gift weighed at least a

hundred pounds in her palm because so much rode on what waited inside. She wasn't all that great an actress so faking a positive reaction was pretty much out of the question.

All right. She'd chewed all the lip gloss off her mouth. No more delaying. Her stomach spinning as if that Komodo dragon was running on a tread-mill inside her, she peeled away the tape away from the blue and silver paper.

She inched the jewelry box out and creaked it open to find… "A watch?"

Nothing flashy or jewelry studded. A simple silver watch with numbers and a hand to tick off the seconds, the kind designed for a nurse. She smiled. Very thoughtful. Not the outrageous gift she was expecting, but nice. She could hang on for a while longer to that sort of sweet sentiment, even if there was a slight let-down feeling inside.

She clutched the heart to her. "Thank you for the watch. It's the perfect gift for a nurse."

He shook his head. "Yes, that may be true but you still missed my point."

"Which is?"

"Time," he said simply.

What? "Time?"

She stared at the gift, his single word bouncing around in her head. Time. She'd spent her whole adult life on fast speed. Most of her relationships were of limited terms. Often the teams she labored with were different for each project. Even she and Sherry only worked with each other on about fifty percent of their assignments and that was just because they both lobbied hard to make it happen.

Time. The prospect scared her more than a little.

Yet when she looked at this bold yet sensitive man, the notion also enticed her as well.

He pulled the box from her and took the watch out. "I want time to get to know each other. Time to romance you the right way so I don't give chocolates or flowers to a woman who would probably prefer a lizard."

Ohhhh. A shiver of excitement sizzled up her spine. A man who was hot, sensitive and he understood her. This was getting interesting. How much more interesting could it get with this time he wanted them to share? "A lizard?"

"See, I'm already learning things about you, amazing, fascinating things."

She looped her arms around his neck. "A man who can fly airplanes, looks hot in a flight suit, kisses like a dream and knows I like lizards? What more could a woman want?"

A wicked glint sparked in his Godiva chocolate eyes. "Just how private is this tree house?"

"If I latch the hatch, no one is coming inside. And since my apartment is a corner unit and the unit on the other side is vacant, nobody can see in."

"Is that an invitation for me to hang out with you a while?"

She stared at him for a long drawn out moment totally meant to torture him just a little before she tapped the watch. "Put it on me."

"Of course." With a slowness that most definitely served as payback for her torture tactics, he slipped the watch up onto her wrist before ending with a tiny *snap*.

She slipped her arms around his waist, her fingers dipping ever so seductively into the edges of his khaki shorts. "Now let's take everything else off."

CHAPTER FIFTEEN

DEREK GULPED IN A HEAVY BREATH of hot cedar-scented air. Take everything off? With Keisha. Out here? Well now that was beyond his best fantasy—times ten.

Then reality smacked him in the face harder than the gust of ocean wind winding through the window. He really didn't want to mess up this second chance. He'd just asked her for time and if they threw their clothes off ten seconds later that didn't sound like he was living out his word.

Hey wait. Was she testing him?

He narrowed his eyes and evaluated her. He wouldn't put it past Keisha. She was a complex woman. He liked that about her, but it also made things tougher for him as he worked to decipher the maze of her mind.

Derek settled back on his butt and rested both of his hands behind him, away from the temptation of touching her.

What a time to notice she'd carpeted the place with AstroTurf so there was no worry of getting a splinter in his behind if they *did* happen to end up unclothed after all. "I'm not sure we're ready to get naked yet."

"Excuse me?" At least she had the grace to look genuinely surprised. Of course that could simply be because she expected *him* to react differently. She reached out to the opening of his polo shirt and scratched a fingernail along the opening, over his skin—heaven help him. "Don't worry. No one can see us here, remember? We can be completely free, out in the open with the sound of the waves and the sky above us. I thought you would like that, given you're a pilot and all."

He stroked her with his gaze since his hands were off-limits for the moment. "Oh, I very much like the idea of making love to you here, thoroughly under the open sky."

"Then what's holding you back?" She flattened her hands to his chest, swaying forward. "It's not like we haven't seen each other naked before."

Nothing like mentioning that encounter to splash cold water on the moment. "We certainly did go at it fast and furious that time, didn't we?"

"I wanted you then, and you've certainly won me over again." Her fingers on his chest worked restless little circles. "You've got charm. I'll give you that."

He gripped her wrists to stop the torment wearing away at his self-control all too quickly. "I want to be more than some guy who charmed you into bed."

She wrenched her hands free and fiddled with the watch. "You really want time."

"Yes." He injected all the sincerity he could find into his tone, trying to make it just the two of them even though the traffic and waves echoed below. "I want us to get to know each other. I found out recently from one of Shane's friends that you hunted a Komodo dragon. Is that really true or just some joke about your fearlessness?"

She rolled her eyes. "Right after the encounter with you, yes, I did. I was in need of asserting myself then. I wanted to feel…uh…unique." Her head dropped and she stared at the watch. "Special."

His heart stung like hell. "I am so damn sorry I took that away from you."

Her head jerked up. "Thank you for the apology, but I'm an adult. I accept responsibility for my own feelings. Besides, I was unconventional long before you." Her eyes glided over him. "It strikes me that I should use this time to learn things about you as well, beyond the jet jock pilot."

Promising. "How about now? A trade-off of info."

"Sure." Her eyes glinted. "For clothes."

"Lady, the more I get to know you, the more I like your unconventional ways. Okay, I'm a gourmet cook and even have my own herb garden. I pay the neighbor kid to water it while I'm TDY." He tugged his shirt over his head.

"I can't even cook microwave popcorn but I have a green thumb." Her shirt followed and glory-be, her bra was emerald green as well.

"My mother and father were active duty Army." There went his shoes and he figured socks could go, too, because he really didn't want this to take too long. He was human, after all.

"My dad died when I was five and my mom's my best friend." Flip-flops went sailing.

"I spent most of my life with my grandma because my parents were always gone and that's how I learned to cook." He shucked his khaki shorts and no way could she miss his erection straining against his underwear. Thank goodness he always packed a condom in his wallet. But only one. Damn.

They would be going inside later where hopefully she had more protection.

"I started boating and shooting the rapids when I was ten. Once I got a taste for adrenaline, I was hooked." She shimmied out of her shorts, but it took forever because she had the longest legs.

Hmm. There were lots of things they could do without a condom so they could hang out in the tree house a while longer.

They stared at each other in their underwear, and he damn well forgot to breathe until his light-headed body reminded him. He held out his hand. She rested hers in his and he realized he needed to take the big step first. She deserved this after the pain he brought on her before.

"I used to think I wanted to wait for a serious relationship until I retired from the military, but there's this woman I just can't forget. She chases Komodo dragons and saves babies in third world countries. And I'm hoping like hell she has time to give this flyboy a try."

His underwear landed on top of his khaki shorts.

She placed her hands on top of his and she didn't smile, but her grip was firm. "I'm a little scared here because somehow it became important to get this really right, but I know what I want—to give that time with you a try. Starting now. But since I'm wearing a bra and panties I guess I need to pony up a second confession. So here goes. I'm a bold woman who takes the initiative in life without hesitation so many times. Except right now, I want you to take my underwear off me."

How could one woman be so exceptional? His body throbbed with anticipation. "My pleasure."

He forced himself to go slow. No sloppy drunken coming together like their other time. With attention to detail he traced over every inch of her green bra until his hands made it around to the hooks in back. *Clip. Clip.* And the satiny fabric fell free, hooking ever so slightly on her shoulders, waiting for him to brush the straps down her arms to reveal—oh yeah—a perfectly pert pair of breasts.

He couldn't stop himself from staring. "You're so damn beautiful. I'm a lucky bastard."

The panties would have to wait because he absolutely had to taste her. Now. He dipped his head to lave attention over one, then the other, her head falling back. Then her whole body bowed backward and he caught her, easing her down onto the floor of their cedar wood haven.

His hands browsed over her flat belly to dip into her panties, a thong that he could wrap around his fingers with just enough pressure to *snap*.

The scrap of fabric fell away as he slid his body over hers.

"Birth control," she whispered against his neck. "I didn't come here planning this."

"My wallet."

She reached for his shorts and with clever hands palmed a packet in less than a minute. "We'll have to leave here soon, you know."

Although it was tough to drag his eyes off her breasts, he looked up into her eyes and smiled. "Don't sell me short, lady."

"Not a chance, Sparky."

The teasing laughter, words and hands played over each other until long past the sunset until the stars started to twinkle over them. He was determined to drive her to the brink again, and again. He wouldn't leave this woman wanting again.

Yet oddly enough, it wasn't just pride. He genuinely wanted to see the pleasure of her orgasm illuminated by the moonlight. And he would. Most likely sooner rather than later, because this extended foreplay needed to come to an end for him.

Even with the tiny fan whirring away in the corner, they still had worked up a light sheen of sweat between them, their bodies gliding against each other as he shifted them along the floor until she rested on top of him. AstroTurf might not be as risky as wood but still wasn't as comfy as a bed and he wanted everything to be as perfect as possible for Keisha.

Moonlight shimmering over her, she smiled down at him as she rolled the condom over him in a seductive stroke that threatened to send him over the edge.

How could he have let her get away before? What an idiot he must have been back then.

Then she positioned herself over him.

He meant to let her take the lead but somehow his body thrust up as she arched down and the tight sheath of her wiped thoughts clean out of his head.

No thoughts. Only sensations of stroking her with his hands while their bodies continued the more intimate caress, up and down. It seemed they left no part of each other untouched.

He cupped the back of her head, drawing her mouth to his for a kiss. He wanted her to feel the intimacy of the moment. It was about more than just sex, and thank goodness, she didn't pull away.

Keisha threw herself into the kiss every bit as much as he did, open mouths with tongues tangling and tasting. Exploring.

Learning.

Yes, learning. That's what they were doing. Working their bodies and hands along each other and learning what made the other moan, louder, until the kiss had to continue to muffle a shout begging for release.

She mumbled his name against his lips again and again, her grip on his shoulder growing tighter until in some distant part of his brain he realized her nails had broken skin—and then he got his wish.

Her head flung back the moonlight streaked over her naked body as her spine arched again and again, holding with the force of her release…until she collapsed on top of him.

With a thrust of abandon, he let himself go. He buried his face in her neck and gritted his teeth to hold in the shout welling inside him. Next time, he would pick a less public hideaway. For now, he simply savored the pulse of his body coming inside her. Finally. Finally.

Until he let himself melt into the AstroTurf, his arms around Keisha while the little fan blew gusts over their perspiring bodies. He nuzzled her ear and whispered simply, "Amazing."

He felt her smile in response. Plenty of answer.

Slowly reality eased in and he started thinking about what he would do with this "time" he'd asked for. Keisha wasn't an ordinary woman. Winning her over would be an ongoing challenge.

One thing was certain. He hadn't chosen the simple route.

SHERRY REALLY UNDERSTOOD how simple it would be to grow paranoid.

Straddling the Jet Ski, she clutched her husband's washboard tummy and held on for dear life. It had taken a crowbar to get her out of the condo, but Derek and Keisha had convinced her they wanted to "play house" with the girls and even Shane had conceded they couldn't stay holed up inside the place forever.

And after the morning they'd had, she and Shane needed this time away. His flight bag had spilled on the table, the divorce papers splaying out there along with other flight plan paraphernalia.

Their eyes had met and she'd read in him the same feelings inside of her. They couldn't stick their heads in the sand much longer.

Right now, she welcomed the open air freedom and chopping through the waves in the Santa Rosa Sound that led to the Gulf of Mexico. Briny spray in her face. Unfiltered sun on her skin. The heat of Shane's back against her scantily clad breasts.

If only the real world could be left behind this easily as the fish jumped and plopped alongside them. The cops had come up with nothing about the attempt to kidnap Cara. David Reis at the OSI had said he'd found some persons of interest but not a thing concrete. For days, zip, nada, zilch. The guy lived three counties over and the cops were keeping a close eye on him. Nothing more could be done.

Although Sherry couldn't shake the creepy crawly sensation that they were constantly being watched. Could she be suffering from some mild form of Post-Traumatic Stress Disorder because of all the harrowing experiences they'd been through in the past two weeks?

Possible. She clamped her legs tighter around the solid strength of Shane's for reassurance as they zipped through the water parallel to the skinny barrier island.

If her nerves didn't settle out soon she might seriously consider speaking with one of the counselors at the Patient Advocacy Office on base.

At least some good had come from these distressing days. Keisha and Derek seemed to have made up. There was no missing the synergy between them.

Farewell allergies.

And what about divorce papers?

Could she and Shane be so lucky as to have a second chance? Second? The Jet Ski bobbled underneath her, almost as if in a divine reminder not to be self-delusional.

They were on about their thirty-seventh chance.

The Jet Ski wobbled again and her stomach started to clench—until the world righted and she realized it was simply a pod of dolphin joining them. The gray-backed mammals raced along on either side, dipping and bobbing. Some leaping. All different sizes. A community. A family.

Their perpetual smiles couldn't help but stir one from deep inside her as well. All negative feelings whisked away like streamers let loose in the wind, left behind as they speeded with their newfound friends.

Shane glanced over his shoulder and smiled back at her. His eyes the sparkling color of the water. His face full of handsome strength that would age well and in that moment she so wanted to figure out how to be around to see it.

The ache returned, a tender ache of longing for something she didn't know how to have. She didn't have the skills to make it happen. And for a woman who'd helped an entire third world village set up a sewage system, that was saying a lot.

The bold magnificence of his face was too much for her, the promise of what they could have had if she'd been a stronger, better woman was too painful. She had to look away, and in glancing over she realized their dolphin friends had left.

Shane steered the Jet Ski toward the barrier island shore along a deserted stretch. They'd gone shell hunting many times, but always with the girls since their Jet Ski held four.

Why had the two of them never thought to take an outing alone? Because they had so little family time. They didn't want to leave the girls with sitters the few weeks each year they all had together.

Yet here they were now. Alone with each other. And yipes, she was overthinking this. Why not simply enjoy the moment and ignore that tender ache telling her they were at the end of their chances?

The Jet Ski thudded against the sandy bottom. Shane cut the engine to idle, and she dragged her water shoes along the shallow ocean floor. The sensation of the water against her body intensified until she could swear she felt the salt gently abrading her skin.

She let Shane beach the craft as was their ritual. *Ritual.* The word stuck in her head. In five years they had built up a number of those she would miss.

She stood in ankle deep water while Shane finished up. "What are we doing now?"

"A picnic."

A statement of the obvious, not a question, but she didn't want to be argumentative. Her eyes gravitated to the small waterproof pack he'd strapped to the back of the Jet Ski. He'd planned ahead.

Thoughtful. She could certainly overlook the fact that he hadn't said something like *A picnic, if you're hungry,* or *A picnic if you want.*

There were so many wonderful and honorable things about a military man. But their clipped statements, orders really, with no explanation of why or query if the other wanted to go along could be really grating.

Actually, if felt demeaning.

But how could she explain that to him without sounding like an ingrate because he planned this beautiful afternoon for the two of them? Arrrrgh! Now she was getting worked up which would totally ruin the day so she stuffed down the feeling and focused on how hot Shane looked right now.

Right now being all they had promised each other. She sloshed her way through the gushing tide until she reached Shane's side on the deserted shore.

She'd been to so many places around the world and still she wondered at the beauty of this location she called home with dunes undulating into the horizons. Sea oats bowed in the ever-present wind blowing across the water. Only the occasional slap of a fish jumping in the water broke the serene solitude.

Slowly, the peace of place drained the frustration of her earlier thoughts away. "It's so…"

"Pretty?" he answered with a surprising guy-sensitivity as he untied the pack from the back of the Jet Ski.

"Of course." She wrapped her arms around her waist while he dropped the blue pouch the ground and knelt beside it. "But I was actually going to say quiet. Nothing but the waves and the birds. I'm so used to the noise the girls make—good noise. I'm not complaining, mind you. But they are rambunctious, normal little ones with their chatter and songs and yes, even their tussles."

He paused unzipping the waterproof bag, staring down at his hands as if unable to meet her gaze. "It's rare that you have time by yourself with me gone so much."

She knelt beside him, the sand and broken shells scratching her knees. "It's rare that *you and I* have time alone."

"Because when I come home we try to pack so many family memories into a short time with the girls."

A sore spot. But he went quiet, apparently not wanting to ruin this rare and possibly final moment between them any more than she did.

Avoidance. Not the best way to fix things. Even their short six-week stint in therapy had taught them that, but for right now she didn't care about appropriate modes of communication. She just wanted to be with him one last time. She wanted to capture a memory of pseudo normalcy to carry with her into the lonely years ahead.

They stayed silent for a moment and she welcomed the second to grab hold of her emotions again. She didn't want to get weepy or angry and stop the flow of discussion.

Finally, Shane reached inside the pouch and pulled out an oversized beach towel. He shook it out and let it flutter to rest behind a dune. She followed his lead and sat on the edge to anchor it while he knelt again and began unloading a feast of…McDonald's hamburgers, a huge bag of potato chips and Diet Cokes.

Food and the smell of sunscreen—the perfume of a Florida panhandle date.

She smiled. He'd remembered. Since she ate so much exotic cuisine while traveling, she enjoyed simple American fare while home. So they sat at their picnic, across from each other and devoured and talked and laughed as he teased her, the playful Shane setting her more serious self at ease.

The meal gone, sun cruising toward the tips of the palm trees, Shane relaxed on one elbow while she hugged her knees, suddenly too aware of how little clothing they both wore.

Nerves pattered inside her. Itchy, she reached to wad up the napkins, chip bag, pitching the remains of their picnic back into the nylon yellow pouch.

Shane clamped her wrist, halting her with his beautiful sunset blue eyes as much as his touch. "We shortchanged each other."

Hearing him admit what she'd been thinking

made it all the tougher somehow, but she'd never been a coward or one to stand down. "That was a mistake on our part."

"One of many we made." His thumb caressed the sensitive inside of her wrist.

"I've been, uh—" like she could really think at all when he was touching her "—I mean it's too late for it to matter now, but back when we were trying to work things, oh, uh…" He'd taken her other hand in his and now she was getting a double dose of that thumb stroke. Who'd have thought her wrists could be such a turn-on? But she had a serious case of the wriggles.

Maybe it had something to do with the way he kept staring into her eyes with his undivided attention. It had been so long since he'd looked right at her, only at her with such soul searching seductive intensity.

Finish the damn sentence. She clenched her fists. "I was thinking we messed up last year. That we missed an opportunity. Six sessions of marriage counseling might not have been a serious effort."

He slid his hands up her arms in a slow and word stealing glide that ended with him cupping her shoulders, those sneaky, sexy thumbs of his now slipping under her bathing suit straps. "I'm thinking I don't want to talk about marriage counselors or kids right now."

Her mouth went all sticky like when she'd snuck

a whole spoonful of marshmallow crème while making fudge for the kids. And then the shiver hit her, a lot like a sugar rush, but times a hundred. She swallowed hard. "What a wise idea."

"What should we talk about?" He caressed her collarbone—beneath her bathing suit straps which made it all the more intimate.

She blinked fast, or at least it felt fast in comparison to his slow blinking assessment. Her eyes fell to his bare ring finger, then to *his* collarbone where his wedding band rested hanging from a black leather string. "What did we used to talk about, back when we were dating?"

Shane stretched out on his side, picking at the pralines he'd surprised her with at the end of the meal—her weakness, damn him. "You mean in those frantic eight whole weeks we dated with two small children underfoot and all the crew gathered around us half the time?"

"Oh. Right." Not much longer than they'd spent in therapy. Rather ironic. Too short a time to build a relationship, now that she looked back. But heaven help her, she'd been so drawn to him and he was about to deploy for war. They'd wanted to be married in case something happened.

She snitched the last praline and nibbled at the caramelized sugar around the pecan, saving the best for last. It was all she could do not to moan. "It's strange how the two things that we have in common are the two things that present the biggest problem in us being able to simply relax and be together."

"What do you mean?" He finished the last swallow of his soda and crumpled the can in his hand.

"The way that we're darn good parents and really good at our jobs."

"Odd how in five years I never considered that." He tossed the can in the yellow sack and snagged a loaf of bread. He pulled out a slice and pinched off a piece to pitch for the birds. "Yet to compromise on those issues would make us less of the people we are, then we wouldn't have fallen in love the way we did."

He tossed a whole slice Frisbee style and watched the seagulls go wild. His good ole baseball arm served him well. He always made the bread go far so the bird never bothered them. If she tried, they ended up with a flock of seagulls overhead pooping all over their picnic like some Alfred Hitchcock movie gone rogue.

The whimsy of it lightened her mood, then saddened her to think of another one of their rituals. Things they knew about each other. The learning process she would have to start all over with someone else if she ever dared try again. Yet, at the moment she couldn't even imagine putting herself through this another time.

"Shane, we talk about the kids, but we don't talk about each others' jobs. It's almost like we love the kids and don't resent the time they take from us. But the jobs—whoa, that's fair game for all-out grrrrr."

"Astute," he conceded.

No time like the present to turn over a new leaf. "So tell me about this new boss of yours. The new squadron commander is actually Australian, right?"

"Part Australian—his father. His mother was an American flight attendant who met the guy on one of her layovers. Word around the squadron has it that some great job offer brought them to the U.S. when Quinn was in elementary school."

"Thus that hint of a hot accent."

Shane cocked an eyebrow. "You think my boss's accent is sexy?"

She traced his mouth with the tip of her pointer finger. "I think your Southern drawl is ten times as hot, so lower the testosterone shield, big fella."

He stared at a piece of bread in his hand. "Why do you ask about where he's from?"

She shrugged. "I just knew that some of the jobs you've held in the past, people couldn't be from foreign countries."

"This isn't one of them."

Wow, he was actually sharing about his job. The rarity of that touched her, and also made her realize how much she'd resented it in the past, but stuffed down that resentment since there really wasn't anything she could do about it. Why not confess it now since she had nothing to lose? "The whole spooky business of what you do weirds me out sometimes, all the things you know and how vulnerable that makes you."

"We're trained." He swung his feet around and sat up to meet her gaze straight on as if realizing the importance of his answer to her. Maybe the man was finally hearing her after all. "We understand, and yes, if some bad guy wanted to get something out of us…there are a thousand ways. But bottom line it comes down to honor."

"A thousand ways?" She shivered in the ninety-degree afternoon.

"In orientations we're asked, straight up, 'Do you have any behaviors that leave you open to blackmail?'"

She wasn't ignorant to difficulties in working overseas. Her job gave her some insights. Still, this question appeared odd. "Why such a broad question? That seems too easy to dodge."

"Sure. It covers questions about excessive drinking to womanizing to 'Do you like to hang out in rest stop bathrooms for hours on end waiting for *companionship?*'"

"Ew." She tossed the half-full bag of bread at him. "Do you have to be gross?"

He draped his arm over her shoulder. "Babe,

that's just the tip of the iceberg of grossness when it comes to the proclivities that could be covered. See, the real question they're asking is, 'If there's a threat to you that your vice could become public, or if you just screw up big time, will you stand strong and continue to serve your country honorably? Or will you buckle and sell her out to stay under the cover of secrecy?'"

His point crystallized in her mind. "Is your country more important than your vice?"

"Exactly."

"And you were able to answer without pause, 'yes.'"

He slung his other arm over her shoulder and linked his fingers behind her neck. "You know me well, my dear."

She cupped his oh-so-handsome face that had given up much to serve his country, even at the expense of his own family. "I've never doubted your honor. You're a good man. You gave up a huge dream in your baseball career to serve. I can't help but admire how hard that must have been for you. How hard it still must be sometimes."

He leaned forward and pressed a kiss to her mouth. Not one of deep passion, a simple, closed mouthed, three-second linger of connection. A hello. But somehow one of great intimacy as they held each other. He pulled back a few inches. Sunscreen and a hint of ketchup in the air. "Thank you.

It's rare we pay each other compliments anymore. I appreciate hearing that."

"I'm sorry for not telling you more often the special things about you. It's defensiveness, no doubt."

"Ditto about the defensiveness, and I'm sorry." His fingers smoothed over her hair, easing her hair a little freer of her ponytail with each swipe, sort of like her slowly slipping self-control. "If ever a woman deserved to be treasured... You are fucking amazing."

She hooked her arms low around his waist because, well, she just loved to cup that cute tush of his. "You sure are cursing a lot."

"I must be feeling strong emotions." His eyes glinted with a blue flame intensity. "I imagine with all that was going on, it's not surprising we didn't have time for the words."

Shane gave her hair tie a final tug and freed her hair. "Near the end there, we barely even had time for this."

He angled his head and guided her mouth to his.

Her self-restraint as uncontrolled as her wind-swept hair at the mercy of the tearing ocean wind, Sherry didn't stand a chance at stopping this fiery kiss from following its natural course.

CHAPTER SIXTEEN

WAITING TWO BLOCKS AWAY from the O'Riley condominium, Dimitri Popov gripped the van's steering wheel in anticipation. If all went well, the first half of his operation would be sealed up tight by the end of the day.

Luckily he had finished up his part of the lectures for the course. He only needed to make periodic appearances to answer questions. So far as the base personnel knew, he was off researching a question for a student. He had his assistant logged into his computer. The log in dates would provide a nice alibi if anyone checked. Not that anybody would have reason to suspect him of all people, especially given his artful disguise. They would think he was hanging out with his female assistant.

Actually, he hadn't lied. He'd said often he had plans to rendezvous with an exotic young thing— and little Cara fit the bill exactly. It wasn't his fault people heard what they wanted to hear.

But damn it all, this job should already be complete, the first payoff already in his Cayman bank account. The new underground faction should already have Cara in their custody so they could begin probing her. One little brat and a highly trained operative couldn't seem to nab her. He had brought a local worker from the cause to assist him this time, Rayhan Abdul-Majeed, leaving nothing to chance this time.

He stared through the leafy trees at the O'Riley residence two blocks away. Great goodness, did these people never allow their children outside for fresh air? He had family back in his homeland and his little ones took daily walks with their nannies.

Dimitri didn't intend to let anything stop him, but kidnapping this Cara child was certainly proving to be more difficult than he had originally expected. So much of his job involved waiting… Watching. O'Riley was a cautious man. Fair enough. Truly, Dimitri could not fault him for that.

At least both parents had finally gone away for the day, leaving the girls in the care of two adults. Too bad they had not employed some teenage baby-sitter he could have easily overpowered. Again, so careful.

He drummed his fingers on the dashboard, his cohort Rayhan beside him. Too bad the Rubistani from the D.I.T. class—Najim al-Hashi—couldn't be won over to their side. But he was so insistent on the pursuit of democracy in his country. Ah, well, he had Rayhan from the local underground.

At least their disguises were solid.

Although disguises in the summer were more uncomfortable than in winter when a person could deck out in parka gear. But for now Dimitri wore a ball cap with a fake ponytail. He'd formed a prosthetic chin. Rayhan had a visor and a prosthetic nose with a Rastafarian wig. They both wore large sunglasses.

They'd also chosen surfer T-shirts and their van bore the logo of a surfboard shop that actually did exist. That should have the police chasing their tails for at least a couple of days.

Of course last night when they had hoped to end this, he had created another clever disguise as a catering company with two chefs. He hadn't even gotten anywhere near Cara thanks to a problem with a police road block and ID checks. He simply wasn't comfortable running the risk.

So now here he waited again wondering what he would do next if this didn't—

The condominium door opened. His heart pounded. He rolled down his window. The conversation could be critical.

The girls sprinted out clutching their matching rag dolls. The African child…

And yes, the Asian girl, Cara.

Both chattered until he almost couldn't tell who said what, his head pounded so. Did not this Sergeant O'Riley demand obedience?

"Ice cream, ice cream!" the younger one chanted

"Going to The Twist! Going to The Twist." Cara danced.

"They have board games to play there. We can stay a loooong time. No more boring old house."

"I love Bubble Gum flavor with gummie bears."

The younger one licked her lips. "I want 'nilla with jimmy sprinkles. Two scoops."

Cara tipped her chin. "Daddy says one."

"Shut up, tattletale."

"Am not, meanie."

Dimitri gripped his steering wheel in a white-knuckled grip. To think, the sitters, Derek Washington and his lady friend just laughed as they loaded the two girls into Washington's SUV. Dimitri bemoaned the fact that the man had such a large vehicle. A sedan would have been easier to run off the road. But only a minor setback.

Part of his training involved car chases. In fact, he actually looked forward to this. He would have two chances—Washington's drive to *and* from this ice cream place.

He would drive them off the road into a deserted area of housing construction put on hold because of financial disputes. Rayhan would use the stun gun to sedate Washington, the woman and the other child.

And finally, Dimitri would have little Cara and that critical piece of knowledge she held in her body from her sojourn to the wrong side of the island.

After that, his team would be free to move on to the ultimate—and explosive—part of their mission.

MAKING OUT ON THE BEACH with his wife.

Who'd have thought that could be such a kick? Shane's fingers teased at the string on the back of her bathing suit. She gave a little wriggle but still he didn't untie the top.

So often **they**'d been about the sex. The big finish.

Now don't get him wrong, he was a huge fan of the big finish. The grander the better. But how often had he taken the time to linger over the beauty of his wife's body?

The sun was dipping lower in the sky so he didn't have a ton of time left since he didn't want to ride the Jet Ski home in the dark. Yet he figured another half hour wouldn't be a problem. This past week of making love every night had taken an edge or frantic urgency off after their stint of abstinence.

Then that growly little voice in his head asked him if this might be the last time? That same insidiously growly voice that tried to taunt him in battle and make him doubt himself into a nosedive straight for an eternal dirt nap.

He pushed it back down with all the other negative thoughts that didn't deserve to see the light of day and focused on sketching along his wife's spine straight into her bathing suit bottom to cup her sweet curves.

Thirty-two years suited her well. She only grew more gorgeous with age, the subtle curves more womanly, the deepening of her voice into a throaty laugh leaving behind the higher pitch of a giggle. He liked her this way. Wanted her this way.

She tugged on the waistband his board shorts with a snap. "Are we going to get rid of these swim suits anytime soon, big guy, or do you plan to torture me all afternoon?"

The tight beads of her nipples against her bathing suit top attested to her arousal, and he couldn't stop the primal surge pumping through him that he'd brought her this pleasure, to this peak of frenzy.

Of course she could say the same for how obviously he wanted her.

With familiar hands he tugged and she shimmied and soon enough their suits rested in a wadded pile on a corner of the oversized beach towel while they lay naked in the late day sun.

She slung her leg over his and fit her hips right into the cradle of his. A perfect fit. His fingers splayed through her hair and he didn't even have to urge or ask, she met him halfway for the kiss. Body to body, flesh sealed to flesh.

Slowly, he slid inside her, stretching her, filling

her. His teeth set on edge as he barely held on to control with the warm moist grip of her encircling him.

Their kiss eased and they took an extended moment to stare into each others' eyes, connected in bodies and sight, somehow as deeply as two people could go.

He wanted to say something but didn't know what. Words seemed trite. So he simply moved inside her and she smiled. Maybe words were overrated after all.

After such an extended foreplay he knew this wouldn't last long. He just needed it to last long enough for her, so he slid his hand between them, lower, and stroked her, gently, slowly until she smiled again. Kissed his chin, nipped his shoulder.

Then she writhed against him. Even though he couldn't see her face he knew the smile was gone, replaced by a tense, more urgent expression echoed by the building frenzy in him as they ground hips against each other. Enough. No more, needing to find…

Her nails scraped down his back as her scream rode the wind along the beach. And yes, he was free to let go and with a final deep plunge, his own shout joined the final echoes of her multiple releases.

They both rolled to their backs, holding hands between them, silently. No words, but for a different reason this time. He was pretty damn sure his vocal chords were temporarily paralyzed along with all the rest of the muscles in his body.

For the flicker of a moment his brain engaged and he realized that yet again they hadn't used a condom. But then they'd never used birth control from the moment they'd gotten married. From the start, they'd both been clear about wanting more children right away.

About four years into the marriage, he'd stumbled on Sherry sitting in the tub, hugging her knees with her face pressed hard against them. She'd started rocking and then he'd known. She was crying.

He'd almost left her alone. She had obviously chosen her solitude. Except something pulled him to sit on the edge and stroke her spine, trying like hell not to think of his mother's multitude of tears. He'd asked Sherry if she was okay. Without looking up, she'd waved him away.

He'd stayed, waited while more of those weeping memories from the past ricocheted around in his head.

Finally, without glancing up, Sherry had said, "Why can't we make babies?"

He didn't have an answer or the perfect comfort, not to mention they'd already started having problems by that point so he wasn't even sure bringing a child into the marriage was a wise idea.

But he really knew that wouldn't help.

So he'd simply said, "We can talk to the doctor.

Or we can talk to one of the overseas adoption agencies." Would it have helped if they'd adopted a third child sooner? Somehow he didn't think so. They would have only brought one more person into this family to hurt when things fell apart. "Whatever you want to do, Sherry, I'll be on board."

She'd nodded, without looking up to show him her tears. But they'd both known they wouldn't do either because it was too late for them.

Lying beside her on the beach now, holding hands, watching the birds circle overhead in the sky where everything was so much simpler, he wondered if this past week had offered them hope.

Or was it still too late and he'd only made things all the worse?

SITTING AT THE TABLE inside The Twist, Keisha twirled her tongue around her soft serve vanilla with a total relish—and total awareness of the effect she was having on the man sitting beside her. Luckily, the girls were totally absorbed in playing checkers and eating their own ice cream, so she could watch Derek squirm a little while longer.

Actually, tormenting him was easier than allowing herself to think about how easily they had fallen into a routine of taking care of Cara and Mally. In fact, it had been fun seeing him roll around on the floor with the girls. Her heart had done a little flip-floppy thing she simply couldn't deny.

He was certainly using his *time* wisely when it came to winning her over.

"Give me my doll." Mally's indignant shout pierced Keisha's musings as well as her ears.

Cara shook her head and tugged back on the rag toy, their game interrupted. "That's *my* doll."

"Nuh-uh, it's mine because mine has a grape jelly stain on her foot. See? You left yours at home, doofus."

Keisha reached to take the doll. "Why don't I just hold on to it until we get back to your place? I'll wash out the jelly stain then. Okay? And don't call your sister doofus. That's a hurtful thing to say."

Problem solved.

Now she was right back to feeling Derek's gaze gobbling her faster than he devoured his melting chocolate double scoop. The outing had been wonderful and the girls had soaked up the time away from the house after so long inside. Sherry and Shane had actually suggested the outing.

The police had deemed the kidnapping attempt a random act after viewing the film. They even had a guy in for questioning based on a van in the parking lot. They thought they might really have the guy.

When she and Derek had mentioned ice cream—after the girls had about gone for each others' throats with cabin fever—both kids sprinted down the hall for their rooms to get ready. Through their open doorways, Keisha had seen them crawling under their beds tossing out toys and mismatched shoes until finally coming up with a matching pair. In a flash, both girls stood by the front door with gleaming smiles and toes wiggling in their glittery flip-flops.

Two hours later, she finished off the last of her ice cream and thought about what she wanted to do *alone* with Derek later. All the while trying not to get too nervous about this aspect of time. That implied long-term commitment. Something she'd never been all that good at and she damn well didn't like feeling scared.

Derek wadded up his napkin, finished with his waffle cone. "It's time to load 'em up, girls. Your parents will be home soon."

The girls moaned just a hint but obeyed with the proper, "Yes, sir." Shane and Sherry had done a good job with their kids. Children took a lot of work.

And *time*.

There was that word again, and her nerves. Part of her wanted to talk this through with Derek and another part of her wanted to take his advice about being relaxed and giving them both the space and time they needed to explore their feelings. Don't push. Don't pressure.

Made sense.

She climbed into the car and buckled her seat belt. Keisha could see Derek studying the parking lot even though they had been reassured again and again that all was well. How much harder it must have been for Shane and Sherry to step away from their girls after a kidnap attempt.

The world was a scary and sometimes perverted place. All the more reason why they wouldn't let those girls out of their sight after all that had gone on lately. She couldn't imagine the ache and worry of being a parent.

They all loaded into the car before Derek looked over his shoulder. "All buckled in?"

"Yes, sir."

"Yep, sir."

He fired up the engine and pulled out of the ice cream stand's lot. He cranked the radio as they drove onto the highway, while the girls chattered and hummed along in back.

Suddenly air seemed in short supply.

This felt too much like a family outing. Keisha forced her breaths to stay even and shallow. She liked Derek. He liked her. He only wanted time, dating. Neither of them had said anything about anything more. They were both free spirits, intent on touring the world.

She had absolutely no reason at all to freak out because they were babysitting for their friends.

So why was Derek's forehead creased with irritation?

"Are you okay?"

"Beach traffic just sucks. All this bumper-to-bumper stuff is for the birds. Let's take a back way home."

At the next traffic light Derek whipped the SUV off the main four-lane highway into a two-lane subdivision under construction. "This will get us there. We'll just have to weave through back roads a while longer, but at least we don't have to worry about speeding vacationers, tailgaters and nowhere to pull off if things get out of hand."

The SUV slowed to subdivision speeds as they passed house after house that looked much the same. How would he find his way out of here? Suddenly she found words tumbling from her that she was dumb, dumb, dumb saying this early in a relationship. "So since we've decided to give this relationship thing a try, are we destined to fail?"

He glanced in the back and lowered his voice, "You mean are we going to turn into a certain other globe-trotting couple we know?"

Oh God, there it was. Out there. Even he'd thought about it. So much for keeping things light and easy. "The thought may have crossed my mind. But on the positive side, there are plenty of people who do make it work. I think by our going into this with our eyes wide open, we're already a step ahead."

"Okay." His fingers tightened around the steering wheel. Not a good sign.

Why, oh why, had she let her mouth run away with her? Were they ever going to get back on the highway and headed home so she could change the subject? "I'm getting ahead of myself when I swore I would take things light." She chewed off the remaining taste of vanilla ice cream on her lips, choosing her words carefully because of the children behind them. "It's just tough. I'm not one to back off from a challenge and, damn it Derek, what we did together was more intense than I expected."

Didn't look to her like the home neighborhood was anywhere out in the middle of this housing construction sight and the road just got narrower. "Like I said. Time," he said absently, staring at the winding narrow dirt road, his four-wheel drive gripping for traction. "A day at a time."

"You're a smart man."

"Keisha, can we table this discussion?" He lowered his voice again. "I don't want to scare the kids, but the van that was tailgating us back on the highway when we were going *to* The Twist showed up again out here on the back way, and he's crowding the hell out of me."

"What?" That couldn't be right. Could it? Maybe it was just a similar van. She glanced in the rearview mirror. It looked pretty distinctive to her—a surf shop van gaining on them with menacing speed. "Why would he show up again?"

"Road rage? Maybe I cut him off unintentionally earlier. I don't know." He checked the rearview mirror consistently as the engine behind them growled. "But he's definitely pissed."

And they were definitely out here all alone. Had they been maneuvered here by the tailgater in the first place?

"Derek, let's get back to the main road." Keisha twisted in her seat to double-check that the girls were safely buckled into their seats, kicking at each others' flip-flops.

She almost wished she'd kept her eyes forward. The back window of Derek's SUV was filled with the looming image of the white van, two men in ball caps in the front seat. The vehicle bore down with menacing intent.

No room for question. They meant serious harm. Her heart thudded in her ears. Could this be the guy who'd tried to take Cara at the aquarium? Or was this just some unrelated act and she was just being paranoid?

Derek downshifted to four-wheel drive, the engine powering through the yard of one of the houses under construction. The suspension popped and bounced, eliciting the first squeaks of surprise from Cara and Mally.

Keisha gripped her seat in sweaty hands. "Hold on tight, girls, okay? Everything will be fine."

The SUV shot out the backyard of the skeletal structure, the van still gaining on them. "Derek?"

"I'm trying my damnedest, lady, but I sure could use a wingman right about now," he said, just as the van rammed them from behind.

CHAPTER SEVENTEEN

DEREK'S WORLD was going to hell in a handbasket fast.

He gripped the wheel of his SUV and struggled to keep the vehicle on the narrow dirt road in the half-built subdivision. The surfer van revved and swerved to the side, accelerating alongside them.

Shit. "Hold on."

The van slammed against the side, once, twice. Derek's muscles tensed and strained to hold the van firm but still the heavy SUV lurched to the side into the soft dirt. He gunned the engine. Tires spewed earth as the automatic four-wheel drive dragged them back onto safer terrain yet again.

He wanted to ask Keisha about the kids but couldn't take even a second's concentration off the looming white vehicle. And somewhere in his mind he registered her soothing the girls with reassurance. God love her for not panicking when she had every right to freak out.

His mind clicked through the identifying markers—surfer shop's name. No license plate on front.

Two men in front. They eased even closer, so damn close he could almost swear he could see the perspiration on their forehead as the late day sun cast its final rays across the landscape.

The driver, with a ponytail, looked like an over-the-hill stoner. The passenger seemed to be trying to pull off a Rastafarian look but somehow the ethnicity didn't fit.

The whole damn thing was wrong.

His instincts screamed they were in disguise.

His shock absorbers squealed even louder as they nailed him from the front, sending him into a spin.

Damn it. Adrenaline fired along his skin as his hands grappled for control of the vehicle and his eyes searched for a way out. He swerved, just missing a pile of dirt next to a backhoe.

Fuck. He needed to drive and worry about the rest later. His perceptions on their clothing did him a damn bit of good as he plowed through a red dirt front lawn, somebody's dream home, while the girls screamed behind him.

Another direct hit from the van to the back quarter panel edged him dangerously close to the drainage ditch. Keisha's gasp—the first one yet—popped sweat along his brow. That deep trench would have spelled the end for them.

"Derek," Keisha's voice penetrated.

"Huh?" He grunted a go-ahead.

"I think if you can make it through two more stretches of dirt road we'll be back on pavement. Maybe around people."

"You sure?"

"No."

"Fair enough. Which way?" God, these housing developments were monstrous mazes.

"Left."

Which would still put him parallel with the treacherous ditch. But he decided his surfer wanna-bes could use a dose of their own medicine.

He nailed the brakes. Cut the vehicle into a spin. Gunned the gas and rammed the bad wig, bad-asses into the ditch.

Without waiting to see how far their van slid down, Derek reversed, turned around and followed Keisha's directions back to paved roads. He glanced in the rearview mirror. Girls were fine, other than wide, tearstained eyes filled with fear—damn those bastards to hell.

Derek looked further. No signs of said bastards yet, but a part of him wanted a piece of their asses right now for daring to risk the lives of these children and Keisha.

He tried to scavenge conciliatory words like Keisha but he couldn't pull anything past the lump of rage in his throat.

So he focused on driving. His brand-new SUV rattled like shit and warning lights flashed like a

Christmas tree, but he wasn't stopping until they were safely at a police station.

There, he would start looking for the sons of bitches and some answers.

SHERRY STOOD ON THE BEACH, the sun sinking low fast as Shane readied the Jet Ski for their return home. They'd put off leaving the barrier island to the very last minute, almost dangerously so, but it had been difficult to give up this time alone together. Such a rare treat, something they should have found a way to do years ago.

Maybe if they'd had the help of parents or siblings, or traded off babysitting with friends to take the kids. Had they figured everything out too late?

Because they'd needed the alone time to work through other problems as well. She waded into the water up to her knees, helping him tie off their yellow bag of supplies. They worked silently in tandem. If only their daily life could be so seamlessly simple.

Although even in the beauty of this day, she had a little grit in her suit abrading her butt, and her shoulder stung a bit from the sun. Even special days had real life itchy imperfections. She was only just realizing she needed to be better at accepting those, too. It was a heavy load to put on herself and those around her—expecting perfection.

But ohmigod, the way they'd come together on

the beach had been the closest thing to perfect she'd ever known and she was going to lose it.

Then a little voice inside her whispered, *What if...*

Before she could complete her thought, the ringing of Shane's cell phone from the waterproof pack interrupted her musings.

"Damn," he muttered, eying the pack and eying the shore as if deciding whether it was worth his while to just ignore the call rather than mess with taking the phone back to dry land.

"It could be the kids."

He unlashed the waterproof sack and made his way back to shore, while Sherry stayed inches behind. He missed picking up in time but he checked the call history. "Derek."

Her heart rate stuttered. "Any messages?"

Shane punched in numbers and frowned. "Damn it, the reception sucks out here. I can't get a signal to pick up for me to check the message or get a call through."

She tugged his arm, staring over at the phone as if she could infuse it to work through sheer maternal will power. "Try again."

"Sherry, I have, and I'm just as frustrated as you are." He gripped the phone so hard she feared he might crack it. "We can stand here all evening and fight the phone or we can hightail it out and get to our girls."

He had a point.

"Okay," she relented, "let's go."

"We'll check on them the minute we reach shore." Seconds later, he fired up the engine with no loitering.

He reached out for her to swoop up behind him, the position somehow all the more intimate this time after how they'd spent their afternoon joined. Lordy, her hormones were a mess. With her arms looped around his waist, she rested her cheek on his back and let her mind ramble along those fantasy roads of what if…

She imagined different ways they could work this out. Compromises they could live with. Except they all seemed so darn hard and one person always had to give up more than the other. She couldn't help but notice how no dolphins journeyed with them this time.

Her eyes stung and she couldn't even delude herself into thinking it had anything to do with the sea spray splashing her in the face.

They reached the other shore in what seemed to be record time. Their special day over.

Shane hauled the Jet Ski in, securing it to the trailer just as the cell phone rang again. Sherry slumped against the minivan and waited to hear who had called. Likely it was just his work anyway, wanting him to come in for something.

Then the air changed. It crackled and snapped all

around him as he stood straighter, his face hard. His eyes an icy shade of blue she'd never seen on him before.

She shoved away from the van and eased toward him. "Shane?"

"Okay," he said into the receiver. "We'll be right there. And thank you."

He thumbed the OFF button and stared at the cell phone for an extended moment that seemed to stretch into a horrific moment.

"Shane, you have to tell me now." She clutched his arm until little fingernail moons cut into his skin.

He looked up. "The girls are fine. Derek and Keisha are fine."

She hated sentences that started like that because it always meant something awful had happened. "And?"

"They went out for ice cream and someone tried to run them off of the road. Derek's car's banged up but everyone's okay."

She started shaking. She couldn't stop, but nothing would keep her from her children. Sherry was in the car, seat belt snapped before the next heartbeat.

Shane settled in beside her and started the vehicle. "We'll meet them at the police station."

"Good." She yanked a sundress over her swimsuit, weaving her arms through the seat belt. "What the hell is the world coming to when people take out road rage on a car with little children inside?"

He stayed quiet.

"Not road rage?" She paused in the middle of slipping on flip-flops.

"The police and the OSI are considering other possibilities."

Horror settled over her in an opaque blanket of all the nightmarish happenings of the past days, most importantly the attempt to kidnap her daughter. She couldn't talk. She could barely breathe. Every ounce of energy within her was drained by simply focusing on surviving to get to her daughters.

An eternity—all of fifteen minutes likely— Shane pulled into the police department's parking lot where Derek's mangled SUV sat parked, dented on every side.

Sherry couldn't peel her eyes away. She'd been so anxious to get to her kids and now she couldn't make herself move away from the horrifyingly mesmerizing sight.

Her door jerked open, startling her. Shane tugged her arm gently. "Come on."

The next few moments passed in a haze for her, police receptionists and formalities. Vaguely she heard voices talking. She simply knelt and held out her arms for her daughters. Once both were wrapped safely against her, nothing else mattered or fully registered.

Some part of her brain heard Derek saying, "Dude, I'm so sorry."

Shane answering, "You have nothing to apologize for. We told you it was fine to take them out for a meal or treat. Even the cops didn't see this coming. You kept them alive. Thank you."

Keisha patting her back.

Sherry thought she chanted thank you to her friends a few—maybe too many times because they gave her oddly worried looks. So she want back to holding her girls and telling them how much she loved them.

Sherry barely took in anything else, the questioning of the police, and OSI Special Agent David Reis. She could only think of holding her girls in her lap and finally, finally taking them home and tucking them safely into their beds where everything would feel normal again.

The ride home passed in a blessed blur. She wasn't ready to deal with the tornado of emotion building inside her yet, swirling faster by the second. She had other, maternal things to attend to first.

Once home, the four walls of her house wrapped around her like a well loved blanket she'd once been given by an old woman in a village she'd lived in for a whole five months as a child. She held on to the sense of security while she fed and readied her children for bed. She kissed each of them on the top of their freshly washed heads and backed into the hall, inching her way into the bathroom and closing the door.

She turned on the sink faucet, sat on the edge of the tub and finally let herself double up and sob. The tears flowed in gulping sobs, nothing pretty or controlled, but wrenching sheetings of tears that filled her nose and clogged her throat.

In some dim part of her rain she heard the door creak open. She squinted through her gritty eyes to see Shane's bare feet on the white tile floor in front of hers.

Her teeth chattered. These past two weeks had just been too damn much. Tears continued to spill over and even someone as practiced as she was at holding them back couldn't control the flood.

He turned off the faucet and knelt in front of her. "There's no need to cry, babe. It's over now. They're safe and home. Tears are only going to make your eyes hurt and drain you. All that emotion's a waste now."

A waste?

A fucking waste?

All the beauty of their afternoon, then the fears for their children, piled on top of her anger. The condensed emotions sliced through like a hot knife into an overfilled water balloon.

She tossed her head back and to hell with him seeing the ravaged and swollen ugliness of her pain. "You told me once that you're ready to battle for your country. That you've even felt your hand rise to volunteer for assignments as if of its own will.

There's a surety in you when you walk out that door and you want the same from me. No tears. Well I'm sorry. I get scared and need to cry sometimes. Right now is one of those times. I've been scared for my children."

Her fists clenched and she pounded her knees. It was all she could do to keep from ripping the shower curtain off its rings in frustration. "I'm not able to suppress my emotions the way you can, and to tell you the truth, I'm not so sure that your way is all that healthy."

"Sherry, baby, we need to keep our voices down for the kids."

Damn it. Damn him. He was right.

She paused to gasp and straightened an orange hand towel hanging on the rack and then thought how damn stupid. She'd been making herself be a Betty Crocker perfectionist after all in so many little ways, creating this perfect little beach theme bathroom with shells she and the girls had found along the shore. She'd called it a science home-schooling field trip at the time.

He shook his head. "Your whole point is that we're different. Okay. I get that. What do want from me and I'll try?"

"I've supported you in the way you are and how you deal with things for years. But where's the support for the way I deal with things? Right now, I'm terrified about the girls and what today might mean. There are times I need *your* support. Not support from my girlfriends. There are moments I need to cry on your chest—"

"Whoa!" He held up his hands. "Hold on a minute. It's unfair to say I haven't held you. When you ask me to, I'm there." He held out his arms. "Fine. If you need to be held now, I'll hold you now."

She rolled her eyes. "You sound like you'd rather swim with sharks."

He flinched, guilt written on his face as clearly as a billboard. His arms fell to his side. "Sherry, I *am* trying."

"I know. But when I ask you to hold me when I need to cry, believe me, I can sense when you're just patting me on the back and *praying* it will be over with fast."

The guilty expression doubled.

"Shane, truly, that kind of obligatory hug hurts more than whatever sent me crying all over you in the first place. Do you understand what I'm saying?"

"Yeah." His jaw tightened as he barked softly, "That I suck in giving you what you need."

"Lower the defenses, Slugger. I'm saying that suppressed *feelings* suck and making me suppress my hurts around you all the time has been destructive in our relationship. You just want my 'happy face' as the kids would say. But that's not real life, Shane. And honestly, I'm only just now starting to understand how that caused me to build up resentment."

"Explain." He lowered the toilet seat and sat.

"Showing you only that Betty Crocker, welcome home face is damned exhausting. I think maybe that's why I started volunteering for extra assignments, to avoid the arguments."

Admitting that to him, her own culpability was tough, but damn it, she was trying to here. And a part of trying included being honest even when it hurt.

He stared at his hands clasped loosely between his knees. "I hear ya. I'm a big one for dodging the fights when I can…" His hands clasped tighter, tenser. "My parents fought, Sherry. They fought hard, and those fights never accomplished a damn thing but hurting everyone within hearing distance of the venom that poured out of their mouths."

"I'm so sorry." The part of her that longed to scoop up children around the world and bring them home with her wished she could have been there for the young Shane as well.

"It's not your fault."

"I know that." She reached to rest her hand on top of his clenched hands. "I'm just sorry you had to live through that."

He loosened his grip and kissed her palm before setting it back on her knee. "After a while, I figured out where Derek lived and his grandma didn't mind an extra kid at her table. Things were happy there, with meals and laughter."

"Like Betty Crocker welcome homes."

"I guess so." Absently he replaced the empty roll of toilet paper with a new one from the basket by the toilet, probably the first time she could recall him actually doing that in their entire marriage. He must be seriously rattled.

She couldn't stop herself from asking the question burning her heart. "Were your parents violent?"

He stayed silent, shoving aside the shower curtain a little farther and easing over to sit beside her on the edge of the tub, their feet side by side on the seashell bath mat.

"Is this delving into those deep emotions where you don't want to go?"

"Like I said before. Those intense discussions never solved anything. But no, they weren't actually violent, other than throwing things at each other once they reached the totally toasted level."

"No. You said volatile fights between two incredibly hostile people hurt everyone around them. That's not who or what we are or what we're trying to accomplish. Strong emotions don't have to be equated with pain." She leaned forward on her knees, gasping for air and needing him to hold her so much, but still he sat there on his side of the edge of the porcelain edge. "But I can say one thing for sure. If you stuff down those strong emotions, eventually it is definitely going to hurt worse than anything you can imagine. I know that, because that's what we forced each other to live these past five years in hiding tears and running from the problems."

"So basically you've spent the past five years being someone you're not."

"That isn't what I'm saying and you know it." How could she get through to him? Was the wall between them so thick as well as high that he couldn't hear her? "I just can't give you a house where I never cry, where we never have a fight before you walk out the door for fear you may die on the battlefield. I know you want your home to be a haven, but I can't make it some nirvana."

Finally he touched her, gently cupping her shoulders as he turned her to him, his eyes every bit as tormented as she felt. "You think I don't know that? My whole job is one fucking war zone. I don't need that at home, too."

"Well, I'm sorry. But I can't give you a house where I have a perpetual smile." The tears started to fill up inside her again so she snatched the stupid crooked hand towel off and swiped it across her face. "If you only want the happy stuff where people never argue, you'll have to find some robot woman. There's more to everyone. Including you."

"Yet when I try, you tell me I sound like some kind of fucking obligatory robot of emotion who would rather swim with sharks than give you what you need."

She sighed when she really wanted to scream—or cry again. "That really wasn't helpful."

And here they were, circled right back around to where they'd started before the terrorist ship shoot-out.

Heaven only knew what had gone on today with the girls. The more time that passed with these bizarre events of kidnapping attempts and missing stickers and such, the murkier things became.

But after this rip-her-heart-out discussion, one thing because very clear.

"Shane, I think it's time for you to move out for good. Leave the divorce papers on the table and I'll sign them by morning."

CHAPTER EIGHTEEN

HANDS WRAPPED AROUND a warm mug of tea, Sherry paced in the small temporary lodging facility—like an efficiency apartment. Last night Shane had insisted she and girls stay indoors, on base. If she wanted him out of the house, then he needed to know she and the kids were protected until they had some answers about all of these co-incidental potential catastrophes landing on his family's doorstep.

He'd been calm. He'd been logical. And he'd been right. Safety was nothing to toy with, especially when it came to their children.

She sagged back against the island separating the kitchen from the living area. The girls had chosen tonight of all times to drift off easily by eight-thirty, leaving her bored and very lonely. Usually she made the most of this kind of time to do paperwork—setting up logistics for other teams heading out into the field, logging data of returning teams, filling out shipping orders for necessities, and of course as always working the grants and donations angles.

Tonight, she simply didn't have the focus required to do her job justice. She clicked the television on low in the two-room place usually reserved for military families moving to or away from the base. A TLF—Temporary Lodging Facility. She clicked through channels, barely paying attention, her mind wandering.

Shane hadn't said as much, but she suspected he or his friends were keeping an eye on her as well. Not that she could sleep for anyone to sneak in and snatch them.

She gave up on the TV and clicked it off. She thought about unpacking her DVD player and catching up on the last two hours of her soap, but couldn't scrounge interest in much of anything. Not with her mind aswirl with kidnappers—and the way she and Shane had left their final discussion about divorce. There would be no miracle cure to put her family back together.

It was all just too much to take in.

Sitting on the sofa, she propped her feet on the coffee table, sipping her mug, listening to the sounds outside. Cars coming and going. The occasional voice, but their stretch of units was pretty deserted, unusual for this time of year.

And scary.

She refused to consider herself paranoid. They'd all gotten beyond that point when some fake-Rastafarian tried to run her daughters into a ditch. A suburban neighborhood in the States could be every bit as dangerous as the foreign locales where she'd often worked. Would she ever be able to relax her maternal vigil?

The girls' bedroom door was open so she could watch them sleep. Although how they'd managed after yesterday's horror on the road, she would never know. Sheer exhaustion and innocence perhaps?

She was running on pure adrenaline and her fourth mug of tea.

Sherry glanced back at the kitchen bar where she'd placed the divorce papers. She thought about the pen in her purse. But wait. Didn't she have to sign them in front of witnesses or something to have them notarized? Or did she just sign them and give them over to him? Regardless, all the details were here, complete with an addendum she'd added tonight with a visitation schedule for the girls. She wanted that for him and them.

How damn heartbreaking to think back to a couple of years ago when they'd discussed how to find a way to make Cara and Mally Holloway officially Cara and Mally O'Riley. No doubt Clint could have been persuaded eventually. He never actually spent much time with the girls, more often just sent his money. It seemed more a pride issue with him than one of love. Whereas Shane's love for them was deep and obvious.

And damn, but the hollowness inside her grew.

A rustling from the girls room snagged her attention. Mally's sleep had been more restless than Cara's. Sherry set down her mug by the television and went into the girls' room. She eased to sit beside Mally, gently, careful not to wake her and smoothed her hand along her back in hopes of soothing whatever nightmares plagued her young mind.

Sherry's hand came back damp.

Mally's nightgown clung to her body with perspiration—and fever. A relapse from her earlier illness? Panic squeezed her heart.

She rushed back into the living room and snatched up her purse. Sifting around her wallet and pack of wet wipes, she found the bottle of children's Tylenol she kept ever-close since the seizure scare and raced back into her daughter's room.

She slipped her hand under Mally's head and whispered in her ear, "Mally, wake up for just a second and take your medicine."

Her request was met with a groggy groan.

"Come on, sweetie, just chew the medicine and you can go right back to sleep."

Luckily, her exhausted child was too tired to disobey and chewed the purple pills before sagging back down on her pillow.

After allowing herself three precious seconds to sag against the door jam in parental panic, she grabbed for her cell phone and called Keisha. No answer at home. Damn it.

She tried her cell…and…three rings later. "Hello?"

"Keisha, Mally's running a fever again and I'm stuck here in this damn TLF alone and I'm terrified she's going to go into convulsions while I have Cara to care for too."

"Calm down." Keisha's voice took on the tone of a medical professional Sherry recognized and welcomed from their work together. "How high is her fever?"

"I don't know. I'm not home, remember, and I don't have a thermometer but she's sweaty and hot." Why couldn't she stop babbling? What she wouldn't give for some of Shane's calm right now. "I do have Tylenol and already gave her some. I'm putting her in a fresh nightgown, too."

Keeping the phone wedged between her shoulder and jaw, she dropped to her knees on the floor beside her daughter's tiny roller bag suitcase and tugged out a polka-dot nightgown.

"Good. You've done just the right thing," Keisha continued with the soothing tones while Sherry changed her daughter into fresh PJs. "There's no reason to panic yet. Go sit with her and I'll be over in a minute."

"But Pensacola—"

"I'm not in Pensacola."

"Oh."

"I'm at Derek's." She paused for only a brief embarrassed second before continuing. "If she has

a seizure, turn on the shower to a tepid temperature and climb in with her. That will bring down
the fever. I'll be there before you even need to
worry."

"Okay. And thank you…" She hesitated, not
sure how to phrase the next her words diplomati-
cally. "Is Derek coming too?"

A three-beat silence passed before Keisha continued, "It'll just be me. He's not out of class yet."

Still in class? Then her thoughts about Shane
and his crew taking turns lurking outside had been
paranoid. She could just shake off the creepy sensation. Nobody was watching her after all. And
speaking of the crew, Rodeo in particular. "This
may be none of my business, but why are you at
Derek's if he's not there?"

"You are a nosy one, aren't you?" Keisha
laughed. "But since we've all had a suck day, I'll
let you in on the gossip. He gave me a key to come
on over and wait for him so we wouldn't have to
drive as far for our plans later."

"You have plans?" Guilt pinched. She shouldn't
have considered Keisha her own personal on-call
medical help. She should have gone to the emergency room like any other mother. "I'm sorry. I'll
just take her to the ER."

"Don't be silly. I'll be there and back here before
he even gets home. He's the one who screwed up
the plans with his late class. I'm on my way. No

arguing. Maybe I can actually meet up with him there."

Sherry sagged to rest on the edge of bed. "Thank you, thank you, thank you, my friend. I really appreciate your help." And for not making her feel guilty because right now, she had truly reached the limit of her emotional reserves. "I'll call the front gate to let them know you're coming so you can get your pass to come through."

"You've been there for me more times than I can count. Friends don't keep score." The line disconnected.

Sherry flipped her phone closed, shoved it in her jeans pocket. She sat limp, drained for…well, she wasn't sure how long because her whole body felt out of whack.

Then a panicked thought broadsided her and she circled around the double bed to check Cara's forehead…

Cool. Something to be grateful for.

She really should call Shane. She reached for the cell again when Cara's eyes fluttered open.

"Mama?" she whispered, blowing a stray strand of silky hair from the corner of her mouth.

Sherry's stroked back her daughter's bangs. She needed to take her for a haircut. They all needed to indulge in a nice normal activity for a change. "What, sweetie?"

"Is everything okay?" She snuggled her doll under

her nose and sniffed, something she always did during their travels as if smelling *home* for reassurance.

"It's going to be. Mally's got the flu again. So I think you should sleep in a different room."

"That means I get to stay in your room?"

"Sure, sweetie."

She lowered her doll and big gap-toothed smile spread over her solemn daughter's face. "I'm kinda thirsty. Could I have a glass of milk first, please?"

"Sure. We'll have something together." She could use another mug of tea and they could stay in perfect view of Mally.

On her way to the kitchen, Sherry swept open the living area curtains so she could see Keisha arrive. By the end of the glass of milk and with only a sip of tea left, the front gate guard called to verify Keisha's request to enter.

Sherry stayed glued to the window, holding Cara's hand until Keisha's headlights from the Ford Escape swooped into the parking lot as she settled two spots down from their door by a family's U-Haul. Keisha disappeared from sight, likely getting her bag with her nurse's gear.

Sherry stepped outside onto the porch, giving her eyes a chance to adjust to the dim halogen lighting, Cara still glued to her side as she'd been much of the time since the aquarium kidnapping attempt. Still no Keisha. Just a scattered few cars, the large U-Haul van and no people in sight. Sherry wondered if she'd given her friend the wrong unit number so she ventured out into the moonlit lot. A lone car swooshed past, then out of sight. Her flip-flops crunching on the gravel, she hitched her bare-foot daughter up on her hip. Lordy, the girl was getting big.

She circled around the back of the U-Haul toward Keisha's car. A creak sounded beside her and before she could fully register the sound, the back of the U-Haul van swung open in a flash. The door blocked the road from sight and she started to back away until—

A bulky man with an askew Rastafarian wig— and a damn large gun held hip level—loomed in the opening. "Make a sound and I will shoot your daughter."

KEISHA FOUGHT AGAINST the drug that had been injected into her by the Bob Marley wanna-be who'd nearly killed her the day before. She certainly hadn't expected to see his fake dreadlocks again when she'd stepped around the back of her car beside a U-Haul van.

Her surroundings were fuzzy and growing hazier by the moment. He'd stuffed a rag in her mouth straightaway then shoved her into the front seat of the large van, further through, roughly into the back where she now slumped on a musty blanket.

She blinked at the parking lot lights streaking through the open back hatch as the Mock-Marley held a gun on Sherry and Cara.

Keisha wanted to scream in horror at what she saw playing out, but couldn't manage with her body so lethargic. What the hell had the man given her in that injection? His thick fingers had been surprisingly adept at sliding the needle under her skin. If her professional guess was correct, she didn't have much time left before she passed out altogether.

His loose pants and shirt set in green, yellow and red stripes rippled like a flag in the wind as he held the gun steady. "Now keep your daughter quiet and climb into the back of the van. Quickly," he said with a hint of a Middle Eastern accent that belied the roots of his disguise. "If you make this public, things will get ugly. Fast. I have many bullets and no problem with becoming a martyr for my cause."

Keisha could see Sherry shaking as she kissed her daughter on the side of her head and set Cara down. Sherry climbed into the back of the U-Haul slowly. Buying time, perhaps? Hoping Cara would run? Praying Shane might finish with that damn class and show up here even though he was persona non grata?

Cara turned as if to bolt.

Sherry must have told her to, but the man in the back was too fast. He thundered to the ground and scooped up Cara by her stomach and flung her in the back before climbing inside after her. Cara squeaked in horror, pain probably too, a second before the man slammed the doors closed.

Only a lone red light rigged in the back corner cast a hellish glow in the metal cavern. His gun steady in one hand, he pierced Cara's skin with another needle from his stash. Keisha tried to peer into the box against the wall where he seemed to have an endless store of drugs at his disposal, but he kept the small trunk-sized container blocked from her view.

And locked.

Their captor faced Sherry full on, his muscular bulk nearly as intimidating as his ugly black gun. "Your stunt with your daughter was very stupid. You could have had an easy sleep like the little one and your friend, but now you will have to pay for your defiance."

While keeping the weapon pointed at Cara, he slid a prepared slipknot of rope around Sherry's wrists. Once he had her hands taken care of he slipped an elastic band over her head and across her mouth, effectively gagging her—then he back handed her across the face. "You now may stay awake and fear."

He kicked Sherry in the stomach with steel toed boots and turned away without the least show of emotion, striding toward the driver's seat. The gag did little to muffle Sherry's moan of agony as she doubled up.

Rage seared through Keisha's veins hotter than whatever he'd pumped through the needle, but there was little she could do. She feared if she appeared too alert, her captor would contain her as well. So she stayed on her musty blanket and watched. Waited.

Cara tried to roll to her mother but the drug was taking effect, either faster acting on the child or a stronger dose because already her lashes began to flutter closed. Her grip loosened on her doll.

Keisha blinked fast to keep her focus in the red haze. Red because of the light, she reminded herself. Not because of the drug. Oh God, her eyelids were getting heavy.

Once the bastard was occupied with driving, she inched her way to Sherry. Not daring to talk so close to the front, Keisha worked at the elastic gag, trying...so damn groggy...

Her fingers fumbled as best she could at the gag as the U-Haul bumped along the road. An idea sparked.

"Shh," Keisha whispered. "Next bump. Roll back."

Then they might be able to talk, further away from the front. Sherry's eyes widened and she gave a slight nod of understanding.

Three potholes later, they'd managed to jostle themselves and Cara into the far back corner of the van. All the while, Keisha wondered how did that goon have access to the base? That made this scarier. The possibilities endless.

Finally, the elastic circle slipped down around Sherry's neck. Sherry doubled up and vomited on the floor, again and again until her body racked with dry heaves.

"Hands," Sherry gagged, "need hands."

Keisha wished she could comfort her but energy was precious. Damn it, why hadn't she thought to untie the hands first instead?

The drug was really messing with her mind, scaring her, loosening holds on her emotions and bringing forward some of the deepest feelings she turned off on a day-to-day basis. Seeing Sherry hold Cara, Keisha wondered if she would have a chance to hold babies of her own. And in the visionary moment, the image became Derek's babies.

Sure she'd had reason to be angry at him before, but she hadn't been wrong about him being an amazing man. Their timing simply hadn't been right then for the kind of relationship she knew they could have created now. If only she could still have that chance.

"Sleepy," she whispered. "Drugs. Fingers can't. Not much time."

The van hit another pothole and Sherry grabbed Cara to protect her unconscious child.

Sherry angled her head closer to Keisha back against the doors. "Are you okay? I'm so sorry."

Keisha dimly registered Sherry moving her arms. Working the rope against the door hinges? Smart thinking.

If she didn't slice open a major artery on her wrist.

Keisha grappled for consciousness. "Not your fau—"

The world went dark.

SHANE STEPPED THROUGH the vault doors after class, down the hall and out the exit into the dark parking lot. The lecture had run late tonight because of a telecon guest speaker from Australia. Shane was antsy. He wanted to park his Jeep within sight of Sherry's TLF so he could stake out the place overnight.

The crew had all offered to take shifts and help. Damn. His chest felt tight when he thought of how his buds had stepped up to the plate for him with support during this hellish time.

At least he'd persuaded Sherry and the girls to stay on base for their protection. That brought him some comfort while he'd waited impatiently for class to end.

The rest of the class milled around him heading to their cars, voices blending in a mishmash of plans to go home to families or head out to grab a bite to eat. Offers to join him on his first watch swirled all around him, but he declined just as fast. He would save their help for later.

He would rather snag something from Burger King and find a fat oak to hide his surveillance. He wasn't in the mood to be social.

Shane reached into his pocket and turned back on his cell phone now that he was out of the vault. Damn it, he'd missed a lot of calls. Fifteen? But all from the same number. Sherry's TLF.

Already his feet started at a dead sprint for the Jeep as he thumbed the numbers into his phone. Only one ring in, an answer but no voice. "Sherry?"

"Daddy?" Mally's voice quivered.

"Yeah, Mally? It's Daddy. Could you put Mommy on the phone please?"

"I'm scared."

Oh God. Scared? So was he. "What's wrong, kiddo?"

"Everybody's gone. I got sick and now I'm all by myself."

"Gone?" And she was sick? She didn't sound like she'd been through seizures. She'd been lethargic for hours after that. He took some comfort in her coherency. "Where did Mommy and Cara go?"

"They all wented outside."

"Go look out the window onto the porch. I bet Mommy's reading Cara a story on the steps because she doesn't want to wake you up."

That made sense. He forced even breaths in and out of his mouth as he sat in the Jeep. A part of him wanted to race over to the TLF, but another part of him thought he might need to tap the help here ASAP so he simply turned on the engine. He was ready to roll, while keeping his eye on his crew in sight if he needed to call for their help.

"I already checked. They're not there. And they're not with the cars. Mommy's van is here and Aunt Keisha's car is here, but she's not here. I'm scared."

Keisha's car, too? Now he was really starting to get that bad, bad feeling right before everything went to shit in battle. He scrambled for control to think of the correct questions to prompt Mally.

"Do you know how long they have been gone?" He tried to think of a good reason for this. They had the nursery monitor with them and were simply a few units down. No big deal. Five minutes could feel like forever to a six-year-old.

"Gone forever. I watched a whole Dora video while I waited and nobody came back. I'm scared by myself."

Shit.

No more growing suspicion. He was totally fucking freaked out. There wasn't a chance in hell Sherry would leave Mally alone for a half hour, no matter what. And he couldn't continue to delude himself she'd taken some walk. Not when he'd been damn clear she needed to stay inside after the kidnapping scare.

But crap, in spite of his plans for surveillance, he really hadn't thought there was a chance these bastards could penetrate the sanctity of the base security.

A sniffle on the other end of the phone reminded him of his priorities and the need to keep himself together, tougher than in any battle he'd ever faced. "You're being a brave, smart girl to call me. I'm on my way to you and we're going to talk on the phone the whole time. Okay?"

"That's good."

"Now hold on while I get some help for Mommy and Keisha and Cara." He cupped his hand over the phone to shout for Derek, the squadron commander—and thank the Lord, David Reis from the OSI had been participating in the lecture again tonight. He shouted for the three of them to come over. "My daughter Mally called and said my wife and other daughter, along with Keisha Jones, stepped out of the TLF over a half hour ago and haven't returned."

Derek blanched and braced his hand on the side of the Jeep. Shane wished he could have been smoother in his delivery of the news but there just wasn't time for prettying up this. Not to mention he was fairly fucking torn up about this himself. "I don't know how valid her account is. They could be just around the corner, but she sounds like she knows what she's talking about."

Reis nodded. "I'm on it. I'll call the base security police. We can give the local police a heads-up, too."

Shane nodded. "Thanks."

Derek's jaw kept working back and forth as he stood silently beside Shane.

Reis's eyes narrowed and settled on Shane. "We're going to find them. I never fail."

Shane's throat moved with a hard swallow. There were times arrogance like Reis's was a damn awesome quality to be valued.

The squadron commander clapped Shane on the back. "I'll follow you over in my car and take your daughter to stay with my wife, before I meet back up with Agent Reis."

Shane started to feel his world settle again as things clicked into place, people were on the move. They would have this figured out in no time, damn it all to hell. "Thank you, sir."

While he held the phone it buzzed with an incoming text on the other line. But he'd promised Mally he wouldn't hang up. He started to ignore the call altogether...and then he saw the number. Sherry's cell phone.

Relief threatened to send him to his knees. "Mally, sweetie, Mommy's on the other line. I promise I will call you right back."

Tension rippled through the three men standing around him. He pressed the button to receive the incoming text. He even felt a smile start inside him at the thought of connecting with Sherry.

His eyes scanned the text and the smile faded

from his soul as well as his face, replaced by horror as he read aloud, "Shane. Cara, Keisha, I R kidnapped in U-Haul van. Off base. Rasti man. Cell on. Track us. Mally alone sick. Have 2 go. Luv u."

CHAPTER NINETEEN

"KEISHA, COME ON, you have to stay awake," Sherry kept her voice low and prayed Shane was taking in every word.

Thank God the cell phone had been in her jeans pocket.

While she had it on, he should be able to hear everything—if the phone's hiding place inside Cara's doll's clothing didn't muffle the sound too much. She didn't want to risk continued texting and have Rasti-man see the glow of electronics. And she'd turned the ringer off in case the line disconnected and Shane tried to call her. It was one thing for the bastard to catch her and Keisha talking, but it would be fatal if he caught her with the cell phone and took it away. Hiding the cell and letting her husband overhear while tracking was the best way. God, her hands hurt from scraping them against the bolt on the door but at least she'd been able to get the text to Shane.

Now she could concentrate on rousing Keisha

again. But quietly. "Fight the drugs. Talk to me. What's going on?"

The U-Haul had stayed parked for what seemed like the longest time while he'd mumbled on the phone to someone before he'd started driving. The wait had made her want to scream, having Shane so near and unable to help. But by the time she'd gotten to her cell in her jeans pocket, they'd already begun to move and she'd become disoriented about time and place. She'd tried to check time on the cell periodically, but the lone red lightbulb in the back of the van made the phone's faceplate nearly indistingshable as the colors blended together.

She could already feel the bruises rising all over her body from jostling around on the hard metal floor. The musty blanket did little to absorb the jarring bounces, so she did her best to keep Cara protectively cushioned in her lap and away from the pile of vomit in the corner.

"I don't have…idea," Keisha mumbled, her words still slurred. "Got to your TLF and he threw me in the U-Haul. I think…this may have cured me…for adventure."

Definitely slurred, but perhaps clearer headed if her humor could peek through this endless nightmare of waiting for the bomb to fall.

"Are you able to check Cara? Her breathing seems so shallow." Sherry forced her voice to stay steady through the mountain of maternal fear as she fed information to Shane. God, she prayed her cell carrier wouldn't drop the most important call of her life. But she had no way of knowing if the connection remained live with the phone safely tucked inside the doll's clothes. "What if he gave her too much of the drug?"

Swaying, Keisha shoved up on her elbow and then to a sitting position. She blinked hard, shook her head fast and finally seemed clear enough to pull herself together and take Cara's pulse.

A brief look over later, she turned to Sherry. "Vitals are steady. Best I can tell." Keisha pressed a hand to head. "Just drugged, but okay."

Sherry struggled to get more information, whispering whatever she could about sounds of boats or cars, but had no idea where they were going. She could hear the traffic outside, like beach traffic with plenty of stoplights. There had been a bridge. Navarre's? Pensacola? Destin? She had no idea. She could only hope that Shane had the base and local police locked in on the cell phone with GPS trackers.

She needed to keep whispering what she could fathom from this hell. "Given what happened at the aquarium, he and whoever he's working with must want Cara. I just don't know why."

Keisha swayed toward her. "Tear a strip from… the hem of your…T-shirt. Your wrist. Bleeding."

Sherry looked down and…crap. She sure was bleeding. And suddenly woozy. Adrenaline had obviously masked it when she cut away the ropes, the crimson lightbulb turning the blood a darker shade, an ominous near black.

She tore off the cloth as Keisha instructed, her friend obviously weaker than she, although not totally out of it. Keisha took the strip from her and apparently training overrode the effects of her drugging. She tied off a tourniquet and bandage with an efficient swoop as Sherry noticed the sounds of traffic fading along with the thin streaks of street lights through the gaps in the doors.

Premonition prickled over her skin along with the sound of crunching gravel or rocky terrain under tires.

The van jerked to a halt. She gasped.

She remembered her phone. She needed to let Keisha know because the kidnapper expected Sherry to be gagged. "Keisha, listen to me. I have my cell phone on and hidden in Cara's doll. Shane is listening to everything and trying to find us. If I can't talk, you keep telling them what's going on. Okay?"

She didn't have time to see if the confusion cleared from Keisha's face before the back door swung open and she saw the outline of two people. One standing tall, one slouching.

Both in military uniform. Neither of them the Rastafarian fella with the steel-toed boots, thank God. Her stomach ached in memory as he stayed in the front seat.

Hope bloomed. She started to bolt upright—

But caution held her in place. She'd been too trau-
matized in too short a time to trust quickly.

Lightning fast she took in details. Cara's and
Keisha's lives depended on her next move. Her
brain niggled at her that something was off about
the man standing upright.

She squinted in the dim light, studying this new
man on the scene, taking in the details of the difference in the uniform of another country. Then
she realized the male beside him wasn't simply
slouching, he was unconscious.

And wearing an American flight suit. Ohmigod.

Another hostage? Someone she knew? Shaking
inside and out, Sherry huddled around Cara. She
also cowered to hide the fact that her hands and gag
were freed—which kept her from having a clear
view of what was going on outside.

Now she couldn't talk. Could Keisha keep up the
steady feed of information?

Bewilderment racked through Sherry's already
shot to hell nervous system as she listened to
Keisha mutter what she could about the newcomer
in uniform. The tall man's face seemed familiar, but
she couldn't place where.

"Here is someone to keep you company." The
guy in the foreign uniform tossed the unconscious
man into the back of van with a string of words in
another language that couldn't be mistaken for anything but curses.

He spit on the ground, then climbed inside the back of the van and slammed the doors closed behind him. His gun in plain sight, he strode past the women into the belly of van.

Once he'd passed them, Keisha crawled over to the unconscious man just as the van lurched forward again. A slight moan reassured Sherry as Keisha grabbed the shoulders of the dark haired man and rolled him to his side, then to his back. Even with his face battered with multiple bruises, Sherry couldn't mistake the airman she'd known for years, a man who'd been like a brother to her husband. A brother-in-arms, in fact.

"Sandman?" Sherry whispered, her voice racked with shocked disbelief.

What did their kidnapping have to do with taking one of the base fliers?

DIMITRI POPOV was doing what they called in America—flying by the seat of his pants.

Keeping his gun in plain sight to subdue their hostages, he walked through the back of the van to the small trunk lashed to the vehicle's floor. If only he could have made his move in the middle of the night as he had planned, but he'd been forced to act sooner when that idiot Rayhan had snatched the girl early—adding the two women to their hostage list. He'd thought he was such a smart one, taking them just because they had walked out of their quarters.

Damn him.

Rayhan had thought it would be no big deal to drive around while Dimitri finished getting the final information from Sandman. Except first the class had run late and then Sandman refused to cooperate.

Suddenly the American flier had grown a conscience. Dimitri eyed the unconscious airman curled in the corner. Beating him had done little to break him this time.

It was time to cut their losses with this one.

Dimitri checked the two women, both huddled around the little girl with her doll in the back corner. He waved his revolver at them once as a reminder before shifting his attention to the intricate lock on the trunk.

Opening slowly, reverently, he looked at the vials inside and the chemical gear suits folded neatly beside them. His hands shook. Sweat beaded on his upper lip. He did not want to be a martyr.

Definitely time for an adjusted plan. Take what victory he could. If he unloaded the contents of the vial and delivered the little girl, surely that would bring him a hefty payoff. So what if the Rubistani cell of insurgents did not get information about the inner workings of the new aircraft that Sandman had promised?

The cell would be angry, yes, because they wanted that CV-22 plan most of all, but they would have to take what they could get. It was *their* person—Rayhan—who had screwed up, after all.

Dimitri resisted the urge to kick the unconscious man again. If there had been more time, he could have used the drugs they'd given Sandman before that had been so effective in making him talk. But once Rayhan had blown everything to hell by prematurely taking hostages, Dimitri knew his window of opportunity with Sandman had been blown.

Hopefully that lapse in time hadn't given the police a chance to find the van. Damned stupid Rayhan.

Dimitri resisted the urge to spit again. His plan had been simple and idiot-proof. Steal into the child's room in the middle of the night. Drug her. He and Sandman would enter the vault at night with his code. Then meet up with Rayhan to get the vials moments later. All in the deep of night when security was low and slower to move once alerted.

They would put on their chemical gear suits, poison the town as a message of Rayhan's group's growing worldwide power, then U-Haul out with Cara in tow.

Suddenly he was burdened with more hostages than he had hands.

Now Sandman would die with the rest. Dimitri only wished he could pour an entire vial directly on top of the useless beast. What a waste of their time he had turned out to be.

For that matter, if the police did track him, they

didn't know Sandman had turned, so he could be used as another bargaining tool. Dimitri stared down at the lethal vials, willing his hands to stay steady. He wasn't as big into martyrdom as Rayhan.

Dimitri had worked his way into this cell to make money and he wanted his payoff. Yes, if they were caught, he would find a way to negotiate and damn Rayhan's alternative martyr scheme.

Sure, he understood the American policy of not dealing with terrorists. But it seemed to him they did grow softer when it came to their women and children. Lucky for him, he had both in his grasp.

"SANDMAN?" SHANE ECHOED Sherry's shocked whisper.

What the hell was he doing there? What did they want with him? In fact this whole thing made little sense at the moment as they sat in OSI headquarters with a hefty contingent from the base and local police in the conference room. Telephone, computers and a long table dominated the space packed full of people all trying to find the van.

They were quickly closing in on a GPS lock on the phone. Unmarked cop cruisers were out, on their way to drive covertly alongside the vehicle until a move could be made while maintaining the safety of the hostages.

Strangely, the van seemed to have driven away from the base then turned back around—which confused them into thinking they had the wrong lock. If they hadn't had the constant reassurance of Sherry and Keisha's voices they would have thought the phone had been ditched onto another car. Her words echoing softly in the room in an unending background simultaneously caressed and tortured him.

His brain kept scrolling through her final text to him.

Luv u.

In the middle of hell, she'd kept her cool, protected her friend, the girls and sent him words of comfort. God knows she must need consoling at the moment. What he wouldn't give to let her cry all over his chest right now.

But he had to concentrate on what he *could* accomplish. Being nose to nose with the authorities in making sure no one dropped the ball at any stage of this rescue operation.

Even with a room full of experts, Shane found he kept his eyes on Special Agent David Reis, the OSI guest speaker who'd come in from Charleston Air Force Base. Shane wasn't quite sure how to describe the feeling except it went all the way back to his baseball days. He hadn't been a record setter in the outfield, but he'd been a helluva hitter. He'd never thought it was because he had any special skill or power with the swing. No. His talent lay in reading body language. He'd always known where the pitcher would put the ball.

Always.

Odd but he'd never thought about carrying that over into other parts of his life until now. And what he read in David Reis's eyes as the man studied the movement of the GPS tracker's unfathomable blipping path told him this was the person to be trusted to find his wife and daughter.

Alive.

David Reis stood, confidence stamped on his aristocratic features. "Look at their path. They're headed straight for the base's beach. My gut tells me they're not going to drive past."

Hurlburt Field had a strip of beach just outside the main gate. Easily accessible to anyone.

The other officials in the room looked to each other as if considering whether this man's gut was worth listening to. Shane didn't even think. He stood as well.

Reis nodded. "Half can still stay here in case I'm wrong. The others head over to the beach. It's five minutes away. Tops. If I'm wrong, we're right back here watching the tracker with you again while the cops follow the van."

If only they knew the reason for this kidnapping. Why his child?

Still the why would have to come later—hopefully. With Reis and the head of Hurlburt's Security Police in charge, they pulled together a contingent in seconds. There was no discussion of Reis holding him back. Shane climbed into the car, only then realizing how the loss of hearing Sherry's voice would sucker punch him.

What if when they returned to the base he never heard her again?

Fuck. He swallowed down the emotions. Hard.

Stare straight through the windshield. Trust this Reis dude.

Shane looked in the rearview mirror and realized Derek was sitting in the back. Shane gave himself a mental brace. He must be more shaken than even he realized if he hadn't noticed his friend climbing into the car as well.

They headed through the night-silent front gate. The base was already on Alpha alert, machine guns on every guard due to the constant threat of terrorism and yet somehow someone had slipped in anyway. They'd already run tapes of traffic in and out of the base and found when the U-Haul had entered in the late afternoon. They were currently tracking the information on the individual who'd rented the van.

So far, all documents had led to dead ends. But with time they could blast through those.

Right now they didn't have time.

Weaving through the cones, Reis finally drove straight past the green light to the strip of beach owned by Hurlburt Field. Reis turned left onto a dirt road that took them out of sight of base and highway, still running parallel of the beach. Water lapped the shore in a calm that so contradicted the turmoil inside him he half expected there to be crashing waves.

An unmarked car slid in behind him while he saw from the corner of his eye a sniper slide into place under the guise of someone out for a stroll with a bag of surf gear. He could hear the hum of a motorcycle in the trees—another cop, he guessed from monitoring Reis's expression.

Deeper they drove into the beachy woods until he saw tucked under the cover of a live oak and two palm trees…a U-Haul van.

The back doors swung open. Sherry stumbled out, an ugly black gun to her head held by a strange man, the Rasti she'd mentioned in her message.

Derek cursed low and long, before ducking his head to mutter to Reis, "The guy with the bad wig of dreadlocks, that's the one who tried to run us off the road."

Shane heard and registered the additional information, but he couldn't tear his eyes off his wife's brave, beautiful—and bruised, damn it—face in the glow of car headlights. She held Cara against her chest. Their child slept, her head tucked against her mother's neck. Shane frowned. How could she be sleeping?

Before he could think further on that, the bastard who'd taken them started talking to them.

"Ah, you arrived sooner than we had hoped. We wanted you here after we made our drop-off. But this will suffice." He stroked the muzzle against Sherry's temple. "Let me speak to the woman's husband."

Shit. He was *expecting* them? And who was this "we" he was talking about? Shane wondered at the word, searching for this other person. He'd heard Keisha's mumbled, incoherent words about another person in uniform right before Sherry had said Sandman. She'd tried to explain about a vaguely familiar looking foreigner in uniform bringing unconscious Sandman, but none of it made sense.

And they damn well needed every edge they could scavenge now.

Shane walked through the wall of people to three steps to the front, fifty feet between him and his wife. He could see into the van, Keisha sitting beside the dim outline of what must be Sandman lying curled unconscious.

Still, Shane's attention stayed primarily on his wife and child. The headlights on Sherry's bruises kept hammering away at his control. Anger fired hotter in him as he forced his boots to stay nailed in place when he wanted more than anything to lurch forward. Attack. "I'm her husband. Tech Sergeant Shane O'Riley."

"Very good." He smiled with his mouth, his eyes soulless pools of evil. His muscled bulk expanded beneath the loose top and pants of green, yellow and red stripes. "What will your government do to keep your wife and child and this other female alive?"

Who was this man with his slight accent that hinted at Middle Eastern roots? And what the hell did he want?

"I am in no position to negotiate with you. You have to know that. I have people with me who can talk to you so this can be settled without anyone getting hurt." He could hear David Reis taking a step closer behind him.

"No." The bastard pushed the gun harder against Sherry's head, her eyes blinking faster the only sign of her fear. "I will only talk to you. I don't want one of your special negotiators who will trick me with fancy word plays or his psychological mind games. Mention another speaker again and I will shoot your wife in the leg."

Shit. Shane held up his hands in a pacifying gesture. "Okay. You want to deal with me, then deal with me. We are both men here. Let's make this between men. Not women and a child. I'll come to you."

"A beautiful speech. But because you value your women so, that's all the more reason I cannot let them go." He smiled. "And your child. She is already lost to you."

Cara? They'd already killed her? A pain roared

so loudly inside him he couldn't see anything but blood red. In some distant part of his brain, he felt hands grip his arms and hold him back. Thank God, because if he'd launched forward without another thought, Sherry would be dead now, too.

He blinked back…tears. And agony beyond imagining. He kept blinking until he could see again and slowly the restraining hands fell away from him.

Sherry shook her head at him, even with the gun at her temple. Right. He had to keep himself together for her and for Keisha. For Mally too so she didn't lose the rest of her family.

Still, his sanity was on wobbly ground. Vaguely, he heard more cars arriving. Support. He had to keep the man talking to give Reis time. "I do not have the authority to grant you anything. You need to speak with our people in power."

The captor shook his head. "I want to talk to you. Everyone can listen. My way or we all die."

Was this man insane? How did he expect to take out everyone? "Who are you then?"

"Rayhan Abdul-Majeed of Rubistan. The real Rubistan that will come back in power. And not just I, but others here who support our cause."

"Let us see the others then." Kidnappers and hostages. He couldn't mention Sandman without giving away the telephone. "We want the cards on the table."

He feared another shock like losing Cara, the weight of it crushing his insides. He was scared as hell it would scramble his thoughts when he needed to stay clear.

The bastard nodded toward the van and slowly Keisha came into view, crawling along the floor of the van until she sat on the edge. She leaned her head against the side, her feet dangling off the edge. Apparently the drug Sherry had mentioned was still in Keisha's system. She wouldn't be of any help in taking down their captors, but she'd done a good job at angling herself out of the line of fire. He suspected that wasn't accidental. Smart woman.

Shane took a deep reassuring look at his wife before turning his attention to her captor. Desperation burned within him to reclaim his family. "Talk then."

It would give the sniper time to gain a possible shot. He still worried about that man in uniform Sherry had mentioned.

"It's not secret we've wanted to introduce lethal bacteria into your world, more lethal and speedy than any bullet. A new bomb of sorts. Your daughters stumbled upon our lab a short while ago. They went over to our side of the island when we were running tests on biological warfare."

His mind raced back to that night when Cara had been singing the song she'd learned from her disobedient trip to the other side of the island. The

General had said there was a terrorist camp in the area linked to the pirate ship shoot-out… And then there had been the attack on the NGO camp…

Shane's brain blazed with the notion of how close Cara and Mally had unwittingly been to that newly set up terrorist camp. "They're so young. It's not as if they understand what they saw."

"It's not what they saw. It's what they were exposed to. We had a lab failure that day with a small leak. Not huge or devastating, but definitely enough to make a lot of our people very sick. Including your children."

"But only Mally was sick." The sudden, unexplained fever and seizures.

"Exactly," Rayhan confirmed, "and from where they were standing, little Cara was actually exposed to far more of the toxin than most. She should have been sick—very sick. Probably dead."

Keisha roused from her slouch against the doorframe, her T-shirt rumpled and sweat stained. No one guarded her, but it would be a gauntlet run to get past Rayhan with his gun. "Her body has a natural immunity to the bacteria."

The evil man smiled, his bulk an additional frightening threat to Sherry, as if he could snap her arm with his fist. "And that's critical to our study. If we examine the child's body, we can find a better antidote to use on the people who deliver the bacteria around your country—and anywhere else we may choose."

Suddenly it was all so clear—the reason they'd tried to kidnap Cara at the aquarium and why they'd taken her now. The insurgents in Rubistan that supported underground factions in the Middle East were planning to use bioweapons on the American home front.

"You can't expect we're just going to let you get away with this. Look how you're outnumbered." The next part pained him but he had to say, "Our country does not negotiate with terrorists."

From around the van, a man, a second man—Dimitri Popov in his country's uniform?—walked with a tray of vials.

No wonder they'd had such easy access to the base. Popov had damn near free run because of his position as a D.I.T. instructor. He'd likely brought the U-Haul on earlier with his base ID and then left in another vehicle. Pieces slid into place as to how they'd managed to pull off their crimes on base.

Betrayal steamed through him. This man had been given access to not only their base, their personnel, the secrets, but to their lives. He'd betrayed treaties and rules of engagement. He'd betrayed the most basic code of honor of the uniforms they wore.

The sound of raised guns clicking echoed behind Shane's head as Reis's backup started to get antsy. This could get ugly too fast. No wonder Rayhan hadn't wanted any of the OSI or other security forces using their negotiating skills to weave through this maze.

Popov extended his hands with the tray of vials. "The bacteria. Unless you do what we say, we start releasing it now into the ocean and the air at levels so high this entire community will be in the emergency room by nightfall tomorrow. All of us will be dead."

"Dimitri Popov. You traitorous bastard. You've been playing us this whole time. Why should I trust you now? For all I know, that's green Kool-Aid."

Popov was from Eastern Europe, for crying out loud, not the Middle East. What the hell did he have to gain from this?

The obvious, most common motivator of all non-zealot crooked bastards. Money.

"What choice do you have but to trust me?" Popov made a furtive move with the vials that sent a collective gasp through the crowd. "I can put it into your town's water system, and the next town while you simply wait…"

Popov's eyes went dark with a wicked glint. He took an eye dropper and squeezed out one droplet onto a low lying bush. The plant slowly started to hang limply, vibrant green spotting yellow. "Not enough to kill us all, but enough to prove my point. We'll likely suffer from the flu by tomorrow. Plant life seems affected more harshly than human life. We are still fine-tuning."

Shane studied David Reis's body language, Derek's next, then back to the bastard with a gun to Sherry's head. Nobody believed the Kool-Aid theory.

If only he had thought to use those same intuition skills to read his wife's eyes with a deeper understanding before now. To see the love she felt for him. To show her the deep, unending love he felt for her.

He refused to accept it could be too late, because he couldn't lose another person. "What do you want, Popov?"

"We will give you this tray of the bacteria to study. That will level the playing field a bit, don't you think? Even if we are ahead of you in having the antidote. In return, you let us fly out of here in one of your country's fancy new CV-22s."

"A CV-22?" Shane could see the "tell" in the man's body language as he actually licked his lips. Popov wanted that CV-22 more than he wanted to spread the bacteria.

In fact, Popov seemed rather antsy around the emerald liquid too.

"Yes, the people I work with are very interested in the inner workings of your cutting-edge new aircraft. And of course we get to study your daughter. We will let the women and the man go once we're in Rubistan."

Like he believed that. Everything inside him rebelled at these terms. Not that it mattered. He knew their terms wouldn't be met.

The best he could do was continue to work as middle man reading the eyes of evil on one side and the eyes of savvy reason on the other. "You know I will need to confer with people about this. You have to realize I can't make it happen on my own."

"Of course." Popov sniffed as if intellectually insulted. "But do your conferring here. We will go straight to the flight line and that is non-negotiable."

Shane began backing toward the contingent behind him, already thinking through possible ways to lure Popov and his cohort into a false sense of security and then overpower them.

Let them think they'd won, while leveling the playing field, putting them inside *his* world. The very CV-22 Popov coveted.

Shane let the rhythm of the waves brushing the shore hypnotize him into a semblance of calm until he could channel his training in time with his steps taking him to Reis. Once emotions were tamed and he was back in the zone, Shane found *it*. An idea. A long shot, low and on the outside crazy ass notion.

Now he just had to pray for a miracle to pull it off.

CHAPTER TWENTY

GAGGED AGAIN SINCE the uniformed man discovered her slipped band and untied hands, Sherry sat with Cara beside her as the U-Haul drove toward the flight line. Somehow Popov and Rayhan's crazy demands had been met with a few apparently well-placed phone calls. Now they were all on their way onto base and to a CV-22. The van was completely surrounded by security vehicles, not that it brought much reassurance with a gun still trained on her and those nasty vials sloshing around in their tray.

Surely there must be a plan in place to take out these two men. A duo couldn't pull off something this large scale—except their test tubes and hostages seemed to tip the scales in the bad guys' favor.

Her daughter's breathing was so shallow now it terrified her. She needed to get her child to a doctor. Now. And what about Mally? She needed to let the doctor know her daughter had been exposed to the deadly bacteria in case—God forbid—her illness could prove fatal.

She'd seen the pain in Shane's eyes at the assumption Cara had died, but they wouldn't let her talk. She'd tried her best with the slight shake of her head, but he hadn't been looking into her eyes then...

Not like later in that amazing moment when she'd seen the reassurance that he had a plan. He would take care of them. And strongest of all, she'd seen comfort. Blessed comfort at a moment when he had to be mourning so deeply. She'd seen his pain, too.

So many emotions.

He'd finally stopped hiding his feelings from her. What a time to truly connect with her husband now when their chances of getting out of this alive were slim.

Time passed in such a blur. She had little idea what was going on outside the moving van that had become her world. A world she now knew contained lethal germ warfare.

A simple wreck could take them all out.

The van jerked to a halt. She gasped, then held her breath. The head goon—the guy in uniform—came from the front through the van. Dimitri Popov, Shane had called him. Sherry had struggled at first to place the name. Finally the vaguely familiar face and name came together, and she recalled him as one of the people from Shane's D.I.T. class. She had seen the man the day they'd played baseball. She didn't recall him joining them for pizza and he hadn't been in his uniform...

God, if only she'd remembered him and been able to warn Shane through the phone. Would it have made a difference? Second-guessing only wasted time.

Popov stopped beside her, followed by his fake Rasti pal so they could both train guns on her and Keisha. The men unlatched the back of the van. Lights momentarily blinded her from the dome lit runway in the middle of the night.

For a second she feared this was the plan. Blind them and shoot. She instinctively wrapped herself around her child. But...

Nothing.

Her captor untied her hands. "Pick up your child."

She grasped Cara with only a second to spare before they were yanked down the steps onto the tarmac. She stumbled to right herself while securing Cara's limp body against her, her daughter's head tucked on her shoulder.

Straightening, Sherry looked past the front of the van and found a gleaming new CV-22, just as requested—with her husband and his crew standing lined up alongside the aircraft in a wall of strength. They waited with their boots braced, holding their helmets, gear bags on the ground.

Pilots, Postal and Rodeo. God, Derek must be out of his mind worrying about Keisha, but his only sign of stress was the clench of his jaw.

The gunners and flight engineer too—Stones with

his bandages off. Padre looking reading to bust heads. And a substitute gunner she didn't recognize but suspected was likely from the OSI in disguise, since Sandman was still in the back of the van unconscious, apparently drugged since Keisha had never been able to find any injury beyond a few bruises.

And her husband. Her honorable, handsome husband who gave up fame and millions on the baseball diamond to serve their country. How could she have lost her way to loving him? Her husband who'd never had a real family and asked only that she try to build one with him.

Why had she spent her life traveling to other continents teaching them to build homes while not devoting some of that time to building one of her own with him? A man she *did* still love. She'd just needed to stand still long enough to hear her heart speak again.

She wished she was as good at communicating with her eyes as he was. She tried and hoped her love for him, her wish to try for real this time transmitted across the muggy patch of asphalt.

Popov kept the gun to her temple while she held Cara, her daughter's head draped over her shoulder. Sherry's arms grew tired, but no way would she pass her child to anyone else. Although she also suspected they had her carry Cara to make it impossible for her to run. As if the warm muzzle of the gun against her head and another against Keisha's neck wasn't deterrent enough.

The best she could do to reassure Shane was pat Cara's back in hopes he would realize she was only resting. Albeit so deeply he likely couldn't see her frighteningly shallow breaths.

What were they going to do with Sandman? She still hadn't figured out the reason for him being there.

Security police encircled the area but kept their distance. She'd expected that, and Popov and Rayhan didn't seem to mind. They seemed to believe they would be allowed to leave in the CV-22.

Perhaps they would. To shoot down the plane would create a crash that would distribute the bacteria throughout the atmosphere. Maybe once they were out over the ocean that wouldn't matter. She seemed to recall Shane telling her of just such a considered plan for getting rid of nuclear matter once.

Popov paused. He pointed to Padre and Rodeo. "You and you. Go into the back of the van and get your useless friend out of there. Take him into the plane and strap him into a seat. Then return to your crew. I will wait here with this lovely lady."

While keeping the gun to her cheek, he grazed a kiss against her forehead. *Revolting.* She swallowed bile behind her gag and tried to maintain her composure for Shane. Even from a hundred feet away, she could see his muscles bunching under his flight suit. Would they have to restrain him as they'd done when he'd thought Cara had been killed?

Wordlessly they strode past, toward the van, Rodeo's gaze meeting and holding Keisha's for brief, heartbreaking second before he disappeared into the van. He and Padre reappeared with Sandman, the unconscious man between them as they loaded him in the aircraft.

Emerging again, they rejoined their places in line.

Popov gave a regal nod, gun in one hand, tray of vials in the other. A simple trip of the step and he could kill Sherry or drop a bioweapon that could potentially take out everyone. "Good. And just so that you know, your friend Sandman was totally worthless. If he had been of help to me tonight and used his clearance to get me into the places I wanted to go, I would have the information I need and I wouldn't have to take your plane. If you need an outlet for all of that rage, you can blame it on him. Now stay where you are and wait for my next orders."

He promptly strapped her, with Cara across her chest, into a seat, Keisha next to her near the open back. The two men never wavered with their guns. She'd been unable to pull off any of those tricks she'd read about in books—going limp, tripping. And the safety class techniques she'd learned… They all sounded so easy in theory, but once the gun was against her head, her child in danger, she could only wrap herself around her baby and pray harder than she'd ever prayed before.

The back hatch still loomed open. As long as she could see land, she allowed herself to hope.

Popov stood at the back and addressed the crew. "You may load up now, but my friend Rayhan will be checking you for weapons. So if you have any guns on you, I suggest you set them aside now. For every gun I find on you when you are in this plane, I will put a bullet somewhere in the body of one of your women."

Wow. She really could read eyes after all because Shane's burned with a hatred right now that actually made her flinch in her seat.

Each of the five men carefully set a revolver on the runway.

Popov nodded. "I expected as much from you. Of course you would try. However it still must cost you."

He nodded to Rayhan. The slap slammed Sherry's head against the side of the plane. She tasted blood. Barely managed to swallow the scream she feared would send her husband launching up the load ramp. Her tongue probed a loose tooth in the back. She winced again, but for once was grateful for the gag. More than that, she was grateful she managed to keep her hold on Cara draped across her.

Popov put his gun back to her head. "Just a little show to let you know your women and children mean nothing to us." He waved his hand. "Now come aboard for Rayhan to check you. Oh, and tell your sharpshooter that Ms. Jones will be standing in front of him the whole time holding a test tube of our 'Kool-Aid.'"

What seemed laboriously slow probably took all of ten minutes to clear the crew into the plane. The two pilots went up front—along with the stranger she didn't know. But wait, Shane sat up front in the flight engineer's seat. Why was the stranger assuming that crew position?

She kept her face schooled not to show the hint of hope inside her as Shane settled into the rear gunner/flight engineer's seat. She wanted to catch his eye and know for sure but he kept his face averted. Likely for the best because they might give something away.

The hatch closed and the world grew darker, engines roaring to life almost as loudly as the fear howling inside her. They couldn't actually be leaving, but she could see her husband's mouth moving as he spoke into the boom mike attached to his helmet. There were no sharpshooters now. No guns but those the bad guys held.

Although at least they seemed to be relaxing their grip now that they had the lone weapons.

The entire craft went pitch black dark except for Shane's glowing panel. Sherry's stomach lurched.

A second later, Shane's screen exploded in sparks, brighter, flashing off a mini-explosion.

SHANE SEARCHED THE DARK for the luminescent dust he'd sprinkled on Popov and his demon pal during the pat down for weapons. Hopefully the explosion inside the aircraft would provide enough distraction for him and the gunners to overpower Popov, his cohort—and secure the lethal vials, because if that bacteria met air, they would all be dead anyhow.

He took one valuable second to slide free the knife hidden in the folds under his seat. He was ever-cognizant of where Popov had set the vials down for a split second to strap his own seat belt. Seeing the vials out of Popov's hands, Shane had called for the pilots to darken the craft and he'd set off the explosion that would create the distraction.

Once Shane had one of the men in his sights, he launched across the belly of the plane. From the tall lean size and the sound of the grunt, he knew he had Popov.

With luck, Padre would take care of the other bastard—while Stones grabbed hold of his huge cahones and secured those vials.

The crew had pulled off some crazy ass maneuvers before, but Shane knew there was zero room for error in this one.

An extra body moved, distracting Shane in his scuffle. Still, his wife's life depended on his focus. He couldn't allow himself to consider grief yet. He plunged the knife into Popov's chest until the man went limp. He'd known from the start, this couldn't be anything but a fight to the death.

A gun went off.

Hell. He landed on top of Sherry and waited for pain. Almost welcomed it because it would mean Sherry was safe.

A ping sounded. Ricochet. All so fast.

Not even a sting. Had anyone been shot? He risked speaking and giving away his position. "Got Popov."

"Got the other guy, too," Padre shouted.

"Vials are in my aching hands," Stones called.

Lights flickered on, powered back up from the pilots in front. Shane looked down at his wife staring back up at him with pleading eyes. He skimmed his hands over her body and she seemed unharmed. She struggled under him, tugging at her gag as Rodeo sprinted past toward Keisha.

"Cara, Cara," Sherry cried, each syllable a knife sliding into Shane's heart.

"Babe, I know."

"No, you don't. She's alive, barely. Drugged too much." She crawled across the floor, searching. "When the explosion happened, she jerked in my arms and fell. Oh, Shane, where is she?"

Alive? Sparks of hope exploded, much like his panel earlier, inside Shane so intense it was almost painful. He'd seen Sherry shake her head, but had thought she was consoling him. Now he realized she'd been trying to tell him Cara hadn't died.

But where was their child now?

And then he realized Sandman wasn't in his seat anymore. He lay at an odd angle on the floor. Blood poured from his side.

The stray shot.

"Sandman's down," Shane hollered as the back hatch cranked opened. He rolled his crew member over to a growing patch of light and found…

Cara.

Sandman had covered her in the mêlée. Shane leaned to press his ear to his little girl's flowered PJs, still barely daring to believe he would hear a faint…*thump, thump, thump.*

His throat closed up, his eyes burning from the acrid air after the explosion. His nose filled too until he realized it didn't have a damn thing to do with the sparks from the blast. He had tears pouring down his face. And if he was crying…

He held out his arm to Sherry and gathered her against his chest while she sobbed right along with him. Cara stirred, her lashes fluttering. Groggy, but awake she reached a shaky hand up to stroke away her daddy's tears before snuggling back on his lap and tucking her head under his chin and drifting off again.

Shane looked at Sherry, really looked at her, into her tear-filled eyes with his own still not quite dry and could only think he would do whatever it took. He wasn't going to lose this woman again.

Heart full and head clear after the last few years of not being able to figure out how to make his home life work. He was going to scoop up Mally, Cara and Sherry all at once the moment he got home.

And right after that, he was burning those divorce papers.

"HEY, RODEO, DO YOU NEED a ride?" Keisha strutted toward Derek outside the base operations building, unable to take her eyes off his tall vitality after a hellish night of thinking she might not live to see him again.

After the debriefing and physicals, they'd all been cleared to leave right at daybreak. Sherry and Shane had offered to take her with them, but she could see their deep need for family time. So she'd sent them on their way to retrieve Mally from Lt. Col. Quinn's wife's care.

Keisha closed the last steps between her and Derek. Quite frankly, she had a need of her own she couldn't deny or write off as simple attraction.

"Seems to me we've done this carpooling route a time or two." Derek strode across the parking lot toward her.

Not smiling. This wasn't a time where levity came easily after all the fear and death, but it was a time for hanging on to each other and life and the blessing of being able to hold his strong hand as they met each other halfway.

"Well, your car is out of commission because of how you saved my life and the girls'." She squeezed his hand, then slid her arm around his waist as he did the same to her.

A deep sense of gratitude pulsed through her over being able to touch him. Even when the drugs had been at their thickest in her system, she'd come out of the fog with this one tangible sensation in her heart and mind. Touch Derek. Live her life fully. Take the risks with her heart that she'd been taking only with her body the last few years.

"I wanted to take out the bastard who had his hands on you tonight," he said with a dangerous edge to his voice, the depth of emotion there leaving no doubt about how much he cared for her and her alone.

"You were a part of the team plan. You put yourself there in that plane, in harm's way for me, for Sherry and her girls." She blinked back tears at the quadrupled fear she'd felt when he had entered the nightmare, in the line of fire. "You've been more than enough of a hero for me these past twenty-four hours, Sparky."

A hoarse chuckle slipped free as he stared down at her as the dome lights flickered off and on in the haze in between time where night meets morning.

"Well that means a helluva lot coming from a Komodo hunter."

She gave him an impish wink, appreciating his acceptance of her strengths. He was a rare man and she was certainly one to appreciate originality. "I was hoping you might come to my place."

"Because?"

She stared up at him with total honesty, no more "allergy" games or time delays. "I really don't want to be alone right now."

Stopping by her Ford Escape, he stroked a knuckle down her jaw. "So anyone would do?"

"I really want to be with *you.*"

"Good." He stopped the caress and cupped her face in his big broad hand. "Because after you scared a decade off my life, I'm not sure when I'll be ready to let you out of my sight."

"It has been that kind of day." She settled into the circle of his embrace and allowed herself a moment of rest against Derek's chest.

Popov and Rayhan had both died in the fight. From the debriefings, it seemed the OSI was already tracking the bigger powers behind their efforts. Keisha realized she would likely never be privy to anything more than what had happened tonight.

As Sherry had often said, military spouses lived in a "need to know" world of information. For a woman used to controlling her destiny, that would be a tough one for Keisha to swallow.

But then after a night like tonight when she'd been faced with the alternative—losing out on the chance to be with Derek—she could find her way clear to make compromises after all.

Life was too precious.

A knot settled in her chest when she thought about Sandman. It could have been any of the crew that had been targeted, any of them in that plane that had been shot in the effort to protect her and Sherry and little Cara.

He hadn't even made it to the hospital. The EMTs had reported to her he'd mumbled apologies to someone named Tabitha before dying. His sister apparently. As best they could tell, he'd been kidnapped in order to gain access to different parts of the base during Popov's demented schemes.

But in the end, Sandman died honorably, protecting Cara from the path of that ricocheting bullet.

What a tragedy for his crew as well. Derek wouldn't have known him as long, having only just joined the crew, but Keisha still stroked her hands along the back of his head in comfort anyway. It had been an awful night for both of them.

"Come on." She tugged him toward her car. "Let's watch the sunrise together on a better day."

He took her hand and walked by her side until they both reached her car and settled in front. She passed him the keys. She felt that most of the drug was out of her system, but she didn't a hundred percent trust her reflexes. She'd been so slow to move in the plane during the final takedown. All those self-defense classes hadn't done her a damn bit of good.

She couldn't wait to rid herself of the blood spattered clothes.

She shivered.

Derek stroked a hand over her head, the warmth of his touch so welcome to brush away the lingering chill of fear. "How much *time* do you think you're going to be needing before it's all right for me to tell you that I love you?"

Her skin hummed with the happy rightness of those words and joy they brought with them. The sensation flooded her veins faster than any mind-numbing drug, bringing with it a power so much stronger than anything she'd known.

She turned her face to kiss his palm, her heart clenching tight in response before it seemed to fill to overflowing. "I think we're both fairly emotional, but hearing something like that right now would soothe my very weary soul."

"I do like soothing you, lady."

"Well, Sparky, a night like tonight puts things into perspective. I always have had a thing for you."

"Now that soothes this soul which happened to have been scared as hell for you tonight."

"Good. Good." She cupped his face. "Say my name."

"Keisha, my love."

"Perfect." She leaned to meet his kiss. Yes, she had a feeling they would be spending a long, long life*time* together.

CHAPTER TWENTY-ONE

EXHAUSTED, BUT SO SWELLED full of relief and love, Sherry sat in the front seat of Shane's Jeep on their way home as the sun kissed the horizon. She barely even noticed their police escort following at a steady but discreet pace behind them. David Reis had insisted on police protection for the O'Riley family until he had more answers about how the base's security had been so heinously compromised.

After the past twenty-four hours of hell, she was totally cool with having her own police detail.

Cara had been cleared by the doctor. They had picked up Mally from the squadron commander's house where Lt. Col. Quinn's wife had been keeping watch over her after taking her to the ER for a once-over. Apparently Mally had an old-fashioned cold this time.

Now, Sherry just wanted to be in her own house, tuck her girls into their beds, and reassure herself of the peek at forever she'd seen in her husband's eyes. She'd been so certain she knew her husband but tonight had been full of revelations. Finally she was ready for compromise.

After their near brush with death—after losing a friend from the crew—life and priorities had a way of coming sharply into focus.

Home had never looked more welcoming than this morning as Shane pulled his Jeep into an empty spot by their door. Their police detail slid into place alongside, where the duo from the Sheriff's department would stay for the first shift.

Toting Cara who was still shaky on her feet, Shane unlocked the condo front door and disarmed the security system. They all four stood in the living room, the silence deafening after the roar of life and death threats.

Mally chewed her bottom lip, furrowed her brow, opened her little mouth… "Fuck."

Shane's eyes went wide, some of the weariness sliding from his blond-god features. "Mally, uh, that's not a nice word."

Mally blinked back at him. "Well, it's what you say whenever the day's been very, very bad."

Sherry smothered a much-needed laugh. She'd really thought he never cursed in front of the kids, but they must have overheard more of their parents' arguments than she'd realized.

A sobering thought that stole the laugh from her lips.

Cara bobbed her head in agreement. "And shit, too."

He turned to Sherry, a smile and bewilderment battling for dominance on his face. "Do you want to take this one?"

"Not a chance, Slugger." She held up both hands. "This one's all yours since we know where they got those words from."

His cheeks puffing with an exhale, he knelt by Mally, Cara still on his hip. "Sometimes people say bad words because they aren't very good at showing the way they really feel inside. I shouldn't say those words. I should let the other person know how I feel by using good words instead. Does that make sense?"

Groggy Cara leaned her head on her father's shoulder while Mally took the initiative. "Grown-ups goof, too?"

Shane stared over Mally's head at Sherry, his eyes holding back none of the regret that apparently pumped through him. "Grown-ups goof really badly sometimes."

Mally nodded. "Okay, I won't say fuck and Cara won't say shit again."

Shane winced. "Good."

Mally wrapped her arms around Shane's neck and pressed a kiss to his cheek. "We'll just tell you we were scared tonight, but we knew our daddy would save us."

He blinked fast, the tears doing nothing to

diminish the strength of the man in his blood spattered flight suit who held two little girls with such tenderness. "I tried my best."

Sherry didn't even bother holding her tears back. This was a night for catharsis.

No doubt later he would have to deal with the way Popov had died, but she knew there hadn't been any other choice. Guns would have been risky in the dark, although they had tried to bring them on board as well. Risking restraint would have left Popov further time to use his weapon—or the chemicals, which posed a far larger threat.

Shane, Stones and Padre had only had one second's chance. Intellectually she understood they were combat trained for just this thing. She'd just never been so close to the harsh reality before.

With the itchy crackle of the enemy's blood still on her clothes as well, she could understand how her husband would need to keep deeper emotions at bay at times. The weight of it all could crush a person's soul. She resolved that even when he needed to face it silently, she would make sure he wasn't alone in those darker moments.

Sherry stepped into the circle of her family and soaked up the feeling of all of them together…until a *snort, snuffle, snort* jolted her.

Shane laughed lowly. "I think Mally's asleep."

Sherry stepped back, and sure enough their youngest was snoring and their oldest had drifted back off as well. They tucked the girls in together, and she no longer took that ritual for granted.

Dropping their grimy clothes in a trail into their room, they climbed into the shower together, both too tired for anything sexual. Yet she savored the closeness as they washed each other with a reverent familiarity, cleansing away the hell and pain of the past twenty-four hours. And maybe even some of the pain from years longer.

Clean and dry from fluffy towels, they dove under the covers in their brass bed.

She settled against his chest, sunshine slanting slim lines through the closed blinds. "I should be sleepy, but suddenly I'm wired."

"Happens after combat sometimes. It's normal, especially after something as bad as this." His arms around her shoulders, he smoothed a hand along her arm. "You'll crash soon enough."

"I'm sorry about Sandman."

His grip on her tightened and they shared a quiet moment together. She didn't look up at him, but rather tucked her head under his chin as she felt his pain in his tensed muscles—expressed differently than she would have, but real all the same. She was learning there could be a middle ground between "Fuck" and bawling her eyes out.

The squadron would have a lot of grieving to do, losing one of their own. The whole business with Sandman was sad and strange. Why had they chosen him? An uneasiness settled in her about the whole thing that she didn't want to explore.

In the end, Sandman had saved Cara's life. That's all that mattered to her and she felt certain Shane would feel the same.

Sherry rolled over and propped her elbows on his chest so she could look into his eyes. "I want to say I'm sorry for something else, for everything really. Not listening the way I should have the past five years."

He threaded his hand through her hair and cupped her head, his eyes as open as she'd ever seen them, even more so than on the runway. All there for her to see. "I owe you the same apology. I want us to figure this out, babe. Compromise and all. But you know it's going to be tough."

"I think maybe that's part of where we messed up before. We looked for simple, Band-Aid fixes rather than going to the root of the problem."

"Any ideas on how to do that?"

Compromise felt easier than she'd expected. But then maturing could do that for a person. "For starters, I'm willing to cut back on travel and apply for more freelance paperwork time at home."

"Okay." He massaged along her scalp, the comfort of his touch warm and wonderful after so much estrangement and distance between them over the past couple of years. "I'll use my leave time to join you on one of your assignments once a year."

She was so caught up in the pleasure of just having him touch her, it took a few extra seconds for his words to register. But when they did… "Really?" Joy tingled through her from the pads of his fingers along her scalp. "You would volunteer to help out?"

"Hey now, I can shovel a latrine with the best of them."

She covered her mouth with her hand, seriously choked up. "We'll have more time together, for us and the girls."

"About the girls… I want us to talk to your ex about my adopting them. Seriously talk, because he's not a part of their lives and we all know it. Those girls are O'Rileys, Sherry."

"I agree." Hadn't she been thinking the same thing earlier? And given how much he and the girls loved each other she was only surprised they hadn't pursued this harder in the past. This had been blessedly easy to settle, but she knew it all wouldn't be so. "We need counseling."

He stilled under her touch, his blue eyes shuttering emotions away. "We did that already."

"A six week, basic communication stint." As much as she wanted to recapture the sweet connection they'd enjoyed just moments before, she couldn't back down as she'd done too often over the past couple of years. "We've got deeper problems than just being apart too much. Your parents have left marks on you. I understand your need for a peaceful life at home because of them and your job, but being Betty Crocker perky all the time is damned exhausting. Try pulling that off for a lifetime. What we've discussed is a big step for us, but I don't think a few words can wave a magic wand over our problems."

His expression opened a hint again, enough that she could see his resistance to therapy. Of course it had been her experience from gossip over the years that all fliers cringed at that word—*therapy*—like it somehow tampered with the immortality they needed to embrace in order to conquer the sky.

She tried again. "It's not just about you. It's about me and my past, too. The places my parents took me to make the island camp attack look like a normal event. And during the few times we came back to the States during my teen years, I had to put on this blasé act. Like it didn't hurt my feelings when I didn't understand pop culture references and jokes. I let myself fall into a pattern that continued through my twenties until I traveled so much because I don't feel like I fit in here." She finally admitted something to him she'd barely dared admit to herself. "I travel to those camps because it's the only place I feel normal."

All the defensiveness fell away from his expression in a flash and he wrapped her in the strong warmth of his embrace. "Sherry, babe, you're so amazingly beyond blah normal. Who the fuck wants boring normal? Sure as shit not me."

Her eyes teared up as she savored more of his touch. "You must really mean it. You said shit *and* fuck."

His low chuckle rumbled under her ear. "I guess I do still have some fine-tuning to do on my emotional outpourings."

They rolled together in downy softness, kissing, touching, holding.

He stroked a hand down to cup her hip and bring her nearer to his side. "Honest to Pete marital therapy, huh?"

"Yeah."

"Yeah."

"Yeah?" She looked up at him with hope bubbling.

"Whatever it takes to keep us on target, babe. Because this time, I'm not letting you go."

She stretched up to meet his mouth for a kiss, her hand grazing over the muscled expanse of his chest. Her fingers hooked on his dog tags, then higher up on the string of leather holding his wedding ring.

Her hand closed around the gold still warm from resting against the heat of him.

He nipped the corner of her mouth, easing an end to the kiss as he closed his hand over hers clutching his ring. "Put it back where it belongs."

Her heartbeat tripping over itself it raced so fast,

she untied the leather and slipped the ring free. She took his hand, the same hand that had saved her, loved her, cherished her children, and she slid the gold band back in place.

He made a fist locking the band tight. "Love you, babe."

"Love you too, Slugger." She closed her fingers over his and leaned in for a slow kiss to seal the moment as well as the emotion.

She knew he would have to take the ring off for flights in the future and all of this was symbolic, but that didn't matter to her. Because she could see in his eyes now that the band would never again languish around his neck. It would always go right back in place—where it belonged.

Just as she now didn't need to traipse around the far reaches of the world to feel normal. She knew where she belonged.

Right here with Shane, in an old brass bed.

* * * * *

Watch for Catherine Mann's next military romance in a special two-in-one collection from Silhouette Romantic Suspense— on sale this November.

REQUEST YOUR FREE BOOKS!

2 FREE NOVELS
FROM THE ROMANCE/SUSPENSE
COLLECTION PLUS 2 FREE GIFTS!

YES! Please send me 2 FREE novels from the Romance/Suspense Collection and my 2 FREE gifts. After receiving them, if I don't wish to receive any more books, I can return the shipping statement marked "cancel." If I don't cancel, I will receive 4 brand-new novels every month and be billed just $5.49 per book in the U.S., or $5.99 per book in Canada, plus 25¢ shipping and handling per book plus applicable taxes, if any*. That's a savings of at least 20% off the cover price! I understand that accepting the 2 free books and gifts places me under no obligation to buy anything. I can always return a shipment and cancel at any time. Even if I never buy another book from the Reader Service, the two free books and gifts are mine to keep forever.

185 MDN EF5Y   385 MDN EF6C

Name _____ (PLEASE PRINT)

Address _____ Apt. #

City _____ State/Prov. _____ Zip/Postal Code

Signature (if under 18, a parent or guardian must sign)

Mail to **The Reader Service**:
IN U.S.A.: P.O. Box 1867, Buffalo, NY 14240-1867
IN CANADA: P.O. Box 609, Fort Erie, Ontario L2A 5X3

Not valid to current subscribers to the Romance Collection,
the Suspense Collection or the Romance/Suspense Collection.

Want to try two free books from another line?
Call 1-800-873-8635 or visit www.morefreebooks.com.

* Terms and prices subject to change without notice. NY residents add applicable sales tax. Canadian residents will be charged applicable provincial taxes and GST. This offer is limited to one order per household. All orders subject to approval. Credit or debit balances in a customer's account(s) may be offset by any other outstanding balance owed by or to the customer. Please allow 4 to 6 weeks for delivery.

Your Privacy: Harlequin is committed to protecting your privacy. Our Privacy Policy is available online at www.eHarlequin.com or upon request from the Reader Service. From time to time we make our lists of customers available to reputable firms who may have a product or service of interest to you. If you would prefer we not share your name and address, please check here. ☐

BOB07

CATHERINE MANN

77118   BLAZE OF GLORY   ___ $5.99 U.S. ___ $6.99 CAN.
(limited quantities available)

TOTAL AMOUNT $ _____
POSTAGE & HANDLING $ _____
($1.00 FOR 1 BOOK, 50¢ for each additional)
APPLICABLE TAXES* $ _____
TOTAL PAYABLE $ _____
(check or money order—please do not send cash)

To order, complete this form and send it, along with a check or money order for the total above, payable to HQN Books, to: **In the U.S.:** 3010 Walden Avenue, P.O. Box 9077, Buffalo, NY 14269-9077; **In Canada:** P.O. Box 636, Fort Erie, Ontario, L2A 5X3.

Name: _____
Address: _____ City: _____
State/Prov.: _____ Zip/Postal Code: _____
Account Number (if applicable): _____

075 CSAS

*New York residents remit applicable sales taxes.
*Canadian residents remit applicable GST and provincial taxes.

HQN™

We *are* romance™

www.HQNBooks.com   PHCM0707BL